This book should be returned/renewed by the
latest date shown above. Overdue items incur ...thout
charges which prevent self-service renewals.
Please contact the library.

Wandsworth Libraries
24 hour Renewal Hotline
01159 293388
www.wandsworth.gov.uk

Wandsworth

Tampa, FL 33602

info@zachevanscreative.com

Printed in the USA.

DEDICATION

This is my love letter to the Black men with good intentions and kind hearts, big smiles and warm hugs, large brains and a desire to be loved, who might have spent the majority of their lives being ignored for these qualities no matter how much they bled from their hearts.

This is my open letter to my nephews, innocent and sweet, who the world judges without seeing the hugs you run up to give me, even now as teens when I thought, at this age, you'd be embarrassed by your quirky aunt. I am grateful for the smiles, the purpose, the joy, and the happiness you've brought to my life.

Dear Black men,
Dear my sweet, intelligent, kind, strong, adorable and handsome nephews,

You are good.
You are loved.

You are treasured.
And all that you endure, my dear?
It will one day bear fruit.
Just keep holding on.

I love you.

NO FEELINGS ALLOWED

A CONTEMPORARY ROMANCE NOVEL

THE BOYS FROM CHAPEL HILL
BOOK 2

K. ALEX WALKER

SAGE HILL ROMANCE

ACKNOWLEDGMENTS

Special Thanks to:
Cover Design - Stefanie Fontecha
Editing & Proofreading - WritePath Editing
Proofreading - Bettye A.

CONTENT NOTICE

For mature audiences.

Contains realistic dialogue (that some may find offensive) and *smexy* scenarios—no less standard fare for my veteran readers who love a steamy, heartfelt, emotional roller-coaster romance. Proceed with an open mind and an even more open heart.

If you're new to my writing...*heyyy.* Welcome, and I'm glad you're here.

No Feelings Allowed touches on the topic of intimate partner violence from a usually unexplored POV, but I promise it's nothing too graphic.

xoxo,
Alex

CHAPTER 1

"So, you're in love with her?"

O.B. Daniels glanced at his best and closest friend, Carson Hollister. "No."

"So yes," Carson said.

They were at Carson's house at Carson's housewarming party. Dozens of friends, Carson's folks, his folks, and their third childhood friend, Miguel Reyes, were all in attendance. All those people and O.B. could see only one. It was Carson's fault this woman had entered his life. She was Carson's girlfriend, Tamika Boone's best friend.

Samantha Norwood.

He'd met her last Christmas Eve at a party he'd thrown for Carson at his nightclub, and the minute she walked in, he'd known he was in trouble.

He didn't avoid fine ass women.

That would be crazy.

But fine ass, accomplished ass, intelligent ass women with nice asses...well, he didn't avoid them either.

Somehow *this* one, this cute little black widow spider, had worked her way past his excuses and fears to set up shop in his heart. She'd even had the nerve to look around at the cobwebs holding the cracks together, all judgmental-like, and then proceed to *begin dusting them away.*

"I don't know what I am." O.B. stared at the woman in question chatting and laughing with Tamika, and each time her eyes landed on him, he came apart a little more. "I don't know what this is."

Carson folded his arms, blue eyes mischievous. "What do you know?"

"That I want her."

"Then go get her."

O.B. shook his head. "I can't."

"Why not?"

"You wouldn't believe me if I told you."

CHAPTER 2

It was no longer a shock to Samantha Norwood's system when she removed one of the many wigs she'd bought during her time in chemo. Her *t.w.a*—teeny weeny afro—was growing back in as soft, beautiful curls. She'd only worn her hair out twice as it was something she wasn't comfortable doing just yet, but she pictured styling it with gel and an off-center part. It would be cute with the pair of large hoops she recently bought.

It *could* be.

She'd been in remission less than a year, and when she wasn't waking up covered in sweat after dreaming her oncologist had made a mistake and she wasn't yet out of the woods, she was scrutinizing her features in the mirror.

Her complexion was finally back to normal, and her cheeks and body were filling back out, but she didn't feel like the same woman she'd been before.

She felt off.

Some days, undesirable.

And a significant part of her feared that change was permanent.

Logically, she knew she shouldn't *need* a man to tell her she was beautiful to feel that way again, but she'd needed to hear the word said with a deep timbre more than she cared to admit.

Her phone buzzed in the other room, and she hopped up to take a peek at it.

O.B.: Hey, you up?

Sam: Yeah. About to take a shower.

She stepped into the shower enclosure and took her time under the hot stream.

O.B. Daniels.

Why couldn't she stop thinking about him?

He was born and raised in Chapel Hill to African-American and Senegalese-American parents, and he'd attended college on both academic and football scholarships at the University of Alabama. After he was drafted, he moved back to North Carolina and settled in Charlotte.

He'd shocked the football nation when he chose to retire, at the height of his career, before the age of thirty as his name had already come up in Hall-of-Fame talk when he'd only been in his second year in the league. According to all the analysts, he would have broken Jerry Rice's record for most receiving yards during his NFL career. This was all according to YouTube, Wikipedia, and the information she was able to glean from Carson and Tamika.

To this day, no one knew why he left it all behind. They'd assumed it would be in his book, but there'd been little to no mention of it.

There was no way O.B. didn't know how she felt, no way he didn't read it all over her face whenever she so much as glanced at him. Maybe he did, and watching her fawn like a teenager over him was fun for him, like when she'd tutored her high school's star point guard, Kelce Majors, in algebra in the eleventh grade. During every session, Kelce would comment about how many times he'd thought about "kissing" her "pretty lips." When he was with his friends in the hallways, he no longer had any idea who she was.

Other than the fact that she was no longer a virgin—*barely*—and was now the founder of a multimillion-dollar gaming empire, she was still very much like that quiet girl who'd routinely disappeared among the general student population of George McLaurin High. The girl with the "soup coolers" who was loved by all her math teachers but ate lunch alone and was too naïve to effectively bully.

Shaking off the memories of her pathetic youth, Sam shut off the faucet, stepped out, and wrapped herself in the plush robe she kept hung nearby.

Her doorbell rang, and even on a doorbell camera lens, O.B. Daniels was perfection.

She slipped her wig back on, disarmed the alarm system, and went to the door. When she opened it, before she made eye contact, she took in his taut, chiseled arms, his flat stomach, and the way his jeans hugged his muscular thighs.

It was late. A little voice screamed for her to suggest that he leave before something happened, but the more it screamed, the weaker the voice became.

"Everything okay?" she asked. "Did something happen?"

He nodded.

"Does it have to do with Carson or Mika?"

"No," he said, head shaking. "Can I come in?"

She sank her teeth into her bottom lip. The threshold of her home was her last stronghold.

"Sure."

He stepped inside.

She shut the door behind him and took a few seconds to rearm the alarm system, needing the extra seconds to prepare herself for looking up at him again—especially now that his cologne had found a home in her nostrils. Plus, there was the way he towered over her, and the fact that she could feel him staring.

He held out his hand.

She stepped forward and slipped her fingers through his.

They walked to the living room where he sat down on her navy-blue sectional and dragged her down on top of him. Something was happening and she didn't know what, but considering it had landed her on his lap with his arms around her, she wouldn't be analyzing it tonight.

"You go back to work tomorrow, don't you?" he asked.

She nodded, cheek rubbing against his shoulder. "Yeah, but it won't be the same as before. I've scaled way back in my duties. It was supposed to be during treatment only, but things are going so smoothly, I'll probably keep it that way."

"How are you feeling about it? I mean, it's been," his eyes rolled to the ceiling, "almost two years in total, right?"

He'd been paying attention.

"Yes."

"You're not putting in a full day tomorrow, though?"

"I only have one meeting." She ran her fingers through the roped strands of his hair. "I got wind of this game that somehow made it to development, and I'd like to address the team responsible. They have their weekly meeting on Fridays, and I'm popping in for a visit."

He shifted, bringing her forehead to his cheek, and although it was an incidental movement, her heart fluttered behind her ribcage —it felt good to be held.

"O.B., you didn't come all the way here to ask me about work," she said.

He released a quick laugh. "You obviously don't check your cameras if you don't know I've been sitting in your driveway for a minute. I sit out there for a while every time I leave your place. Even when I have somewhere to go. This time," he shrugged, "I couldn't convince myself not to come back to the door."

All the lights in the lounge at the front of the house and living area were off, but she could see the outline of his face in the glow from her bedroom.

"Why?"

"To talk to you. Look at you. Be around you." His heart thrashed underneath her palm. "You did something. I wake up thinking about you. I go to sleep thinking about you."

"You came here to ask me to sleep with you," she said, deciding to head him off at the pass. "That's why you're flirting."

"You think this is me *flirting?*"

"Then what is it?"

"You wouldn't believe me if I told you."

She switched positions so she straddled him and hooked her fingers behind his neck. "Try me."

He opened his mouth.

Closed it.

Lips parting and sealing, it went on for an agonizing minute before he finally found whatever words he'd been searching for.

"Okay, so I do want you," he said.

She groaned. "Here we go."

"But hear me out."

"Is this a competition type of thing?" she asked. "You and Miguel talked and bet on which one could get me in bed first?"

Last Christmas Eve, she'd jokingly asked him and one of his best friends, Miguel Reyes, to help her fulfill a bucket list wish she'd made while undergoing chemo. She'd never expected them to agree, and she'd blamed it on them both being drunk...until it happened again. And again. If her father ever found out she'd had two men working her, at the same time, even though there'd been no full on sex, he would send her to hell himself in the front seat of his Cadillac.

O.B. had the nerve to look upset. "Uh...no. Why? Did you sleep with Miguel?"

"Would that be any of your business?"

"Yes."

Desire, which had been a foreign concept for so long, swarmed through her like she'd swallowed a beehive.

"Do you want me?" he asked. "Do you want me like I want you?"

Actually, I love you.

"That depends," she said.

"On?"

"*How* you want me." Her attention fell to his mouth. "Is it a sex thing...or something else?"

"Like I said, you did something." He tapped his temple. "Something that makes you stay up here. With that being said, I would be a lying man if I said I didn't think about having you in the *biblical* sense."

Her chest heaved underneath the robe. If it hadn't been for the thick, fluffy fabric, he would have seen the way her nipples had turned into pebbles.

"And if I want you the same way?" she asked.

He jolted back. "What?"

"You're...why do you sound surprised?"

"Because you're supposed to say 'No, O.B., I only see you as a friend.' That way, I'd tuck my tail and leave and resign myself to getting over whatever this...thing is I have when it comes to you."

Only a man who regularly broke hearts was this good at penetrating them. If he'd charged in and demanded that she "give it up," she definitely would have sent him packing. Somehow, he knew that, so he'd used this method—getting into her head. Making her feel desired and wanted.

She kissed his cheek. "Come to bed with me tonight."

"Samantha," he groaned, eyes closed, "I can't do this to you. Don't let me do this to you."

"But I want you to do it to me, the way only you know how. Come on, O.B. You know I want you."

"I really can't."

It was what he said, but his hand fiddled with the tie on the robe. She angled her hips so that her heat pressed directly against his erection. He pulled in a harsh breath, dove for her neck, and sucked hard.

She held onto his shoulders for support against the onslaught of his tongue. "Why not? You don't want me?"

"Of course I do, but I won't be able to stop." He sucked again, and when she cried out, he soothed the spot with a long lick. "You've got me all fucked up in the head, you know that?"

He was trying to get a rise out of her. This was a man who'd once walked out to his car and found several different pairs of panties on the hood. He wasn't fucked up in the head. He wanted something he hadn't had yet...and she currently wasn't mentally capable of doing anything to stop him.

His warm palm grazed the skin on her stomach, sending a buzz through the length of her body, rough against smooth. She arched her back, pushing her breasts toward him, and the robe fell away, exposing both mounds for his view.

"Sam, Sam, Sam." He gripped the back of her head and their mouths came together. She thrust her fingers through his dreads as he stood, carried her to the bedroom, and laid her on the mattress.

The robe fell off somewhere along the way.

Her skin was still damp in some places. Her nipples were so hard, it was close to painful. She ached for him. She'd never understood the phrase before, but her body pulsed, begging for his touch, his tongue, and for him to sink all the way into her.

He straddled her, a knee on either side of her body, and pulled his shirt off over his head. He'd been out of the league a little over a year, but it didn't appear he'd given up the workout routine. His arms had cuts that showcased muscles everyday men couldn't have possibly possessed, and it all looked so *smooth*. She wanted to reach up and touch him, but she didn't dare move with the way he stared at her.

All the skin, from his left shoulder to his wrist and across one side of his chest, was covered in ink. She had a rose vine tattoo that started underneath her collarbone and extended down her left arm, one of the first things she'd gotten once her divorce was finalized.

He left the bed, eyes still locked with hers, and stepped out of his pants and underwear. "See?" He nodded downward. "My dick's already hard. Just thinking about you and my shit gets hard."

It took her a moment to comprehend the statement. She was too busy trying to figure out where he thought he was going to put that thing.

"So, you know I'm divorced," she prefaced.

His fingers traveled along her slit, his focus between her thighs. "Yes."

"And you know it took some years before it was finalized. During that time, I was hyper-focused on my career. Plus, I didn't want to jump into something else before I closed the chapter on my marriage. Right after that, I had to deal with *Lou*."

His expression softened. He hated talking about her illness almost as much as she did, so he'd helped her find something else to call it. She'd had leukemia, so they called it "Lou."

"I haven't made much time for intimacy."

He looked up. "You haven't had sex since your divorce?"

"No."

She'd been waiting for a second marriage, but when Lou showed up, she'd realized how silly it had been to wait, so she'd made it her mission to get some once she was in the clear. After meeting O.B., he became the only man she'd wanted that "some" from.

"Samantha, I'm sure plenty of men have wanted to fuck you."

"Feeling has to be mutual for it to happen," she reminded him.

He slipped a finger inside her. On command, her body arched. He then tried two fingers and her body suctioned them, tight, which made his head fall back and his eyelids flutter.

"*Jesus.*" He'd murmured the word so low, she almost didn't hear it. "This isn't going to end well."

"For who?"

"Either one of us if I mess around and fall in love with you."

She swore she heard her heart sigh, all breathy and rushed like an enamored southern belle.

"O.B., you don't need to say things like that." Lie number one. "I promise I won't get all emotionally attached." Lie number two. "I know you don't like that sort of thing."

"Oh, you 'know' that?"

He lowered his head, his breath warming between her thighs and rolling over her sex. Then, his mouth connected.

Oh, God.

That tongue.

That damn tongue.

In an instant, he'd pushed her legs wide, parted her with his fingers, and flicked his tongue over her clit. When his tongue wasn't playing with the little organ that promised death by ecstasy, it slipped inside her, taking turns with his fingers. His mouth treated her like a piece of fruit, and the way he groaned his pleasure and lost himself in his ministrations made her want to get a taste of herself. She'd never imagined any part of her body could be this sweet and yet, he made her feel like a starved man's first meal.

"You are so good at this," she said, fingers and toes slowly curling.

His laugh vibrated against her flesh. "Helps when your woman tastes the way you do."

"I'm ready for you."

She assumed he would rise, slip on a condom, and get to business.

Not this man.

He lavished and licked while stroking her with those two fingers until she was nothing but a creamy, shuddering mess. When he finally rose, he was already wearing a condom. She didn't see when he put it on, but for the last minute or so, she'd seen nothing but the back of her eyelids.

He climbed over her, and she held her breath in preparation. But he kissed her instead, so sweet and tender, she whimpered and thrust her arms around his neck. He smiled against her mouth, raised her hips, and sunk his way in.

"*Ahh...Samantha.*"

Even if she'd had sex two weeks ago, this was still a lot of man to handle.

"I'm hurting you, baby?" he asked, voice strained.

"No, I just," she moaned, part pleasure and part pain, "have to get used to this again."

"I'll go slow. Tell me if I hurt you."

And he did go slow, giving her his length inch by inch. While he burrowed his way into her body, he resumed those tender, head-spinning kisses, and with each kiss, her muscles relaxed. He could make any woman feel loved with a kiss. Fall in love from a simple kiss.

"*Fuck*, Samantha." He kissed the side of her face, her cheek, her mouth. "I knew you'd be like this. I *knew* it would be like this."

She was so full with him, it was like he was in her throat.

He eased out just as slowly, pulling out only part of the way before pushing back in. This time, there was only pleasure.

"There it is." She nodded. "Oh, you feel so good, O.B."

He groaned, eased out, and thrust, several times, until she'd relaxed enough for him to catch a rhythm.

"Say my name again."

"O.B."

"Tell me you want this dick."

"I want this dick. I love this dick, O.B. You feel *so good*."

"You've been wanting this too?"

He could barely get the words out, and she couldn't believe it was her body bringing so much pleasure to this large, beautiful man.

"Yes. I've been dreaming about it," she said, barely getting the words out herself.

A moan rolled like thunder in his chest. His pelvis crashed against hers. She'd never had it this good. She'd had no clue it could be this good. Pleasure rippled through her in small explosions all building toward one massive release. O.B. was right; this wouldn't end well, but he was wrong when he'd said it wouldn't end well for either of them.

"Samantha," he groaned. "You're beautiful."

Her heart gave an unexpected tug.

"And you're...*this pussy is so damn good*...perfect. Baby, you don't know how much I wish..." His words trailed off, but she was so gone, she thought she'd heard him mumble the words, "could be mine."

He steadied himself on his elbows so that only his hips pivoted, driving into her steadily. This man had to be in the Guinness Book of World Records under Most Skillful Stroke. His body control, his pace, his attention...no wonder he broke hearts. No wonder he was walking dynamite.

"O.B., I'm gonna come."

"*Mmm*." He sucked on her bottom lip. "Come for me, Samantha."

Then there was way he said her name...

She shattered into pieces.

As her climax made its way through her body, she held onto him. He paused, his temple pressed against hers and their chests touching. Words left his mouth, but she wasn't in the state of mind to comprehend them.

Then he was moving again, pulling every last bit of the orgasm from her body. Not long after, he grunted, body stiff as he jerked and pulsed at her entrance. She marveled at the grimace of pleasure that covered his face, as if he was spilling his entire soul.

Don't fall in love, Sam.

Pull back.

After a few moments, he lowered. She wrapped her arms around him, fingers again in his hair. He kissed her jaw, her mouth, her neck, and the warm space between her breasts.

When they separated, she held her breath. After all that, she'd now have to spend the night wrapped up alone in cold sheets. If she hadn't been raised the way she had, perhaps she would have been able to accept this for what it was without feeling like hot wax would be torn from her spine the minute he left.

He went to the bathroom.

When he returned, he climbed into bed next to her.

"You're staying?" she asked.

"Samantha, I couldn't leave you right now if I tried."

She wanted to know what it meant. She wanted to analyze the statement, make a diagram, but he felt so good against her, she fell asleep the minute he drew her close.

CHAPTER 3

A meeting room table full of men and women lay in front of her, and yet Sam wasn't the one who had sweat on her brow. While she'd stepped back from her duties at the company, she didn't completely relinquish control. She couldn't. She loved the industry too much. She did, however, reduce her responsibilities to where she only had to be in the office once per week and attend one virtual meeting a month.

What had started out as a video game obsession when she was a child, she'd turned into a gaming software giant on par with Electronic Arts, Epic, and Rockstar. She'd named her company *Two-Twelve* after a Bible verse her father used to hammer into her, before she understood what role society expected her to play based upon the vagina it also seemed to prohibit her from talking or thinking about.

Two-Twelve's first game, an open-world, action-adventure release following the journey of Hannibal of Carthage during the Second Punic War, thrust the company from startup phase to investors leaving drag marks in concrete to get a piece of their success.

Her father used to complain about her obsession with video games when she was younger, reminding her that she should have been reading her Bible to learn how to be a good wife.

He still complained. It was just in a different way.

"Samantha, don't cause trouble. A married woman should be concerned only with how she may please her husband."

"Samantha, a married woman is bound by law to her husband as long as he's living. John came to me and repented his sins. Yet, you still walked out on your marriage."

"Do you really expect another self-respecting man to want you now? Leviticus 21:13."

Her initial plan had been to retire before she was forty and travel the globe with the love of her life, but the *love of her life* turned out to be something she still couldn't refer to as a man.

John Grant had started out as doting and sweet. Caring. She'd even believed that her father, although intense in his delivery, had been onto something when he introduced her to John.

They married when she was eighteen, him twenty-five. She attended college to get her engineering degree as a married woman while he worked day and night to grow his congregation.

And he'd succeeded.

It was virtually guaranteed he would have become as renowned as he'd become due to his good looks and "charming" personality. However, the higher he climbed on the rungs of his career ladder, the more insidious he became, eventually morphing into a faithless snake.

He'd tried using scripture to get her to "fall in line" because she'd decided to pursue a business opportunity with a fellow engineering grad instead of tucking away her degree to wait on him barefoot and pregnant. When *that* didn't work and she'd chosen to focus first on growing Two-Twelve, without a child in her uterus and with her shoes still on her feet, he'd taken to using his fists.

One time.

He'd hit her one time, and once she'd gathered her bearings, she'd retaliated with punches, scratches, and bites. She'd then grabbed whatever things of hers could fit in a gym bag and left that same night, letting him know she wouldn't be his wife for much longer.

As the pastor of one of the largest churches in the southeast, it had taken her a while to navigate her way out of the marriage—when her father wasn't interfering, John was refusing to grant her a divorce for one reason or another. After she'd threatened him with public humiliation, complete with *receipts*, he'd agreed to finalize their split.

She'd seen that moment as a chance to start over, live life on *her* terms. Then, leukemia entered her life, which her father had warned her was punishment from God for leaving her husband. If that had been the case, then why had He healed her as well?

"President Norwood, thank you for dropping in." Her newly appointed Head of Game Design and Strategy, Joshua Thames, pushed his glasses up on his nose. "It's nice to see you back and in good health."

She sent him a warm, genuine smile. "Thank you, Josh. I appreciated all the well-wishes, visits, and gifts from everyone while I was in treatment and recuperating."

Although an otherwise brilliant businessman and strategist, he had the plight it seemed so many in their industry shared—over-reliance on authority figures' opinions to the point that it shattered their confidence.

Most of them had grown up introverted and shy.

Many of them still were.

Joshua was more on the tall and lanky side, his hair low, dark, and tightly curled. Though designer and a lovely shade of blue, his suit could have been tended to a bit more by his tailor. His life, like that of the majority of the people in the room, revolved around gaming, the gaming industry, and gaming hardware. Of course they had additional interests—family, hiking, parkour, baking—but gaming was their soul.

Sam gestured to him. "This is *your* meeting, Josh. Go ahead."

They both knew she was goading him, setting him up like bowling pins while wielding a ten-pound ball. And there was no quiver or hitch to her voice. If only she could do the same in the world of romantic relationships.

"Uh..." He lowered his gaze, swiped his finger over the surface of his tablet, and pushed a button to cast his tablet screen to the virtual image hovering over their table. "Well, the new game that everyone made a push for is one that's never been done. It's about...colonial times."

"Let me help you out." Sam leaned forward, hands clasped. "It's a slavery game."

Every shade and skin tone in the room turned different hues of red.

"Don't get me wrong, Joshua, this could have been designed with poise and tact, but I'll leave you to tell me what actually happened." She reclined in the soft, faux leather chair. "Tell me about the slave trade portion of the game where the gamer can decide how much of his 'cargo' to off to save money. Or the part where the true hero of the game is actually a slave master who," she crooked her fingers, "'turned good.'"

Another member, Travis, spoke up. "We wanted to reflect authenticity."

"Travis, I prefer a little bit of sugar when you hand me a cup of bullshit."

He bristled.

"I came in here with the intention of not only shutting this down, but sending you all out on your asses. This isn't just an oversight. This is a complete lack of visionary depth. It's, in a word, idiocy."

Someone gasped.

"You had the opportunity to be *raw*." She punched her fist. "You had the opportunity to be so poignant that players were forced to look in the mirror and spot their flaws, their true natures. You had the opportunity to make something that would have been imprinted in our history. For God's sake, there wasn't even a mention of a rebellion. Look at *Mercenary's Bond: Blood and Freedom*. It's nowhere near perfect, but it's a framework. It took a chance on something otherwise overlooked. How the hell do we, instead, create something along the lines of that one game that turned slave ships into a Tetris board?"

The gasper struck again.

"Mario, if you burst into tears..."

It was too late.

"Miss Norwood," he sniffed, "I'm so sorry. I didn't want *no* part of this, ma'am. I'm from Mississippi, and when I went back home and talked about the game, people I used to go to school with started talking about how many lashes and whippings they was gonna give out once it was released. I spoke up, but nobody really listens to me."

She went soft inside but kept her expression out of her feelings. Mario was good-natured and kindhearted, and his sensitive nature helped put heart into the games' stories and subplots. He was also one of the brightest, if not the most brightest, person on his team, but he often didn't get credit for it because of his vernacular.

21

"Destroy it," she ordered. "Destroy it today. If I so much as hear about it again, you're all going to be fired. Is that understood?"

An energetic chorus of affirmatives moved around the room.

They knew.

They *knew* it was crap.

The fact that it had even made it this far...they were damn lucky. Not only had she been set on firing them, she'd wanted all those responsible for the disaster blacklisted to the point where they couldn't go to Best Buy and buy a Playstation when she was done with them.

"Now, Jamaica, you had something."

Jamaica Borneo stood, tugging self-consciously on her cardigan and pencil skirt. She turned, one hand on her lower stomach as if hiding it from judgmental eyes, and smiled. A dimple emerged in one of her cheeks, and Sam's thoughts went immediately to O.B.'s dimples, his smile, his eyes, his skin, his hair, his d—

"Miss Norwood?"

She shook off the image. "Go ahead, Jamaica."

She and O.B. had done what they'd done and now, it was time to move on. It didn't matter, *at all*, that he hadn't called her since he slipped out that morning. It didn't matter, *in the least damn bit*, that he hadn't so much as texted her when he'd texted her every morning up until the night they'd spent together.

It was what she'd wanted, wasn't it? What he'd said, about how hard it was to leave her, had come from a man flushed with oxytocin and high off endorphins.

"Sorry," Jamaica said.

Sam raised a brow. "Sorry for what?"

"Surprise!"

A crowd had slowly been gathering outside the conference

room's glass walls. One of their executive members, Emilia Yoon, wheeled in a large, rectangular cake. On it, in curly handwriting, were the words, "You Don't Know How Much We've Missed You."

Tears welled up in Sam's eyes and spilled over her cheekbones. "Please tell me then that the game wasn't real," she said.

Mario laughed. "Not in the slightest. Don't you know us by now, Miss Norwood?"

She pointed at him. "Good acting."

"Why, thank you."

There were so many people, they had to move the celebration to the cafeteria, which had a banner at the entrance with the same message printed on the cake.

Since everyone had either known her long enough to know Sam Norwood didn't like too many eyes on her, or they were new but someone had told them, no one asked her to give a speech. They simply ate, had a good time, and pummeled her with hugs. Some even cried, and it warmed her heart to know she could be loved by this many people.

"Miss Norwood?" Jamaica joined her, leaning on the wall next to where she'd retreated for a moment to recharge. "Can you please thank O.B. for helping us put this together?"

She looked around the room.

O.B. did this?

"O.B.?" Sam asked. "You mean, O.B. Daniels?"

"Yes, ma'am. We were already going to do something, but it would have been smaller than this. He said you deserved something bigger even though an hour into a celebration with this many people and you'd be pulling your hair out."

"It's finally growing back." She patted her wig, a black bob with feathered bangs. "I won't be pulling out my hair anytime soon."

Jamaica's smile faded. "I'm sorry you had to go through that."

"Thank you, Jamaica, but I can assure you, I'm good now."

"Can I still hug you?"

Sam opened her arms, and Jamaica stepped into them and squeezed tight.

When the fatigue of having not worked a full day in nearly two years hit her, Sam gave the room another round of thanks, went to her office to get her things, and headed to the front of the building to call a car. The distance from the building to her house wasn't *that* far, but the doctor's office where she was diagnosed was nearby. Each time she got behind the wheel of her car, she had flashbacks of that day, and it made it impossible to drive to work.

O.B.: By now, you've got my surprise. Did it make you smile?

She didn't answer.

It wasn't that she didn't want to or wasn't planning to, but she needed time to make peace with the reality of their situation. He would never be hers, no matter how much she'd prayed for it.

"Excuse me, ma'am, I'm looking for my future wife," a male voice said. "Have you seen her?"

"Miguel! What are you doing here?" For all her hemming, hawing, and pulsing over O.B., she had to admit Miguel Reyes looked damn good in his tailored, gray designer suit with a white dress shirt underneath. A glittering tie bar that matched the diamond studs in each of his ears held a dark blue tie in place.

He, Carson, and O.B. had grown up in Chapel Hill, and O.B.'s father often took credit for "how well they turned out" because of his influence in their lives. Miguel now played wide-receiver for Carolina, and he'd been one of O.B.'s former teammates.

He walked over and wrapped his arms around her. "I'm glad I caught you."

"Everything okay?" She returned the embrace, indulging a little since it wasn't everyday she was hugged by a man who felt this solid or smelled this good. "I ended up staying longer than I planned."

He stepped back and shoved his hands in his pockets. "Yeah, yeah. Everything's fine. Carson was trying to catch you before you went home. He's throwing a dinner and said he needs you to be there."

Carson had asked her, not too long ago, "If one wanted to hypothetically propose to Tamika, what would be the best way to go about doing so?" She'd told him that Tamika was the kind of woman who preferred no fuss. An evening at home with friends was the perfect setup.

"I can take you." Miguel pointed behind him at his car, a rust-colored Bentley Continental GT. "I have to head that way anyhow."

He extended his elbow, and she hooked her arm through it.

According to Carson and O.B., the Bentley was one of Miguel's largest purchases to date, except for the house he'd bought in Dilworth. He'd picked it up after signing a major contract extension as a "selfish" reward for his success in the league, but she didn't really see anything selfish about it. The team wouldn't have offered an extension if he hadn't earned it.

The top was up and the interior cool. It was supposed to be a nice evening in the high sixties, but she appreciated not having to worry about her wig being blown off her head in the middle of the journey.

"Are you staying for dinner?" she asked, relaxing against the soft leather.

He reached across and covered her hand with his. "Nah, I have a meeting to go to."

"You look nice, by the way."

"Really?" His face flushed. "Thanks, babygirl."

They traveled in silence along the interstate, Miguel's thumb moving lazily over the back of her hand. When she grew tired of rows of trees, green signs, and cars swerving haplessly between lanes, she redirected her attention to his profile.

He smiled. "Like what you see?"

"Miguel, you already know how good you look."

"Nice to hear it from time to time." He slid a glance her way. "Especially from you."

"Miguel—"

"Why him?"

She'd never lied to him about her feelings and where they stood. And, while she did feel *something* for him, what she felt for O.B. just happened to be more potent.

"Is it because I'm Dominican?"

Sam snorted a laugh. "Uhh, no. You're fine as hell."

"So then, what's the problem?"

"I wish I knew what to tell you."

"I think I know what it is." He brought the back of her hand to his lips. "You think you'll be the one to change him."

She didn't want to change O.B. As a matter of fact, she liked a lot of things about O.B. outside of everyone else's version of him, which mainly highlighted his sexual proclivities. What she wanted was for him to mean the things he said to her, or not say them at all.

"I don't have that kind of pull," she argued.

"I'm not too sure about that." They exited the highway and headed toward Huntersville, just outside the city, where Carson and Tamika's new house had been built. "He's definitely different with you. Your biggest hurdle isn't O.B.'s asshole tendencies, though. It's Jerica Waters."

26

"That one actress?" she asked. "What's she have to do with this conversation?"

"She has everything to do with this conversation. Jerica Waters is the reason O.B. can't move on." He turned the car onto Carson and Tamika's street. "Jerica has a hold on him neither me nor Carson understand. It's almost as if he's afraid to completely let her out of his life."

He stopped in the driveway in front of the two-story Craftsman. A colorful wreath hung on the door, and Sam's stomach tightened when she spotted the blue Maserati parked out front. Of course, O.B. would be there. If Carson intended to propose, just like he wanted Tamika's best friend to be there, he wanted his. Had it not been for Miguel's meeting, he'd likely be there as well.

Miguel dragged his lips through his teeth, top then bottom. "Looks like your man's here."

"Stop." She swatted his forearm. "Don't tease me."

She reached for the door handle, but he grabbed her chin, turned her face back to his, and pressed his lips against hers in a soft kiss that certified she was crazy. This man was a sweetheart, but his heart wasn't the one she craved.

He leaned back.

"He's watching us, isn't he?" she asked.

"Yep."

"You're so bad."

"I'll see you later." He kissed her cheek. "Be good."

She laughed, stepped out of the car, and made her way to where O.B. stood in the driveway, the expression on his face that of a man out for murder.

Miguel waved and drove off.

"What was that?" O.B. asked.

She brushed past him. "Hello to you too, Mr. Daniels."

O.B. DIDN'T TRY TO TAMP DOWN THE PRIDE HE HAD FOR his boy. He'd had more than enough money to help Carson out over the course of their friendship, on several occasions, but Carson always chose to support himself. With the exception of the couple of times Carson *had* accepted help before he'd gotten the job at Boone Publishing, his best and closest friend had wanted to dig himself out of every hole he'd created.

Now, Carson was living good.

The house wasn't gaudy; that wasn't Carson's style. There wasn't any marble anywhere to be found and no baby grand piano. He had all that shit in his own house because he'd handed the interior design off to a professional. If it wasn't for regularly scheduled maid service, it would all be covered in dust.

"I had a basketball court put in out back," Carson said, leading him through a wall of accordion doors. "You can come out here and shoot around on those many lonely nights of yours you spend, baying at the moon, wishing for Sam to—"

"What did I tell you about being loud with my business?" O.B. glanced back at the house. "You know your woman has those damn owl ears."

"Mika can't hear us."

"Still," he flicked his earlobe, "I don't want her hearing you and thinking I'm hung up on her best friend."

"But...you are."

"I know, but I don't want her thinking it."

Sam was beautiful. Pretty and cute and effortlessly gorgeous. Whenever she opened her mouth, it didn't matter what came out; his ears soaked it up like a sponge. She was also sweet in a way he wasn't used to. She talked *to* him instead of at him, saw him as capable of more than just how good he made her look, and she was the first woman, in a long time, who didn't make him question his sanity or his worth.

He hadn't expected her to say yes the other night. He'd needed her to give him a reason to keep their relationship from getting more physical than it had already been.

Because he had a problem.

That problem became a reality the minute he fit inside her body like her pussy was the mold his dick had been created from. No two people should ever fit that well together.

There was attraction between them. Strong attraction. He could see it in her eyes whenever they were together, and his attraction to her slipped from his pores and hair follicles. If he wasn't careful, it would leak from his mouth whenever he spoke.

"O.B., you sure you're okay?" Carson asked, somehow several steps ahead of him.

"Yeah." He stretched the muscles in his neck. "I'm good."

They walked out to the court where they were able to get a one-eighty view of the property, and it was like the house had been built with Carson in mind. It was homey. A place for a family. Carson was only twenty-six and somehow already knew he wanted a wife and a kid or two.

O.B.'s attention flicked to the car pulling up in the circular driveway.

Miguel's Bentley.

He wasn't like Miguel or Carson or most normal human beings. When he fell, he broke his damn nose. He went all in, losing control of his heart like he'd fallen asleep at the wheel. It came from witnessing the love that made up his parents' marriage. His father was one of those romantic, old school types who was just as in love with Bridgette Daniels née Diao as he'd been on his wedding day—a point his father never failed to emphasize.

Growing up with a man who treated his wife like a treasure, his daughters like the most precious things in his life, and his son like the other half of his heart had resulted in a son who, when he fell, became hell-bent on giving a woman the world.

It was why he didn't fall.

Why he *worked* to make sure he didn't.

But, right now, his heart didn't seem to care. It had flopped onto its belly to write "O.B. ♥ Samantha," surrounded by daisies, in chalk on the basketball court.

"Did Guel change his mind?" he asked.

"No, he can't stay." Carson grabbed a basketball from a wire enclosure and sank a quick three-pointer. "He just grabbed Sam before she left the office for the day."

Why hadn't Sam just rejected him?

"O.B.?"

Now, Carson was halfway across the yard, basketball gone.

"Shit. I'm coming."

Carson headed to the kitchen to get Tamika while he detoured to the front door. When he stepped outside, he saw Miguel's mouth pressed against his woman's, but by the time he started forward, she'd already pulled away.

She and Miguel exchanged a few words.

Then she was walking toward him.

And she looked so damn good.

Carson said Miguel had picked her up from her office, but if she'd gone to work looking this good, how the hell did anything get done at her company? Her dress hugged every curve, and the belt across the middle further emphasized just how many of them there were. It was also the sexiest shade of red he'd ever seen in his life. His complexion wasn't much deeper than hers, but he'd never looked *that* good in red.

"What was that?" he asked, head going light when she paused in front of him.

She shook her head and brushed past him. "Hello to you too, Mr. Daniels."

He went inside, shut the door, and grabbed her wrist. "You okay? Did they not give you my...*the* surprise at work today?"

She glanced at where he held her, and the look on her face made him release his grasp. That and the fact that with one tug, she'd be up against his body. Her soft would be pressed against his hard, and he was sure Tamika and Carson wouldn't appreciate him hiking up her dress and plowing into her in their foyer.

"They did," she said. "Thank you for that. It was very sweet and thoughtful. Very you."

His chest swelled. "You deserve it."

"If you say so."

So, she *was* upset about something.

Tamika entered the room, and it was as if neither he nor Carson existed any longer. The two women hugged tight, and O.B. studied their exchange with his head cocked to the side. Both had amazing bodies. Sam's ass was one of his favorite things about her with her breasts coming in third. His number one favorite part of her was her mouth.

From what she'd told him, she was still regaining weight from her illness and treatment, and it both hurt and pissed him off that she'd ever had to endure cancer, chemo, or radiation.

He looked up to find Carson watching him. He'd expected a

warning look—it was obvious he was thinking about Sam and Tamika naked and touching on each other—but Carson shrugged and ticked his head to the side, like he'd been picturing the same thing.

Tamika and Sam finished their greetings and catching up, and they parted just enough for Carson to walk up behind Tamika, wrap his arms around her waist, and plant a loud smack on her cheek.

"Ugh, please." O.B. rolled his eyes. "Y'all are making me nauseous."

And he was happy as hell for them.

First, Carson had convinced Tamika to sell her place and move in with him in the custom home he'd had her help him design. That had been Phase I of his plan. Then he'd given her full reign about what to do with the interior so that she'd feel like she was at home whenever she walked in. Phase III would be carried out tonight.

Carson glanced at him.

O.B. nodded.

"Sam, you want to see the basketball court?" Carson asked. "Baby, let's go show her the court."

Tamika craned her neck back toward the kitchen. "But, the food—"

"O.B. can keep an eye on the food."

"O.B.?"

O.B. spread his fingers across his chest. "I'm a dog, not a kid. I can handle some chicken."

At the mention of the word dog, something that looked a lot like hurt flickered over Sam's features.

Tell me what I did.

Please.

He watched them go, watched Sam's valleys and curves walk away from him, and reminded himself he had a promise to keep.

He tore his gaze away from their little group and put one foot in front of the other until he made it to the kitchen. Carson had given him a camera that looked exactly like the base for a phone charger, and he plugged it into the outlet in the kitchen island then verified it connected to his phone. When he was done, he tested the angle. As long as Carson didn't intend to propose to Tamika underneath the table, everything should be fine.

"And it stays warm all year round," Carson all but shouted, alerting him that they were on their way back.

Carson rounded the corner first, and O.B. sent him a quick nod to let him know everything was in place.

"Come on, Mika." O.B. pulled out a chair from underneath the dining table. "Get off those feet."

She drew down the corners of her mouth, impressed, and took a seat.

Perfect.

When Sam was close, he hooked her around the waist and tugged her down onto the chair next to his seat, his knee brushing hers.

"You're really just going to manhandle me?" she asked, not-so-discreetly moving her chair away from his.

"That's a good color on you," he said. "Isn't it, Mika?"

"I said the same thing when she tried it on." Tamika sent a wink Sam's way. "You look beautiful, best friend."

Sam, smiling, lowered her eyes.

While Carson set out the food, Tamika offered to pour the drinks. O.B. didn't stop her or step in to help, considering the direction the night would be heading for her in a moment. He needed her out of earshot for a few minutes.

"You're mad."

Sam looked at him like she'd intended to respond but changed her mind at the last minute.

"Tell me what I did."

Please.

Tell me how I hurt you.

"You didn't do anything, O.B. I'm mad at myself."

Carson and Tamika made their way back to the table.

"So, O.B.'s got a pretty busy weekend planned next week," Carson said.

He glared at Carson until their eyes met and gave a slight shake of his head. They'd sworn there would be no Jerica talk tonight, and when Carson had asked him why not, he hadn't been able to answer. It was that reluctance to answer that made it so that there was currently Jerica talk.

"That sounds like all of your weekends," Tamika teased. "What makes this one special?"

"He's Jerica Waters' date for her movie premiere," his meddling ass friend continued. "O.B. and Jerica have history, and this is the first time in years they're going to be seen together. She posted that he was her date, and it got something like one-hundred thousand likes in twenty-four hours."

O.B. grabbed the nearest bottle of wine and added more to his already half-filled glass. "Carson, you can't keep secrets for shit."

"You two getting back together now that her marriage fell through?" Carson asked.

He imagined himself sticking his fork through Carson's shoulder. "She called me, asked me to attend, and I said yes. End of story."

Which it wasn't.

Not quite.

Jerica had asked him to attend the premiere with her *before* he met Sam. She'd asked him while straddling his waist with her breasts in his face and her engagement ring on her hand. One of those breasts had been in his mouth at the time.

Jerica was, essentially, Sam's opposite. She had sex appeal and owned it. The woman rode dick like a dick conductor. She flaunted her assets, both the natural ones she'd been born with and those he'd paid for. In no environment or situation could she ever be mistaken for shy, quiet, or introverted. In certain environments, however, she'd been mistaken for stable, caring, and understanding. It was funny the things people hid behind closed doors, himself included.

"Well, did you want to talk about your plans for next week, Sam?" Tamika asked.

Sam slipped a thick piece of honey-garlic roasted carrot between her lips, and O.B.'s mind took him places it was dangerous to go to if his intent was to avoid lifting the table from his crotch. Any man interested in women who saw Sam's lips had to think about, at least once, how they would look swallowing his dick.

God, she's so pretty.

"It's not big news like a movie premiere or anything," Sam announced. "I just have a date. My first real date in a long time. I promised Mika that I would at least *try* the dating scene before I considered the other thing."

O.B. tore into his chicken. "What's the 'other' thing?"

"A business arrangement with one of our," she motioned to herself and Tamika, "colleagues where the agreement is we go half on a baby."

O.B., choking, grabbed for a napkin.

"A business arrangement for a baby?" Carson asked, obviously trying not to smirk. "How does that even work?"

"I froze some eggs a while back as a sort of insurance policy. It was right after my divorce, and there are actually a few men who me and Tamika know and have worked with who wouldn't mind being a donor."

O.B. swallowed a bite of food, this one making its way down his throat, although it went down like stripped wire.

"Like a sperm donor," he said.

She shrugged, eyes on her plate as she chewed that single piece of carrot to death. "It's done in our circle a lot more than you think. Me and the proposed father would meet in advance to agree on certain financial and familial terms. For instance, he might want a child but not a marriage. In turn, we'd share custody—"

"That's way too clinical. A kid needs a chance to have a *Daddy* in its life."

"They would have a father, *O.B.*"

"A 'Daddy' is not the same thing as a father, *Samantha.*"

She sucked her bottom lip into her mouth. He watched that lip as it slipped into her mouth, as her teeth worked it, and as she slowly released it, wet. So wet. As wet as her pussy had been, wrapped around his dick, warm and snug like a Christmas scarf.

He eased further under the table to hide the brick behind his zipper. "A 'Daddy' or a 'Pops' is different," he explained. "I wouldn't have turned out the way I did without the role my *Pops* played in my life. He's there whenever I need him. He taught me that the world was going to attempt to convince me what being a man meant, a Black man, but it was my job to ignore the bullshit and listen to him. He told me, 'When you become a father, play with your kids and kiss them goodnight, even your sons. Tell them you're proud of them. Love on them.' His father didn't do any of that with him, so he made sure to raise me the way he wanted to be raised."

His father, his namesake—it was the only excuse for his wreck of a name—had been right. Whether or not he asked for it, he was bombarded with different opinions about what it meant to be a man, even from the women he dated.

One woman had told him men who used spoons were

"pussies," so she only dated "real" men who ate with forks or their hands. A former teammate of his didn't cry at his own little brother's funeral.

He felt most comfortable and most proud being the man his father raised him to be, and his father had to have done something right. His only hangup was that he didn't, whatsoever, want to fall in love, ever again, in his life. Love made him do stupid, irrational shit. Then again, so did fear.

"She's considered that," Tamika said, in defense of her friend. "But the dating pool's a little shallow. I had to hook up with a guy fifteen years younger than I am."

Carson clutched his chest. "The whole dagger, Mika?"

"But I'm good with that," Tamika quickly added. "I love you, Carson, but Sam, she's...well..."

"Not as bold when it comes to romantic relationships," Sam finished. "But, I think I'd prefer an arrangement. I've been in some messy situations, and if I'm not careful, I could end up getting involved with a man who'll be," she glanced at O.B., "nothing but a waste of time."

That fucking stung.

O.B. set down his fork. "And how would 'a man' be that?"

"Pretend to be into me."

I'm not pretending.

"And by the time I realize it's all for show, it'll be two years later, and I'll have nothing *to* show for the time I wasted on him."

"You think it's time wasted?" he asked. "What if you enjoyed your time with him?"

"Doesn't matter. He was only in it for the ride."

"And you're sure about that?"

"It's not that hard to tell." She set down her own fork. "Let's take you for example, O.B."

O.B. leaned back in his chair, chest puffed up and his arms spread wide, prepared to catch whatever she was about to throw.

"You date tons of women," she began. "You've slept with tons of women. You'll never settle down, and you're entitled to that lifestyle, but how many of the women you date or sleep with are probably waiting for that next day call or text only to realize they'll never hear from you again?"

Fuck.

He didn't text her.

Or call.

He'd fucked her and disappeared the next morning. What made it worse was, before they'd had sex, he'd either text or call her every morning. From her vantage point, it looked like now that he'd gotten what he wanted, there was no longer anything about her worth spending time on.

Tamika cut in. "Even if the women know you're only in it for a good time, you're telling me no one ever catches feelings?"

He lost his appetite for both chicken and alcohol. "Feelings have been caught before," he admitted. "*I've* caught feelings before. And yes, maybe going into a few of them, I didn't make my intentions clear, so they never got that next day text or call when it was possible they'd been waiting for it."

Carson draped an arm behind Tamika's chair. "What intentions are those?"

"I may have forgotten to make it clear that the sex was just for fun."

"Fun?" Carson pressed. "You sure?"

"Yep. Nothing more."

Sam's brown eyes flickered with the realization of what he'd just claimed her to be. He saw the war going on inside her head, saw her replaying the things he'd said and the way he'd acted, trying to piece

38

everything together. None of it would make sense. It would have only made sense if his words were representative of his actions.

"Let's change the subject," Carson suggested. "Sam, I hope your date goes well, and I hope it's not with somebody who'll waste your time. Hopefully, it's a man who'll mean what he says. You deserve that," he cut O.B. a sharp look, "and more."

O.B. was the only one close enough to hear Sam say, "Too late."

CHAPTER 4

She had to get away from this table.

Away from this man.

This was completely her fault. O.B. never lied about who he was. His very own best friend had warned her about him, but she'd still let her heart get involved because of the way he'd held her, looked at her, and the things he'd said to her. Why did she think she could sleep with *him* and walk away? A human male, maybe, but not a whole masterpiece.

Sam was about to push out her chair to leave when she noticed Carson nervously glance at O.B. O.B. pulled out his phone, opened up an app, and pressed what looked like a record button.

"Mika?" Carson took Tamika's hands in his. "So you know I think you are the most amazing, wonderful, and sexy woman in the world, right?"

"You tell me all the time," Tamika said. "And I love you for it."

The rest of Carson's speech was drowned out by Sam's heart

pounding, her racing pulse, and the blood in her ears. If she was this excited, she could only imagine how Tamika would feel once she caught on to what was happening.

Carson reached into his pocket and pulled out a blue box.

"My boy went to Tiffany's," O.B. whispered, in Sam's ear. "I helped him pick out the ring."

Carson sank onto his knee in front of Tamika. Tamika slapped her hand over her mouth, eyes shimmering.

"Do you think you could be happy for 'a couple of forevers' with me?" he asked.

"Of course." Tamika nodded. "Of course I can. Yes."

"You haven't even seen the ring yet."

"I don't need—"

Carson opened the box.

"Oh, it's beautiful."

Sam hopped up and hurried to give her best friend a long hug. When she released, she and O.B. good-naturedly toasted to the happy couple, and she swallowed her water before excusing herself to the bathroom.

O.B. caught up to her quicker than she'd expected. She'd heard he was fast, but she'd only seen him in action in videos on the internet. Videos she'd watched like porn.

"Samantha." He hooked an arm around her middle and drew her back against him. "I'm sorry."

"You don't have anything to be sorry for," she insisted.

"Yes, I do. For one, I'm sorry for being a sorry excuse for a human being. My inconsiderate ass couldn't even think to text you?"

She'd never wanted a text more.

"O.B., let me go before they see us."

He stepped closer, his pelvis pressed against the curve of her bottom. "Something going on between you and Miguel?"

"Wouldn't be any of your business."

"Of course, it's my business." He kissed the back of her neck. "Go out with me later."

"No."

"Please?" He pushed into her, and a whimper betrayed her and snuck from her throat. "I want to take you out. I want to make you smile."

"No."

"I'm sorry, Samantha. I'm a dog, yes, but you're my favorite kind of bone."

She dragged herself out of his grasp and faced him. "There is something *clinically* wrong with you."

"Sam, I didn't mea—"

"If you're trying to hurt me, for whatever reason, congratulations. You have. Maybe it makes you feel better."

"I don't..." He rubbed the back of his neck. "That's not—"

She held up a hand. "Here's the thing. I promised you I wouldn't get attached, and I didn't. I already had feelings for you before we got in bed together, and I was the stupid one to cross a line I knew I couldn't handle. Regardless of that mistake, I didn't promise to be your pseudo-sexual-emotional punching bag, and I'm not going to be. So...just stop and leave me alone. Please."

She headed down the hallway and stepped into the bathroom where she hid until it was no longer obvious she'd been crying.

She stayed for dessert and would have stayed longer, but Carson and Tamika were a newly engaged couple. They wanted to jump each other's bones so badly, their desire perfumed the air. That desire was why she and O.B. were currently across the room, in the foyer. To avoid getting caught up in their *vibrations.*

"I can take you home," O.B. offered, reaching out to poke her in the side.

She stepped away. "I'll call a car."

"Sam...please?"

Carson must have picked up on something going on between them because he headed over. "I can take you home if you'd like, Sam," he offered.

"It's fine, Carson." This was his and Tamika's night. If that meant riding home with the man who'd called her "fun" and "bone," both in the same evening, then that was what she'd do for her friends. "I'll go with O.B. Stay here and love on your fiancée."

Carson grinned. "Has a nice ring to it, doesn't it?"

"And now, Tamika has a nice ring too."

She squeezed him in a tight hug, hurried over to do the same with Tamika, and followed O.B. out to his car.

They didn't speak on the ride to her house.

He glanced at her at stoplights, and she glanced at him underneath streetlights. What was the purpose of making a man this good looking? What had God been trying to prove, that He could attain perfection? Every brown, chiseled square inch of O.B.'s body had been created for the benefit of people like her who couldn't help but gawk. What the hell had she been thinking, that he'd somehow mysteriously fall for her when he had women like Jerica Waters in his back pocket and behind his zipper?

Jerica looked the part of a baller's girlfriend with her golden-beige complexion, exotic features, and dyed blond hair, the roots dark. Jerica was what most men expected if a friend told them they were setting them up on a blind date with someone beautiful. Maybe she *should* have let herself be more open to something with Miguel, but she'd seen some of his exes as well.

Next to them, she felt like a bumpkin.

She didn't feel the same way about herself as she had before. The Sam from before, although she wasn't ever going to be the loudest person in the room, had been able to work that room with a quiet confidence. Back then, looking in the mirror was never a chore, and it had been easier to appreciate her smooth brown skin, dark eyes, and full lips. The Sam from before wouldn't have worried about having to "stack up" against women like Jerica, but when chemo killed the abnormal cells in her body, it seemed to have killed her confidence right along with them.

The guard at the entrance to her neighborhood waved when he recognized O.B.'s car, double-checked to make sure O.B. was inside, and opened the gate. Because he was O.B., he stopped to have a chat

"Henry, my man, how you livin'?"

Henry Fordham grinned and tugged on the front of his cap. "Can't complain, son. You look good."

"I have to if I'm trying to be like you when I'm forty."

Henry, laughing until he wheezed, slapped his thigh. "Son, you need to stop. You know I'm pushing sixty-five. I'm close, but I can't retire yet, though." He bent lower to peer inside the car at Samantha in the passenger seat. "Not until I'm sure whoever takes over here will take care of my little Sam-Sam."

Her face flushed. Ever since she hit the age of thirty-five, it became even more endearing when older folk she respected referred to her in an affectionate, parental sort of way.

"I appreciate it, Mr. Henry," she said.

"O.B., I know you get this question all the time," Henry prefaced, "but we're really not going to see you out there on the field anymore?"

Sam studied O.B.'s face. According to Tamika, not even Carson knew the real reason O.B. had left the league. The reason he gave reporters, and had even put in his book, was that his heart had no longer been in it, but his face was ten times brighter than she'd ever seen it as he chatted with Henry. His eyes sparkled. There was no way he'd lost his love for the game. Something had pushed him away.

O.B.'s smile dulled. "No, sir. I'm afraid not."

"Man, I don't know. I don't think we're about to see another ring for a long time."

"You still have my boy, Reyes, and I heard they're starting that one kid who came out of Oklahoma. I saw some of his film. He's mobile *and* accurate."

"I hear you." Henry gave his cap another tug. "Still, man. You have a gift. You were made for ball, let me tell you. I'm just grateful I got to watch you play. Me and my Pops, who passed away last year, it was one of the ways we spent time together, you know? I appreciate everything you've done for this city, and I know, if he was still alive, he'd tell me to tell you the same."

Sam held in her gasp when O.B.'s fingers found hers, slipped between them, and squeezed.

"I really, *really* appreciate that, Henry," he said.

They shared a silent moment, Henry looking down at his shoes and O.B.'s focus slowly moving back to the front windshield.

"You two children have a good night, and if he gives you any problems, Sam-Sam," Henry bent, eyes finding hers again, "let me know. I know his mother taught him how to treat a queen."

O.B. gave her hand another squeeze. "Samantha's more than royalty. If you can put in a good word, though? Convince her to say yes when I ask her to din—"

She smacked his shoulder.

"Damn, Samantha," he said, rubbing at the spot they both knew was nowhere near sore. "That really hurt."

Henry burst out laughing, and they wished him a good night as they pulled through the gate.

Although the drive to her house wasn't much farther, Sam

slipped her hand away from O.B.'s and settled it on her lap. She'd held his hand too many times in her dreams to feel comfortable doing it now. Plus, she was exhausted. Holding his hand only tempted her to lean on him and hope he wrapped his arms around her waist to pull her close.

He stopped the car in the driveway and shut off the engine. "Do you need me to walk you in?" he asked.

"No, I'm okay." She grabbed her things and opened the passenger door. "Thank you for the ride."

"I—"

"Good night."

To reassure him there were no hard feelings, just hurt feelings, she leaned across the seat, kissed his cheek, backed out, and shut the door. Unfortunately, several forty-pound weights fell onto her shoulders before she'd made it even halfway to the front of the house.

After promising herself she would take things slow, she'd stayed later at the office than anticipated. If it hadn't been for a recent appointment with her doctor, terror would have been interlaced with her sudden fatigue. Here she was, months into remission, and some days, she felt almost as terrible as when she'd been in the thick of things. If it wasn't fatigue, it was brain fog. If it wasn't brain fog, it was nerve pain. The PTSD never quite went away.

"O.B.?" she called, hoping he could hear her from the car. As far as she could tell, she hadn't heard him pull away. "Do you mind giving me a—"

"I've got you," he said, somehow already next to her.

She unlocked the door from her phone, and he carried her inside all the way to the living room sofa. Once she was situated, he locked the front door and returned to her side. Before she knew it, she was in tears and, silently, he held her until the moment passed.

Sam leaned back, swiping at her eyes with the back of her hand.

"Sorry about that," she said.

"Samantha, you don't have to apologize." He glanced at the kitchen. "Do you need a glass of water? I can get you a glass of water."

He went to fill a glass without waiting for her answer.

When he returned, he handed it to her, and each time he chose to sit next to her instead of heading for the door, applause released in her chest.

She raised the glass to her lips, took a few sips, and set it on the coffee table. O.B. studied her, worrying his bottom lip between his teeth, and lifted her feet onto the cushions to slip off her shoes. Then he let her know he'd be right back, disappeared in her bedroom, and returned with a cotton cami and pajama pants.

Leaning against him for so much support it was mildly embarrassing, she allowed him to help her out of the dress, and he deftly slipped the cami over her head and the pants up her legs.

"Better?" he asked.

At first, she smiled. "Better."

Then she was crying again.

This time, when he tried to reach for her, she raised her hands to stop him. If he held her tonight, she'd start to expect it, and it would be agony when it stopped. It was funny, her telling him she had "feelings" for him when it was so much more than that.

"Back when I was in college, I had an appendectomy," he said, scooting on the sofa until he'd propped her feet on his lap. "After the surgery, I told my doctor I felt fine, and that I didn't need any down time because I couldn't afford to have a busted appendix mess up my draft chances. He told me that, even though it was mild surgery, I would have to take it easy. Guess what the first thing I did was?"

"Not take it easy?" she asked.

"Exactly."

"And what happened?"

"My body essentially told me to sit the fuck down." He grunted out a small laugh. "Turns out, your system responds to being cut open as a whole-body experience. Healing takes a toll on you mentally, emotionally, and physically."

Condensation running down the side of the glass of water momentarily grabbed her attention. It was a simple gesture, getting her something to drink, but she'd heard that many women had called this man heartless. He could be something of a dick, yes, but she didn't see heartless. Guarded, but not heartless.

"How long have you been keeping that in?" he asked.

She leaned into the cushions. "Probably a year or so."

"You haven't cried in a year?"

"No, I've cried. It just comes in snatches. I think my brain knows giving me everything at once would be too overwhelming, so it throws it at me at random times." She studied his face. "Honestly, it happens most when I get frustrated."

"What frustrates you the most?"

"Not being able to walk to my house from your car. The times I don't feel like myself." The tears started up again. "The fear that I'll never feel like myself again."

"Samantha, can I hold you? I won't make it awkward. At least, I'll try not to."

If all she had was this night to cry in his arms, it was better than all the nights she'd cried with only her blanket and sheets tucked around her.

She nodded.

He drew her onto his lap like he'd done the other night, wrapped both arms around her, and she rested her head on his shoulder.

"You feel good," she said.

He laughed, soft and gentle. "Can I be honest?"

"Nothing's stopped you before."

"I...deserved that." He smoothed the pads of his fingertips along her forearm. "I was a complete ass to you today, and if there's one thing I'm sure about, it's that anything I do that hurts you, it's never because I want to. I never want to hurt you, Samantha."

"So what were you supposed to be honest about?"

"This." He squeezed her against his midsection. "I've thought about this."

"Holding a woman? You're O.B. Daniels. From what I understand, you've held your share of women."

"You," he clarified. "Holding you. I've thought about it. More than once."

"I don't think we should...you know. Ever again."

He shifted, Adam's apple bobbing as he swallowed. "That's fair."

"It's not because I didn't enjoy it. It's just..."

He knew.

She didn't have to finish or repeat it.

"Samantha?"

"Yes, O.B.?"

"I wish it wasn't me."

And that single admission almost made her start crying again.

"I think very highly of you," he explained. "I put my foot in my mouth today, yes, but I really do. When I stopped by your building to help set up the welcome back party, I went to your office and saw all the game cartridges on the wall, starting from the first one Two-Twelve put out. I saw all the awards, and Layla let me know you had more, just not on display. Baby, you have a picture with Michelle Obama."

"It was our first sensor bar, gyroscope type of game." She snuggled into him, and he tucked her in further. "Michelle actually reached out to us and said she loved our work, admired me for what

I've accomplished, and wanted to collaborate on a program to get kids to move more."

"Did she smell good?"

"You know she smelled good. Like cocoa butter, roses, and *auntie*."

He laughed.

"I don't understand why you wish it wasn't you, though?" she asked. "I mean, I'm not expecting you to feel anything for me. You, literally, don't have to do anything with the information I gave you earlier. It's just that, lately, waiting or holding things back hasn't really been my thing. Not sure why."

He didn't laugh again, like she'd hoped. Instead, his right leg bounced.

"Were you scared?" he asked. Like in the car, like it was a reflex, he reached for her hand. "Was Mika with you when you found out?"

"When I found out, yes. When my doctor brought it up as a possibility, I was alone and scared out of my mind. It was the last thing I was expecting to hear although I'd had my suspicions."

"Did you have to go through chemo alone?"

"Not on most days. Some, yes, but Mika...she's amazing."

"That she is."

She swatted his chest. "So then why do you give her and Carson such a hard time?"

"It's fun." He grinned, trying to be his normal, playful self, but something had obviously hurt or unsettled him. "But you know I love Carson. I thought I was trying to protect him from falling for Mika and having her drop him on his ass. I never expected them to be where they are now."

"They're unnaturally cute together."

"Right? Makes me sick."

Each time he tightened his hold, she died a little more on the inside.

Eventually, the bouncing of his leg slowed, and it wasn't long before she started yawning and breaking down her nightly routine in her mind to see what she could skip to save time on tonight.

"I should probably get to bed," she said.

He sighed, his chest expanding and shrinking. "Yeah. You're right."

"O.B., I won't ask you why, but when you tell people you left the league because your heart wasn't in the game, that's not true, is it?"

He waited a beat before answering. "No."

"Something forced you away."

"Yeah."

"Knew it." She yawned again. "I watched your videos on YouTube. Whatever it was, I hate it already. I would have loved to see you play at least once. You're amazing."

He stood, lifting her at the same time, with ease. "You're only saying that because you're desperately, hopelessly in love with me."

If only he knew how close he was to the truth and how much she wished he wasn't. It wouldn't be impossible, but it was going to be difficult to get this man out of her system. She hadn't even met her date yet, and she was already sizing him up, comparing his smile and height to O.B.'s. If this guy didn't have at least one dimple, she wasn't sure she could imagine a second date.

"I pretty much hated you earlier," she teased. "But that didn't stop me from thinking you're great. I don't know if I get a version of you no one else ever sees, but you're a good person in my eyes. A great athlete, and a good person. I envy the woman who gets your heart."

The next thing she knew, he was pulling the covers up over her body, and the bed had contoured to her form. When she heard the sound of clothes being shed and then felt his warmth behind her, she pressed her hand to her chest in an attempt to manually slow her racing heart.

Before she drifted off, she heard him whisper, "You don't have to." However, by then, she'd forgotten the topic of their conversation.

CHAPTER 5

"Something wrong, babe?"

O.B. looked up from his phone into Jerica's light-brown eyes, which were locked on him, her eyebrows narrowed above long, thick eyelashes. Bold red lipstick colored her full lips, and her stylist had opted for dark, sultry makeup around her eyes. She'd had her hair straightened, and she currently wore it pulled back away from her face in a simple yet elegant low ponytail.

She was beautiful,

He would always find her beautiful.

Those eyes had drawn him in when they'd first met, but it was those same eyes that had never truly stopped haunting his dreams.

"No, nothing's wrong," he said. "Just checking on something."

He tucked the phone into his blazer. Sam's birthday was a couple of months away, so it wasn't like he had to find a gift for her *right* then.

"I haven't had the picture posted yet," Jerica announced, wiggling her phone in his direction, the screen facing him. "You know the one we took in my suite? Erin'll post them tonight. At least, she better. I bet they get, like, ten thousand likes in an hour."

This was the movie role she was convinced would catapult her career in a more serious direction. So far, nearly all her roles had been in movies with ensemble casts and simple, straightforward, predictable plots. She wanted to star in the Saving Private Ryans and Schindler's Lists of their generation. It was one of the first things she'd told him when they met, so he'd dropped a ton of money on acting lessons and helping her build her image while gaining connections in the industry.

She left her side of the limo, sat next to him, and leaned her head on his shoulder. "I'm glad you decided to come with me. I'd love your feedback on how I did after we watch the screening."

He draped an arm around her. "I can do that."

"I miss this, baby."

A long time ago, that single sentence would have been enough to stir his blood and make him push up her dress to help himself to a buffet between her legs. He would then fuck her until she was hoarse and her complexion turned from golden to red, and he'd naïvely assume that meant things were back to normal. That things were better. After a week, he'd realized he was still caught in the emotional loop in which she'd kept him prisoner for years.

"Do *you* miss this, O.B.?"

"What happened with Landon?" he asked. "You two were together for like two years but married for less than a month. How does that work?"

She snorted. "They weren't two great years, no matter what the photos showed. I mean, he had an orgy at the All-Star Game."

That was something he could say he'd never done—he'd been with multiple women at once but never an orgy. He was too selfish to share that much intimate space with someone else, which was how he knew Sam had to be some sort of witch or sorceress to convince him to share any part of *her* with Miguel.

"Didn't Landon propose to you at the All-Star Game?" he asked.

Jerica's head bobbed. "Yep. You get my drift, then."

"Jerica, you were still having sex with me while engaged to him."

"That's different." She pouted, glossy lips poking out. "We have history."

"Maybe you need to stop going after ball players."

"He played *basketball*."

"*All* ball players."

She kissed his jaw. "Except for one."

The top part of her dress, which had barely concealed her breasts in the first place, fell away, revealing a chestnut nipple. The dress had been kept in place with fabric tape, so he knew this little nip-slip was orchestrated.

Jerica had a natural, nicely-shaped ass, but her stomach, breasts, and arms were the work of a skilled plastic surgeon in California. Sam had beautiful breasts, which were the perfect weight in his mouth, and the type of ass it was virtually impossible not to worship. Not only was her ass like an apple he wanted to sink his teeth into, he could grip a handful and squeeze the hell out of the plump, round flesh.

He'd asked Tamika, in ways he hoped hadn't been too intrusive, if she believed Sam's illness had changed Sam in any way. It was after the first time he'd caught Sam looking at herself in the mirror at Carson and Tamika's. Though he'd seen nothing wrong with how she'd looked, she'd studied her body with unmistakeable disappointment. She wasn't as thin now as when they'd first met, and back then there'd been a tired element to her eyes, but the woman had always been, and would always be, gorgeous.

According to Tamika, the entire ordeal had tanked Sam's confidence, and he'd witnessed it that day he'd caught her looking in that mirror.

It was why he constantly told her that *he had her.*

That he'd be there for her.

If it hadn't been for the woman next to him, it could have been more. Sam made him feel like the man he'd assumed he'd lost years ago.

Jerica rubbed his growing erection over his tuxedo pants. "I missed him too."

Jerica's hand on his dick with Sam on his mind made him harder, and he closed his eyes, head falling back against the seat.

"O.B.? Should I tell the limo driver to take another lap around the block, baby?"

Jerica unlatched his belt, unhooked the button on his slacks, and pushed her hand inside his waistband. Grip firm, she stroked him like a woman familiar with how he liked to be touched while kissing his neck and pushing her exposed breasts against his arm.

"Want me to suck it for you, baby? Or do you want me to ride it?" She spread the moisture that dripped from his tip with her thumb.

"That feels so good, Samantha."

The hand stopped moving.

"Who the fuck is Samantha?"

O.B. opened his eyes. "What?"

Jerica scurried back to the other side of the limo. "O.B., I don't pretend to be naïve about you fucking other women, but what the fuck? You're thinking about somebody else when *I'm* touching you? I swear to God—"

The limo jerked to a stop.

He stuffed his deflated erection back into his pants, hooked the clasp, and latched his belt. Jerica readjusted her clothes, lifted her chin, and someone on the outside opened the limo door.

He exited first.

Jerica took his extended hand, stepped out, and threaded her arm through his elbow.

This part, they were good at.

They had experience going out in public places, pretending to be happy and in love despite leaving behind limos and hotel rooms that had to be cleaned and readjusted by assistants before the press got wind of the chaos inside.

"Jerica! Jerica! Over here!"

She squeezed his forearm, relaying a silent message.

Behave, or else.

They faced the cameras, flashing lights going off one after the other. He'd been a "sensation" during his college years, which was what had kindled his popularity. When he entered the league, that popularity exploded, throwing him into "celebrity" status. Apparently, he'd had the perfect mix of skill, good looks, and personality without the expected arrogance; since childhood, his father had drilled into him that a big head wasn't necessary and to let his talent do the talking for him instead.

Not too many players crossed over from football to celebrity status, and he wished he hadn't been one of them. While the perks were nice—he enjoyed the major media appearances to speak about causes he cared about and five-star service at hotels, events, and airports—he hated having to go to the ends of the earth for a little seclusion. At least, back home in North Carolina, people didn't rush him even when they recognized him. There were occasional requests for pictures and autographs but, for the most part, he was treated like a respected human being worthy of space and privacy.

"Jerica, does this mean you and O.B. are back together?"

"Jerica, O.B., you two look hot!"

"You two are perfect for each other!"

"Hashtag couple goals!"

It all made his stomach turn.

They posed for pictures before heading over to where Jerica had agreed, beforehand, to have a few words with designated entertainment reporters. Afterward, he hoped they went inside the theater and that was that.

For now, he would play the role.

It always felt like he was playing a role, whether it was as Jerica's longtime love, O.B. the partier, O.B. the player, or whatever title everyone else decided suited him. There were only a few moments where he felt like he could shirk all the shit and be himself, but it was in those moments he'd panic because he'd been playing roles so long, he had no idea what "being himself" looked like anymore.

"Jerica, honey, you look *gorg!*" Danielle Petersen from Celebtainment News stepped into their path. "And I see you came with the absolutely fine Mr. O.B. Daniels on your arm. You two are couple goals for sure."

Jerica leaned against his side. "Danielle, O.B. and I are here only as friends."

He sent a smile Danielle's way. Danielle blushed until she turned the color of Sam's dress that night at Carson and Mika's.

"So Jerica, tell us a little bit more about your role. I've been looking forward to *Asylum* ever since I first heard about it."

Jerica explained that her role was about a woman whose asylum status is rescinded right after she gives birth. Her baby goes missing from the hospital, and it's a race against the clock to find her baby before I.C.E. agents catch up to her. If she did a decent job, O.B. could see it changing her career the way she hoped.

"So sorry to hear about things not working out with you and Landon." Danielle *tsk*ed, and her mouth curved downward. "He doesn't deserve you."

Jerica flicked her wrist. "I'm a strong woman, Danielle, and strong women simply learn how to cope and get through and bounce back."

"What's past is past?"

Jerica slid a gaze O.B.'s way.

He smiled at her, right on cue.

"I don't know," she said. "Sometimes, the past isn't always a bad place to return to."

They did the spiel of the different designers Jerica wore, from her earrings down to her shoes. Then, Danielle set her sights on him.

"O.B., when will you let America know why you really left the league at the height of your career? No one can get you to talk about it, but maybe you'll be able to shoot me a quick word since you're here with your longtime love and feeling good?"

He smoothed the front of his tux. "I've already given an answer."

"We heard talk that it was because—"

"Unless it comes out of my mouth, Danielle, take it with a grain of salt."

They thanked her and started off, but Danielle had one final question.

"Are you getting into the gaming industry?"

He turned. "What?"

"You were spotted with Samantha Norwood of Two-Twelve

games, the first Black woman to found a *gaming mega-empire,* several times since the start of the year."

Jerica's raptor claws descended into his forearm.

"They've been making moves to break into the sports gaming industry to rival titles like *Madden* and *Fifa*. Is that your next venue? Are you consulting with them?"

"I didn't know you were into gaming, Danielle," he said.

"Trust me, I'm here for all the black girl magic." Danielle tossed her auburn hair over her Los Angeles-tan shoulder. "And Samantha Norwood, she's *beautiful,* smart, and successful. She's a powerhouse. We need to be doing more features on women like her. Women creating legacies."

"I agree that's she's very beautiful and one of the smartest people I know," he said, trying and failing to hold back a smile with Goliath strength. "She would be a great person to start with, but my good friend, Carson, is marrying Samantha's best friend. That's why we've been spending time together."

The last thing he wanted was to have Sam's name spilled all over media tabloids.

Danielle motioned to his face. "That's a huge smile you've got there. Is marriage on *your* mind, O.B.?"

Jerica's nails moved south, piercing the skin on his wrist.

He shrugged but didn't offer anything further.

"Thank you, O.B.," Danielle said, beaming. "You two have a nice time inside."

They did three more interviews before they entered the theater. Not every actor from the film would be in attendance, some of them preferring not to see themselves on the big screen, but the majority of the main cast was there.

Jerica left him to schmooze her way around the room.

He escaped to a refreshment table in the back, grabbed a napkin, and pressed it to his bleeding wrist.

Nothing, at all, had changed.

"O.B.?"

In front of him stood one of Jerica's costars, Matt Lane, who played her love interest in the film as well as one of the agents assigned to locating her character.

"Have we met?" O.B. asked.

Matt waved both hands in front of his face. "No, not at all. I just...it would mean so much to my boy if you'd sign something for him. He's one of your biggest fans, and I swear I'm not just saying that."

"Yeah, of course." O.B. tossed the napkin in a nearby trash bin. "I'm always amazed by the young fans. Some of them know more about football than I do."

Matt, laughing, brandished a Sharpie and a small piece of paper. "His name's Sam."

O.B.'s heart raised its head and looked around. When it didn't spot the Sam it belonged to, it returned to its chamber.

"How old is Sam?" he asked.

"Seven. He's been watching you since your college days at Alabama. It's because of you he wants to play football instead of being a 'boring actor' like his dad."

Young Sam appeared to conveniently be nearly the same age as his professional career, which meant there was no way he'd watched him while he was at Alabama.

"Want to take a picture too?" O.B. returned the paper and marker. "He might not believe you actually met me."

Matt's eyes opened so wide, his eyelids disappeared. "Hell, yeah."

They flagged down a server passing by who snapped a couple of photos and then took one for herself. Once she left, Matt stared at the image on his phone.

"Man, I can't thank you enough for this. Sam is going to be so happy. Do you mind if I post this on my timeline?"

Jerica waved.

"Not at all," O.B. assured him. "Nice meeting you, Matt. If you'll excuse me."

She found her seat, and he eased down next to her. Anger vibrated from her in waves that threatened to shake the floor. Then again, they were on the West Coast. Everyone would simply assume it was an earthquake.

"I looked her up," she whispered.

He decided to play dumb. "Looked who up?"

"Samantha Norwood."

"Oh."

"She's a little out of your league, isn't she?"

"That depends on what you think I'm doing with her."

She smiled with each word, in case anyone was watching, but vehemence shined in her eyes. "I don't see why a woman her age and with her level of success would want to fuck around with you. You couldn't find your way around a pussy using GPS."

Pussy was the one thing he never needed directions to navigate, which Jerica knew from experience, and there was no shaking his confidence on that front.

He'd forgotten about that evil little lip twitch of hers and the way her eyes drew to slits when she plotted murder. His skin burned where she'd cut into him with her nails, and he couldn't help but wonder *what* about this he'd ever found irresistible. It was like he'd loved Jerica the way some people loved meth—the high brought a certain kind of rush, but at the end of the day, all his fucking teeth would go missing if he didn't give up the habit.

"Jerica, you were married not too long ago," he reminded her.

She lowered her voice further. "That doesn't mean I would have stopped messing around with you."

"I'm not sleeping with a married woman, even if it is you."

"Were you really doing it? When I was touching on you, were you really thinking about her? Tell me the truth."

He was thinking about Sam now.

He *never stopped* thinking about her.

"Let's talk about this later," he said. "The movie's starting."

The iconic lion's roar boomed through the surround sound, and the lights dimmed.

As the film played, O.B. found himself surprised at how invested he became in the plot. Jerica committed to her role as Nohely Mejia from South America, and he believed Nohely's pain when she found out her baby had been taken. He loathed the main I.C.E. agent, and it stung a little when Nohely had to make the hard decision to leave her son behind. After everything she'd gone through to find him, it seemed unfair she couldn't take him home. At least, the couple who adopted him appeared to have his best interests at heart.

When the credits rolled, he stood and clapped with everyone else.

Jerica stood, wrapped her arms around him, and leaned against his side. "Did you really like it, babe?"

Thankfully, he wouldn't have to lie to her. "I did."

"The cast has to go on stage for a Q&A thing. Then, we're going to the after-party, okay?"

He had no interest in going. "Okay."

There was a short intermission between the end of the film and the Q&A, so he decided to give the refreshment table a try, although it looked disappointing from a distance.

He grabbed a plate smaller than his palm and helped himself to bacon-wrapped jalapeños, pinwheels with some sort of flavored cream cheese, and stuffed mushrooms, steering clear of anything that looked like raw fish. A passing server handed him a flute of champagne, and he posted up in a corner to devour the bite-sized food. Hopefully, the after-party was just a stop-through and he'd be able to leave early to get a more substantial meal.

Jerica answered questions, but her gaze landed on him every few minutes. At least, it seemed that way. His attention pivoted between her and his phone.

O.B.: Do you eat raw fish?

Those three dots lingered for what felt like years.

Samantha: That's a very random question.

O.B.: Do you?

Samantha: Is this sexual?

O.B.: No...

Samantha: I've tried sushi, but I wasn't a fan. Didn't care for sashimi and I won't touch smoked salmon.

O.B.: That's what I thought.

Samantha: Why?

O.B.: I'm at the movie premiere and some of the hors d'oeuvres are hard pieces of bread with smoked salmon on top.

Samantha: You mean, crostini?

O.B.: What's that?

Samantha: The hard pieces of bread.

O.B.: Why don't they just call it bread?

Samantha: Should you be texting me? Don't you have a date who needs your attention?

O.B.: I had a question. I can't ask you a question?

Samantha: About raw fish, though?

O.B.: I saw the fish and thought of you.

Samantha: 😳

O.B.: Dammit. Not in that way. I mean, it made me wonder if you ate raw fish.

Samantha: Go back to your date, Orylin.

O.B.: Please don't.

Samantha: You're in my phone as Orylin Brian Daniels.

O.B.: When I get back, we're changing that immediately.

Samantha: I happen to like your name.

O.B.: You're literally the only person who has ever wanted to tell that lie.

Samantha: I have to say, I'm impressed you spelled hors d'oeuvres right.

O.B.: That was all autocorrect. Can I call you later?

Samantha: I don't know. Can you?

O.B.: Fine. *May I* call you later?

Samantha: That's not what I meant. But yes.

O.B.: A whole yes? Not a yep, yeah, or whatever? You must miss me.

Samantha: I kinda do.

O.B.: 😊

He put away his phone, swallowed the rest of the food in two bites, downed his champagne, and reclaimed his seat. A smile remained glued to his face during the rest of the Q&A panel.

THE AFTER-PARTY HAD NOTHING BUT DRINKS.

Jerica kept him glued to her side all evening. Even when she was deep in conversation with notable actors, she kept her palm attached to his. Once she finished meeting and greeting, she led him over to a

VIP area. When he sat, she scooted onto his lap, laid her head on his shoulder, and yawned.

"My feet hurt. I have *maybe* twenty more minutes here in me."

"I'll call the limo and make sure they know to meet us out front."

She raised her head. "How many stops will it be making, you think?"

"The limo?"

"Yes." She giggled. "What else?"

"Two stops," he said. "Unless you have somewhere else you want to go."

"You're not coming back to my hotel?"

"No."

"O.B., what's going on?"

Sam wasn't his woman, and he wasn't Sam's man, so there was literally no reason he couldn't go back to Jerica's hotel. But, he'd turn Jerica down a million times over if it prevented him from hearing Sam tell him, ever again, that he'd hurt her.

"Jerica, I'm hungry and tired. I want to go back to my room, eat a steak, and relax."

Heat spread along his thigh. "So, I'll come to your hotel."

"Not tonight."

"Do you still love me?" she asked, the disappointment so heavy in her voice, he knew she was playing it up.

"I always will, probably."

"Then, why not?"

"I just want to eat and chill, Jerica."

"Is it because of Samantha?"

Yes.

Hell, yes.

He didn't respond.

She fiddled with his blazer. "Will you at least kiss me goodnight?"

"Sure. I can do that."

What else could he say?

"Jerica, I can't have sex with you because my dick currently only works for a woman I'm not even dating. A woman who, the minute I'm alone in my hotel room, I'm going to call because I've been counting down the hours until I hear her voice again. Let me tell you a story about her lips..."

They stayed for another half hour before piling into the limo. She fell asleep against his side, and he removed his jacket and draped it over her shoulders. He had the driver take them to her hotel first so he could make sure she got in safely, and she requested that he walk her up to her suite. Outside her room door, she propositioned him one last time.

"Are you sure, O.B.?" She wrapped his arm around her body and placed his hand on her ass. "You remember how you like to grab my ass while you're fucking me from behind?"

Of course, he did.

"Remember the time I sucked your dick on that hotel balcony in Barcelona for our six-month anniversary?"

He wouldn't ever forget it.

"Jerica, you were married not too long ago," he reminded her. "I think you need time to sort things out before we go any further. You know we're like gasoline and fire when we're together."

Bleach and ammonia.

Hell, Mentos and Coke.

She dropped her chin with a quick nod. "You're right. When we get back together, I want it to be for good. It was you I should have agreed to marry, O.B. Not Landon."

The last thing he needed was Jerica with power over his last name or children.

"Well," she sighed, "good night, then."

"Good night."

"Kiss-kiss."

He touched his mouth to hers, and she slipped her tongue inside. Her hand went behind his head, and he allowed her to indulge. For someone who she claimed couldn't find his way around a pussy, moans dripped and trickled from the sides of her mouth.

"Yes, that's it." She sucked on his bottom lip. "You feel it, don't you? You want this pussy, O.B. You'll never ever be done with me."

An image snapped in his mind.

He drew back. "I really have to go, baby."

The endearment softened her.

"Fine." She poked out her bottom lip. "I'll see you tomorrow."

He made sure he saw her safely enter the suite and started back down the hall.

The minute he got back to his hotel, he ordered a grilled steak and a baked potato. Then, he took a quick shower so that after the food arrived, he would have no further distractions or interruptions.

He set his meal on the terrace dining table overlooking the city. If New York was the city that never slept, Los Angeles was its first cousin. Towering buildings checkered with lights in the distance brightened the sky. The outline of the mountains that had been visible during the day hid once the sun went down. It was a decent view for what the room was worth, but he was a nature man. He loved looking out of the window and seeing the Smokies, parks with bridges made out of brick, still lake waters, or fall in the form of the changing leaves of hundreds of trees on a hillside.

Which gave him an idea for Sam's birthday.

He pulled out his phone.

O.B.: Are you decent?

71

Samantha: Yes.

O.B.: Never mind. I'll call you later.

He waited for a snarky, teasing comeback but got nothing.

O.B.: Can I FaceTime you?

Samantha: Are you eating?

O.B.: Maybe.

Samantha: Why do you always FaceTime or text me when you're eating?

O.B.: Because I'm happy when I'm eating. Seeing your face or talking to you is a bonus.

Samantha: 🌚

He toned down his smile while the phone rang, the pit of his stomach stirring in a way he chose to blame on hunger. When her face finally appeared, the sensation changed. He'd seen her before he left two days ago and yet, he missed her.

It was late back home, but she was dolled up and wearing a curly unit with bangs that flitted each time she blinked.

"You look cute," he said, opening up his potato.

She was in the living room from what he could tell. The deep blue of her sectional and a rustic clock on the wall near the hallway served as a backdrop. Blue was another good color for her complexion, and he wondered if she'd be opposed to him buying her a few outfits. If so, he would tell her they were from Tamika.

"Thank you." She smushed her bangs against her forehead. "So do you. Did you have a good time at the premiere?"

"As good a time as I think a person could."

"How was the movie?"

"You know what? Not that bad." He blew on a forkful of potato and popped it into his mouth. It still burned, and she giggled at his agony at having to push it around in his mouth until it cooled enough to chew.

"You could have called me when you're done with your," she squinted at the screen, "steak and potatoes?"

He took another bite, making sure to blow longer this time. "Not really."

"You couldn't wait until after you finished eating to call me?"

"Nope."

"I won't even ask why."

It wouldn't take much longer for her to figure out that his flirting wasn't harmless, but he wasn't sure she'd ever figure out why he couldn't do anything more than flirt. On one hand, he wanted to take the secret to his grave. On the other, he wanted someone to know everything. At least one person.

"What was the movie about?"

He explained the plot between bites of his meal. Her eyes rolled to the ceiling and her head bobbed as she listened. She added her own commentary, and it didn't surprise him she knew a little about immigration law in the U.S., which she said had come from game research.

"Now that you know all my business," he pushed his empty plate away and leaned back in the chair, "what did you do tonight and why are you still up?"

Her gaze flicked in the direction of where the TV hung. When she looked at him again, it was like seeing her that first time at Carson's party. They'd assumed he hadn't worn socks with his outfit, but he left the house in socks. They blew away when she walked in. Drunk O.B. had said something along those lines.

"I actually," she scrunched her nose, "stayed up waiting to talk to you."

Another massive smile threatened to breach, so he licked his lips. "Is that why you're all extra *cutified*?"

"Oh, no. I had my date earlier, remember?"

No, he didn't.

"The guy's a mutual colleague of mine and Mika's. He's the founder of an advertising tech firm, Forbes list, all that."

"White guy? Black guy? Dominican?"

She chastened him with a look.

"What? You're into Dominicans."

"White guy."

"Was something wrong with him?"

"Not at all." Her gaze flicked, again, toward the TV. "He was extremely handsome, tall, a gentleman, and had the prettiest blue eyes. He just...I think I jumped the gun. I might not be as ready as I assumed for this whole dating thing. Before I met...let's just say, a couple years ago, he would have been an A-plus. I would have already been looking forward to our next date or still out right now talking and walking around downtown Charlotte. I haven't felt like myself lately, and it's starting to show."

O.B. picked up his room service tray, set it outside his door, and climbed into bed, one hand behind his head. She knew he would stay silent until she shared. She knew he actually wanted to know.

"O.B., can I ask you a juvenile, stupid question?"

"That's only fair since I ask you juvenile, stupid questions regularly."

"Would you say I'm attractive?"

He almost dropped the phone. Attractive, yes, but it was a pretty mild word. There were at least a dozen more he could use to describe her, and he'd still only toe the line.

"Yes. I'd say you're beautiful. Gorgeous. Cute. Sexy. Bad. Fine. Pretty."

With each word, her chest rose higher.

"Do you need more?"

"No." A slow smile stretched across her lips. "But thank you."

When her gaze flicked to the TV again, he decided to ask her about it. "What are you watching?"

"Hmm?" She pressed her lips together. "Nothing."

"Samantha, are you watching something nasty?"

"No. I'm watching...football."

O.B. glanced at the time on his phone. "There's no football on right now, here or over there. Is it, like, a replay game?"

"It's a game I found on YouTube. Carolina versus Seattle from five years ago."

"Five years ago? I was playing five years ago."

She nibbled on her top lip. "I know."

He had to stop himself from reaching for his chest to soothe what wasn't, in the slightest, a painful ache.

This should have been the woman he'd met seven years ago. He would have thought he was the shit, dating a grown-ass, fine-ass thirty-year-old woman. Knowing Sam, she probably would have encouraged him to grow his investment portfolio. Barring no serious injuries, he would have still been playing ball. If she was interested, they might have already had at least one child. They would have definitely been married, and there would have been zero instances of her having to go to chemo alone. Tamika said she never found a bone marrow transplant donor. That would have been a different story if she'd been his wife.

"How do you do that?"

He realized he'd been staring and blinked, finding the side of her face. "Me?"

"Yes, you. Like...do you remember any of your plays?"

"For the most part."

"So, this Seattle game. I mean, you caught that ball one-handed, after it bounced off the defender, and got both feet down in the end zone when I'm pretty sure the human body shouldn't be able to contort like that."

She flipped the camera for him to see the TV, pressed rewind until the video stopped right before the catch, and let it play. He had full recollection of it—how it felt, the deafness of the stadium, the Legion of Boom defense. The corner, Lamar Andrews, one of the top defensive backs in the league at the time, *wore him out*. It was one of those games where the refs let them bump, run, and shove. Their quarterback had avoided targeting him for much of the night since Andrews led the league that year in interceptions. Not even he knew how he made the catch, and it wasn't until he'd seen the replay that he'd even believed it.

"What if I came back?" he found himself asking.

"Come back where? Charlotte? Wait," she sat up a little straighter, "were you thinking of not coming back?"

Like he could live in a different state than she did.

"I mean, what if I came back tonight?"

"You think you'll get a flight this late?"

"I can try." He was already up, headed toward the room phone. "If I make it in tonight, I'll come straight there. It'll be late, early there, but can we sleep in and watch more games together tomorrow. I can give you the play-by-play."

"Really?"

Jerica would be pissed since she expected to see him tomorrow at some point. It was a risk, but he didn't want to go to sleep without holding Sam.

"Yes, really."

"Okay, then." She did a little wiggle, a little happy dance. "I'll see you then. Call me. I'll come pick you up."

"You sure?"

"I can drive to the airport. It's not in the same direction as the doctor's office. Plus..."

She didn't have to stay it.

He couldn't wait to see her either.

The minute they hung up, he called the concierge desk.

"Hello, Mr. Daniels," a sultry, feminine voice answered. "This is Amber again. It was nice meeting you at check-in. How are things in your room? Do you need someone to come up and—"

"Are there any flights from LAX to Charlotte tonight?" he asked.

"I can check right away, sir."

Keys tapping filled the dead air. While Amber searched, he collected his things.

"Sir, there is one, but it's leaving the airport in forty-five minutes."

"That's fine." He tossed his clothes in his carry-on and didn't care how they landed, as long as everything fit. "Book the flight, check me in, and arrange transportation. I'd like to be out of here in under five minutes."

The hotel was high-end, and he was staying in one of their most expensive penthouse suites. It came with hidden luxuries, an on-call personal assistant being one of them. All he'd had to do was make a couple of social media posts about his choice of lodging while he was in LA.

"Yes, sir. Should I send someone up for your bags? I can even come up mys—"

"No, I have just the one."

"Okay, Mr. Daniels. The car will be outside when you come down."

"Thank you."

He ended the call, did a final sweep of the room, grabbed his stuff, and headed to the lobby.

CHAPTER 6

Sam kept one eye on the attendant at the airport who'd told her, twice already, she couldn't park along the curb, but there was literally *no one else* there.

He didn't have to trip so hard.

Obviously, with the way she squeezed her fingers and bounced on her toes, she was waiting for somebody important. Somebody she couldn't wait to see, even though she'd *just* seen him a few days ago. Did she care that all this time spent with him only made her fall further, putting her at risk for an even greater broken heart?

Mildly.

Somewhat.

Was it crazy that she allowed their flirtatious exchanges to continue, knowing they meant more to her than they did to him?

Possibly.

Probably.

But, right now, it didn't matter.

There he is.

His locs hung around his face and spilled over his shoulders, down his back. There was a rugged, disheveled quality to them, like he'd slept on the plane. His lean yet muscular frame filled out a black T-shirt and sweatpants that sat low on his waist. Men always talked about women in sundresses, but they didn't know the power they wielded in a pair of sweatpants with the right kind of treasure underneath. She'd been on the receiving end of said treasure, and her body had asked, several times, why it had been so long since it was last acquainted with the Black masterpiece walking her way.

She bounced on her toes and waved.

A broad smile stretched across his face, and he waved back.

Unable to wait for him to reach her, she headed toward him. When they stopped, inches apart, he towered over her. The sun would rise in the next couple of hours. He *could* have waited until the next day to come home, but she was glad he didn't.

He dropped his bag, bent, and lifted her off her feet. She locked her arms around his neck and her legs around his waist. The attendant from before called out to them, but she ignored him. She'd been *waiting* for this.

Her gaze fell to his mouth.

He trapped his bottom lip between his teeth.

"Excuse me, ma'am?"

That damn attendant.

"We're coming," O.B. said, eyes on her. "Give us a minute, please? I haven't seen my girl in a while."

"Liar," she teased.

He shrugged.

She didn't kiss him.

Instead, she let him lower her to the ground, and he followed her to the car.

She'd taken a catnap after their video chat to make sure she was prepared for him. The way she saw it, they could have breakfast, watch the videos, and sleep throughout the day—if he was interested. His body could still be wired to do *something* after having to perform on Sundays for so long.

"Feel like picking up some breakfast on the way back?" he asked. "Little Egg is on the way to your place...unless you want to come to mine."

She'd been to his place before, but her body hummed like going to his place guaranteed a night with him.

"We can do that." Because she regularly laid her edges on the go, she had an extra scarf on hand. There was no way she was comfortable enough to go without one in front of him. "What's on the way to yours?"

"Café Dawn. You ever had them?"

"No. They any good?" She slipped behind the wheel, and the car bounced with his weight lowering onto the passenger seat.

"They're decent," he said. "Want me to order something for you?"

"Sure. You know what I like."

She pulled away from the curb and waved to the attendant when they passed.

"Damn." His head reared back, and a smile curved along one side of his mouth. "I do. When did I learn you so well?"

"I have no idea."

"We spend too much time together."

"Probably."

They looked at each other, smiled, and Sam returned her attention to the road while he ordered their food from his phone.

O.B. ABSENT-MINDEDLY MASSAGED SAM'S FEET, HIS BACK pressed against the soft headboard of his king-sized bed. She lay on her back, perpendicular to him, her face turned toward the large TV on his wall. After breakfast, they did end up falling asleep, and even though she knew they were at *his* house, for a few disoriented seconds after she'd woken up, she'd thought she was alone. She'd been sleeping alone for years so didn't know how she'd acclimated to having him in bed next to her so quickly.

"The easiest defensive formation to start with is the blitz," he explained, putting pressure on each of her toes in sequence. "That one's called a zone blitz. The hope is that, putting enough defensive players in the quarterback's face can overwhelm the O-line and open up a lane for a defensive back to get in for a sack."

"And a defensive back is like a corner or a safety, not a linebacker."

"Yes. Do you remember why?"

"They play farther away from the line, and corners usually play deeper than safeties, right?"

He pressed into her instep with his thumb. "Yes. I told you that *one* time and you remembered. Shit's crazy."

When she was invested enough in a subject—in this case, a person—her brain sopped up all the information it was given and made sure there were no leaks. O.B. could have been explaining the process of fermentation and she would know how to make kombucha before the end of the day.

"How would you be useful during a blitz?" she asked. "Because you were a...wide receiver."

"A wide receiver is crucial during a blitz *if* the quarterback can escape it. If you send that many defensive players toward the quarter-back and past that...remember what the line's called?"

Her eyes rolled around in her head. "Line of...scrimmage?"

"God, that's such a turn-on." He squeezed the arch of her foot, and her back involuntarily bowed in response. "So, yeah, if you send that many defensive players *and* if the quarterback can escape the blitz, he's in a prime position to make a big play in a virtually empty backfield. He can either find a receiver who's wide open, or one who only has one defender on him. In my case, I was dangerous one-on-one because there were less than a handful of backs in the league who could beat me in a jump ball situation."

Her lip tugged. "Cocky much?"

"Stating facts."

His phone lit up on the nightstand, the fourth time it had since they woke up. She knew it lit up because the phone case had a lip edge and the light from the screen reflected off the top of the nightstand.

The first time, he'd glanced at the screen, flicked the switch to place it on silent, and set it face down. The calls came through on his watch as well, but he didn't so much as glance at it.

"That's her, isn't it?"

It took him a moment to meet her eyes. "Yeah."

"Did something happen between you two while you were out in LA?"

"You mean, did we have sex?"

Yes.

"Not necessarily."

"No," he said as he left the bed, grabbing his phone in the process. "We didn't."

He left the room.

She lowered the volume on the TV and moved as close to the door as possible without putting herself in the compromising position of getting walloped in the head should he suddenly walk back through it. Unfortunately, she picked up only snatches of his conversation. He'd walked farther than anticipated.

"Jer...you can't...no...worry..."

Two words made her ears perk up.

"Nothing...Samantha."

There was a long break of silence, and then footsteps. She scrambled onto the bed, lay down, and paused the TV like she'd been waiting for him—and so he didn't notice she'd lowered the volume. When he entered, the relaxed look that had been on his face since the airport was gone.

"Need me to go?" she asked.

He cocked his head to the side and stared at her, obviously baffled. "What? No. You stay. I'll let you go when I'm ready."

"Didn't realize I was being held captive."

He returned to his spot and resumed the massage. "Well, you know now."

Miguel: I suggest you check Jerica's page.

O.B. LEFT THE ROOM, LEFT SAM NEARING CLIMAX BY FOOT massage—which he'd really needed to see—and did as Miguel said. He went to Jerica's page and instantly wished he hadn't.

Neither Carson nor Miguel knew, but there was a part of him that believed they speculated something had been rotten in the Waters-Daniels relationship. Miguel's text had confirmed his suspicions.

To everyone else, what she'd posted looked like support for

victims of domestic violence. To him, it was a threat. A reminder that if he didn't call her back, if he didn't do her bidding like he'd done since they met, she would destroy him.

If she'd simply wanted his money, he would have been fine with that.

If she'd threatened to tell the world he was a lying cheat, he could have handled that as well.

This, he'd devised no defense for.

He'd read the image post only once, but once was all it took for the words to remain cemented in his brain:

Why didn't she leave?
Because she was scared.
Because she was tired.
Because the fear of leaving didn't outweigh the fear of staying.

She'd littered it with several domestic violence hashtags.

He'd never called a woman outside of her name in his life, but as he picked up his phone to return her call, he had to swallow several variations of, "Bitch, what the fuck is wrong with your crazy ass," while her phone rang.

Smugness dripped in her voice. "Hey, baby."

"Jerica, you have to stop this."

"Stop what?"

He breathed through a snap of anger in the event she had him on speakerphone. His anger was only ammunition.

Jerica had a one hundred percent African-American defense lawyer father and a South African-German mother, yet she'd come out damn near lighter than Carson in the wintertime. It didn't matter if he portrayed his anger with a cool, calm head. As long as it came from him with his skin and his presence, he would look like a beast baring its fangs instead of a man interminably caught by a twisted, manipulating mental mousetrap. How could someone who weighed eighty-pounds less than he did have this much control over him?

He softened his tone. For Jerica, he needed to be velvet and cotton and silk. "Baby, what's wrong?"

"You didn't answer my call," she answered. "I got worried about you. You didn't tell me you left LA last night."

"I didn't get a chance to."

"It's...a little past two there. What were you doing between your flight back and now?"

"Sleeping."

"By yourself?"

"Yep."

A door closed on her end, and the dragon hiss he'd become all too familiar with reared its head. He almost asked what had kept it when it hid from him with the proficiency of a two-year-old playing hide-and-seek.

"I don't think you understand," she prefaced, racing past the point of seething and going straight to menacing. "Me and you, we're a forever deal."

The declaration gave him an instant headache.

"So, choose your words wisely and do not lie to me. Did you leave last night to go back to Charlotte to be with Samantha Norwood?"

O.B. glanced at the closed bedroom door. "No."

He'd known he would like Sam. He'd known he would like her more than a little bit, and he knew that spending time with her further complicated things between them. With other women, it had been easy to remain detached. Yes, he'd broken hearts, but those women had no idea the hornet's nest they would have walked into if he'd decided to pursue anything serious with them.

Each time he'd tried to push Sam away and that flash of hurt had crossed her face, no matter how well she thought she hid it, he'd seen it. And he would sooner toss himself chest-first onto a sword than hurt her again.

"You better not be fucking lying to me. All I'm trying to do is love you and show you how much I love you, and you're out here acting funny."

"Jerica," he fell back against the nearest wall he could find, "you can't just be out here posting shit like that."

"Oh, so you saw it?" He imagined her pretty face curling into a sneer. "Is that why you finally called me back? You thought I'd tell the world your little secret?"

Jerica was crazy.

Insane.

He was a huge advocate for mental health awareness, especially among Black men, so he was cognizant of avoiding certain words to describe someone's mental health status. However, there was no medication for what Jerica had. There was no doctor, no specialization. She was an entirely new diagnosis, effectively treated only by a team of psychiatrists, hypnotists, and a couple of female correctional officers with bats, who'd had a shitty day.

He couldn't figure out if it was a personality disorder, a dent in her brain, or her growing up with a father who'd never used the word *no* toward his children or their mother. Whenever Jerica heard the word, a switch went off and she turned into a hybridization of Medusa and the woman from *The Exorcist*.

At twenty-two years old, he'd assumed his job had been to be respectful of Jerica's emotions. To be understanding when she blew up and lashed out when stressed. Growing up, school-related stress had often made his sister, Raina, moody and irritable. Though Raina never got violent, he'd justified Jerica's behavior by telling himself Raina and Jerica were two different people capable of different wheels of emotion.

With nothing else to go off of, he'd assumed their relationship was *normal*, so he'd done the only thing he'd known to do to get through it—swallow his misery. Support her. Focus on football. Eventually, it wasn't enough, so he told her they would have to break up.

She'd said she was fine with it, that she wanted to see other people too, but they *had* to get back together at some point. She would only agree to their relationship ending if he came back to her when he was bored. Like a boomerang.

He didn't agree.

The rage had moved over her face in waves, and then she'd broken down in tears. Heavy tears. Jerica had given him enough apologies to fill a novel and yet, those tears...it was like she was going to die.

She'd then dashed to the closet.

Annihilated by guilt, he'd run to check on her.

The minute he crossed the threshold, she wailed on him.

At the time, he didn't know what she'd struck him with. In the aftermath, he saw her clothes, still on hangers, on the floor, and realized she'd torn off one of the metal bars from the closet system.

It wasn't the scratches or the broken skin that had set him off. It wasn't the nips of pain that had spread wherever the metal bar collided with parts of his body. It was the blow that caught his hand, as he'd tried to take the weapon from her, and broke three of his fingers—pinky, ring, middle. The fingers on his left hand. His dominant hand.

In that moment, he let his anger get the best of him.

He'd grabbed the bar, tossed it, and pushed her back against the wall. He didn't remember, to this day, the moment his hand went around her neck, but it had. And Jerica was almost as pale as Carson in the wintertime.

There, on her neck, had been the bright red evidence of his lack of control.

She'd called the police, cried and put on a show.

They took pictures.

No one asked him about his fingers.

They'd been ready to take him, in handcuffs, until she stopped them. Until her father showed up and requested that they file no charges because Jerica had asked. Her father, who was on golf buddy terms with the Chief of Police.

They'd unlatched the cuffs, and the incident never went public. However, her father kept the pictures as an unspoken warning.

Jerica, behind her father's back, had smiled at him and dealt the final blow to his self-esteem—she'd mouthed, *"Gotcha, bitch"* as her father had walked the police officers to the door. Ever since then, for the sake of his image and his career, whatever Jerica wanted, Jerica got. He could weather being seen as a cheating, lying bastard, but he never wanted to be seen as a man who beat women.

It wasn't until the next day at practice that his fingers were tended to. He'd always found it strange that his coach never asked what happened and had simply made sure his fingers were set and wrapped, and he'd ended up missing only two games.

After practice, he'd sat in his car for hours, prolonging the moment he had to see her again.

When he finally went home, she was apologetic. Damn near penitent.

They'd had sex.

And it would be three more years of pins and needles, mood swings, demands, unexpected bursts of violence, and empty, tearful apologies. Now, he'd somehow found himself back in it.

"You don't have to worry about Samantha," he reassured her, and he didn't have to see her to know her tears were as shallow as a backyard hose dripping water on pavement.

"Will you come see me soon?" she asked. "I'm sorry I did that. I'll take the post down. I just...I was so worried about you. I can't lose you, O.B."

"Don't take the post down, but...don't do that again. Please? It's not fair. How can you say you love me if you want to hurt me?"

She sniffed. "I'm sorry."

"We'll talk later, okay?" Sam's shadow moved underneath the bedroom door. "I have to go help Carson with some wedding planning stuff."

"You think he'll let me be your plus-one?"

Carson, without knowing all their relationship details, hated Jerica. *Hated* Jerica. He would sooner invite Satan.

"I'll ask him."

"Okay." She sniffed again. "I'll see you later. I love you, and I really am sorry."

"It's okay, Jerica. I forgive you."

"I love you, O.B." She waited a beat. "I said I love you, O.B."

"I...love you too."

After they hung up, he counted to twenty-five and then headed to the bedroom, making sure his steps were heavier than usual to give Sam a chance to pretend she hadn't been eavesdropping.

When he stepped back into the room, he paused a moment to look at her. To take her in.

Anyone but him.

It should have been someone else but him.

He returned to the bed and resumed Sam's foot massage, one-half of his mind still on his conversation with Jerica. The way things currently were, he wasn't convinced he wouldn't forever be a slave to her demands and requests. Over the years, he wondered how many wonderful women he'd had to give up, not only for his protection, but theirs as well.

And he couldn't tell a soul.

"O.B., are you okay?" Sam asked, slipping her foot away, which he'd stopped massaging at some point. She rose onto her knees and laid her hand on his forearm. "You can talk to me, if you want. You know *I'll* be here for you."

He tilted his head to better admire her eyes. "Why do you say it like that?"

"So you'll know that, if no one else is," she shrugged, "I, at least, will be."

"Why?"

"I care about you."

"Why?"

"Because of the way you care about me." She held fast to his gaze. "You're a good person. You know that, right? I mean, even dogs have their days."

He felt himself smile. After the conversation he'd just had, he didn't think it was possible, but he felt the tug on his cheek.

She smiled right back.

He tipped his chin at the TV. "Your nosy ass can go ahead and turn the volume back up before you press play."

Her smile stretched wider, and she raised the volume and started the video.

He pulled her to sit between his legs, and she lay back against his chest. He then reached for her hand and laced their fingers together.

Definitely.

Sam definitely would have been his wife if she was the woman he'd met seven years ago.

"Now that," he pointed at the TV with their clasped hands, "is called a spread offense."

CHAPTER 7

Between the sleep she hadn't gotten much of last night—she'd stayed up half the night fantasizing she'd spent another night at O.B.'s place instead of going home—and running around with Tamika doing wedding *stuff* all day, Sam would be surprised if she made it to five o'clock without face-planting on a sidewalk somewhere. Tamika was trying to cram twelve months' worth of planning into four since she and Carson wanted a Christmas wedding. The families were on board, and the concepts Tamika had come up with so far were like a winter fairytale.

While she and Tamika ran around interviewing wedding planners, Carson and O.B. worked on their wedding registries, getting the wedding website up, playlists, and finding a DJ.

They were all waiting for him to officially ask O.B. to be his best man. It would be no one else, so they weren't sure what the hold-up was. Tamika's primary concern was that O.B. *would* be Carson's best man, which meant his bachelor party theme would consist of meat, beer, and strippers with *tig ol' bitties*. The agreement was that if

Carson had strippers, she could have strippers *and* get slapped in the face by another man's penis. Carson didn't think the terms were fair, but Tamika hadn't budged so far.

While they waited for the latest wedding planner, Sam's phone vibrated.

Orylin Brian: You know that one song that goes *Last night, I was inside of you?*

Sam: Um...where exactly are you going with this?

Orylin Brian: Carson and Mika's wedding playlist.

Sam: They DID NOT leave that up to you.

He sent her a GIF of Patrick from SpongeBob SquarePants sneakily rubbing his hands together.

Sam: They're going to uninvite you. Wait, disinvite. What-ever. They're going to tear up your Save the Date.

Orylin Brian: Can't undisinvite the best man.

Sam: He finally asked? About time. Mika's not sure what he's waiting for.

Orylin Brian: Not yet. Is Mika afraid his bachelor party will have strippers? Because his bachelor party WILL have strippers.

Sam: You know about the agreement? If he has strippers, she can too?

Orylin Brian: That's fair.

Sam: And get slapped in the face by a 🌶️?

Orylin Brian: WTF? What kind of freaky shit is she into? And why didn't I hit on her first?

The final planner they were meeting for the day entered the waiting area. The woman, who was a dead ringer for Shari Headley from *Coming to America*, clasped Tamika's left hand between both of hers.

"You must be Tamika," she said. "I'm Jess. Can I call you Mika?"

Tamika sent her a friendly smile. "Yes, I don't see why not."

"And who is this sexy gumdrop?" Her gaze flicked to Sam. "Maid of honor? Wait, you have to be a matron of honor. Let me see...no wedding ring? How's that possible?"

"Samantha," Sam introduced. "But you can call me Sam."

Because O.B. calls me Samantha.

"Sam and Mika, Mika and Sam," Jess sang. "Come on back. I have everything set up from the details you sent me."

"Already?" Tamika asked, hurrying after Jess. Sam had to hold onto Tamika's arm to keep up with the wedding planner's long strides.

"Oh, I work fast, honey."

They entered an office space decorated in pale blues, pinks, yellows, and greens. Jess requested for her assistant to bring them champagne, and Sam settled for ginger ale. She hadn't done much drinking before her diagnosis, considering her father had called it the "devil's piss" *after* filling his system with it in the seventies and eight-ies. Now, she was too afraid of what it could do to her body to so much as touch a drop.

Jess lowered into a fuzzy chair behind an oversized pink desk with a glossy surface and gestured for them to sit in two purple guest chairs on the other side. In front of them sat an iPad each and, as Jess spoke, whatever she brought up on her computer came up on the iPads.

So far, the entire experience was impressive. Plus, Jess was amiable enough.

"Now, when you sent me the email with your timeline, I almost died," Jess said, frantically clicking the computer mouse. "I mean, your vision in, what, just about four months? And you want a Christmas wedding instead of the June weddings we see coming through here time and time again? I *knew* I had my work cut out for me."

A selection of venues appeared on the iPad screens. Sam picked up the tablet, made herself comfortable in her chair, and accepted the flute of ginger ale passed over her shoulder.

"But then I looked at the signature tag in your email, and even if you'd given me two weeks, baby, I'd still make it happen."

"You're familiar with Boone Publishing?" Tamika asked.

"Familiar?" Jess' eyes widened. "Boone has published some of my favorite books of the last decade. Plus, I make it my business to learn about as many powerful women as I can. Will you indulge me a bit?"

Tamika accepted a flute of champagne. "Of course."

"Okay, so one of my top ten..." She tapped her left index finger. "*Vampire at Antietam* by Joyce Hardy."

Tamika's sip of champagne nearly dribbled from her mouth. "Whoa, that's one of the first ones we put out. Jess, you're taking me way back."

"That started my love affair." She tapped another finger. "Okay, next we have *Snake Skin* by Judy Henry Williamson. That one resonated with me because I spent most of my life feeling like I was living in a body whose skin I needed to shed in order to be my true self. Without worrying about stereotypes and whatnot, you know?"

Sam and Tamika nodded, understanding.

"Another good one," Tamika said. "That was, what, six years ago?"

"You are really involved, aren't you? I figured, being the head of everything, you'd just sign the checks."

Tamika shrugged in modesty.

"Okay, well, a more recent one...*Ruse de Guerre* by Carson Hollister. I love that book more than I love my mother."

Sam's gaze flashed to Tamika just in time to see Tamika's smile spread from one side of the room to the other. She had to stop herself from searching through her purse for her sunglasses.

"What just happened?" Jess glanced at Sam. "I did something."

"That's my future husband. Carson Hollister, he's my baby." Tamika unlocked her phone, opened up her photos, and handed the phone to Jess. "Look."

Sam sipped her ginger ale, studied her friend, and wondered what it felt like to love and be loved in a true, open, and honest way. Love without subterfuge. And she wondered if that would ever be a possibility for her.

Orylin Brian: Are you and Mika still with the planner?

Sam: We're with the last one. Why, are y'all hungry? Cause I'm staaaarving.

Orylin Brian: We got something quick to eat. Carson said not to say anything to Mika.

Sam: I'm saying something to Mika.

Orylin Brian: That's why your ass is starving now.

Sam: Go away.

Sam giggled, drawing a look from both Jess and Tamika.

"It's nothing," she quickly said. "Carry on."

"Well, I'm happy for you." The honesty on Jess' face either meant she was an amazing salesperson or genuinely kindhearted. "And, if you look at these venues, the one that I think will best suit you if you want to stay in town is the Biltmore House."

A small presentation came up on the tablet.

Tamika oohed and ahhed, hands clasped beneath her chin.

"*If* she wants to stay in town," Sam said. "What if she can do overseas?"

Jess straightened in her seat. "I'm glad you asked. Now, if you truly want to go for the fairy tale, Christmas wedding feel, I present to you the Archerfield House in Scotland. The winter cycle is the same as it is here, and your guests can stay right onsite."

Tamika's eyes grew big.

Jess continued the presentation, going through the different preparations that would go into making the wedding of Tamika's dreams. The main caveat was that Tamika would have to make a decision before the end of the week if she was considering overseas because of her tight timeline. Even knowing who Tamika was, Jess presented the price tag with a subtle display of nervousness.

"Carson and I *did* agree to stay on a budget, regardless of what we can afford," Tamika mumbled, staring at the pricing sheet. "I can get a little carried away."

Sam reached into her purse. "Then you've just saved a crapload of money. Jess, do you need a deposit today or—"

"What are you doing?" Tamika grabbed her wrist. "Sam, you can't be serious."

"I can afford this in my sleep, Mika."

"That's not what I mean."

"Mika, these past few years...hell, this last decade has been *very* trying for me. Who was there for me, every step of the way? You've been there for me since the day we met, and I've always dreamed of being able to do something major for you one day. I owe you my life, so spending this money is nothing compared to what you've already given me."

Tamika's eyes filled. "Jeez, Sam. I wasn't expecting to cry today. At least, not over this."

Sam turned to Jess. "Whatever she wants. This is my sister."

"Yes, ma'am." Jess dabbed at the corners of her own eyes. "Wow. You're not much of a talker, but you're a powerful one."

Tamika picked up her phone and stood. "Let me check in really quick with Carson."

She headed to the back of the room.

Jess excused herself, and Jess' assistant refilled Sam's glass with more ginger ale.

Orylin Brian: Samantha Candace Norwood.

Her heart gave a tug.

Sam: Yes, Orylin Brian Daniels?

Orylin Brian: Am I eavesdropping correctly? Mika wants to get married in Scotland?

Sam: Yes.

Orylin Brian: Our wedding party is going to tip the demographics of the entire country. Are you sure they've ever seen this much black folk all at once?

Sam: Stop. I can't laugh this hard in a public place. And haven't they hosted the Olympics?

Orylin Brian: *Winter* Olympics.

Sam: Oh. Nvm. Hold on. Let me send you some photos.

She sent photos of the venue and Tamika's theme for the wedding. Tamika had originally wanted red, white, and royal blue, but after compiling inspiration photos, it had looked entirely too American patriotic. So, she'd changed her Christmas theme to silver, black, and white with pops of red. What Jess had created—fairy lights, holly, pinecones, and poinsettias all combined in a sophisticated elegance—was like she'd stepped directly into Tamika's mind and gave life to her concepts.

Sam: Nice, right?

Orylin Brian: Damn. It really is.

Tamika and Jess returned at the same time, and Jess waited for Tamika to sit before reclaiming her seat.

"Carson's on board," Tamika informed them. "He said to do whatever makes me happy as long as he gets to be the one standing across from me."

Jess released a long *aww.*

Sam thought back to her own wedding, held so close to her eighteenth birthday she'd barely been legally able to sign her own marriage papers. It was held in her family church, which was to be expected, and the décor had been simple bordering on plain. Her father had warned her that the day was for holy matrimony and coming together before God. To overshadow that with anything gaudy or colorful was sacrilege.

If fate granted her the chance to do it all over again, she wanted something beautiful and bursting with as much pops of color as the love she felt inside for her groom.

They finalized the planning schedule, and Sam handed her American Express card to Jess. When they finished, Jess gave them both warm hugs and walked them to the front of the building.

The minute they stepped outside, Tamika's stomach released a loud growl, and she pressed her hands to her belly. "Carson said they're just about through with his half of stuff to do for the day, so we can grab something to eat. We're meeting up at Lettuce-Eat for lunch. Since he's with O.B., they got a private dining room."

Tamika and O.B. teased each other every chance they got, but Sam had enjoyed watching how their relationship had grown as Carson and Tamika became more serious. It alternated between an older sister giving her younger brother a hard time, and a younger brother who derived comfort from pestering his older sister.

"They got something to hold them over," Sam said, making good on her promise to double cross O.B. and Carson. "Carson said not to say anything, but O.B. told me."

"A strainer can hold more water than O.B. can keep things to himself." Tamika frowned. "I can't believe Carson betrayed me over some food. We were supposed to be hungry together."

Her car alarm chirped, the lights flickering as they neared, and the pause that fell between them as they got into the car meant she was gearing up to ask the question Sam had been waiting for her to ask for a while.

Tamika started the car, checked the rearview mirror, and pulled out of the parking spot, headed for the main road.

"Something going on between you and O.B.?" she asked.

Sam shifted in her seat. "Why?"

"Sam, you don't just convince two men to eat your pussy one time and then nothing happens after. Something's up."

"Well, for starters, it wasn't just one time."

Thankfully, they'd come to a stoplight because Tamika choked half to death on a gasp.

"More than once?"

"Yeah. They did it...several times."

"Did you do the whole threesome thing?"

"No." *Maybe I would have if O.B. wasn't one of them.* "At the end of the day, I couldn't go through with it."

O.B. controlled her from the tip of her head down to her toes. If she'd gone through with having sex with them both, at the same time, two minutes in and Miguel would have sensed something wasn't right. He would have seen, on her face, that she'd blocked him out, against her will, and in her mind it was just her and O.B.

"I don't think I'd be able to handle those particular two," she confessed. "They'd break me in half."

"Trust me, I get it." Tamika clicked her blinker and went left when the light turned green. "I love my baby, but I'm not blind. O.B. and Miguel are *fine as hell.* I should've asked Carson if he'd be down to share *me* with one of them."

"If you had," Sam fiddled with her seatbelt strap, "hypothetically, which one would you choose?"

Tamika went quiet for a moment, deep in thought. "See now, that's a hard one. There are several variables to consider, like which one Carson is closest to because it influences whether he'd go through with it or not. And I've never seen them naked, but something tells me O.B. and Miguel have those monster dicks. Then Miguel's got those damn sexy lips, so you know that man can eat some pussy."

The interior cabin fell to an almost deafening silence.

"I'm right?" Tamika asked, a smile sparking on her face.

"Yes." Every occasion with the men came back to the forefront of Sam's mind, creating a deluge of sinful memories. "He's definitely an expert in the subject."

"But O.B., now, he's a whole experience," Tamika went on, changing lanes. "He's got those lips, those eyes, that body, that hair, that smile, those dimples. That fucking tongue, *Jesus*. If Miguel eats pussy, O.B. *engulfs* it. You know he sucks on the whole thing, lips and all. Like, he *gets in there*. He's one of those that'll grab your thighs if you try to run away and just bury his face in it."

Sam squeezed her thighs together. It was dangerous to have this conversation, see O.B. right after, and then attempt to stick to the agreement that she'd been the one to propose.

"Then to be fucked with that tongue? Lord have mercy."

Sam wiggled her phone. "FYI, I'm recording this for blackmail later."

"Ha! Carson knows he's," Tamika shivered, "more than enough man for me. But back to O.B. Now, can the brother eat pussy?"

Sam closed her eyes, pressed her head back against the seat, and tried to remember exactly why she'd ended the physical aspect of her relationship with Orylin Brian Daniels.

"Yes."

"Yes or *yes?*"

"Yes." She held up an index finger. "But, it's different. Miguel, he has a PhD in cunnilingus. O.B., it's like he got his first taste in college, got hooked, and could spend the entire night between your legs and be as happy as a fish. Miguel has a method that's practical, enjoyable, and effective. O.B., he's...hungry."

Tamika made a noise in her throat and flicked her tongue along the corner of her mouth.

"Hmm. Well, damn."

"I wish I could channel the feeling into you."

"Girl, me too. But, to answer your question, Carson and O.B. are best friends, so he'd feel more comfortable with me being up under somebody he knows. Carson being O.B.'s best friend means he might be opposed to seeing O.B. plowing his woman. So, I'd go with Miguel."

"Really?"

"Not because of expertise," Tamika clarified. "It's just that, Miguel seems like the type you can sleep with, have a good time, and then go back to your life, with your man. You'll never forget the way he sucked on your clit and looked into your eyes and made you feel like you were the only woman in the world for him. In that moment, in his arms, you were in love. But O.B., he'll fuck away your whole soul. One night together and you'll start thinking about marrying his ass. He'll fuck you until you only see in grayscale. You'll be outside his door talking about 'O.B., let me have your baby' after one night, and I'm pretty sure Carson wouldn't be okay with that."

Sam held back for as long as she could before she burst out laughing. Tamika swung into an empty parking spot at Lettuce-Eat then turned to Sam, grinning.

"Am I wrong?"

"No, but you are very specific."

"There's a reason O.B.'s left behind a trail of broken hearts." Tamika shut off the engine, but she didn't move to get out of the car. "Jerica's a lucky woman if she somehow managed to snag O.B.'s heart, and he can't seem to get her to let go."

Sam continued to laugh, but the statement struck her in the middle of her chest.

"Sam?"

"It's not a big deal, Mika."

Tamika scanned her face, seeing everything, like she usually did. "How bad is it?"

Sam stared out of the passenger side window. Anyone not familiar with the area would, at first glance, assume they were driving through a residential area, but that was Charlotte. That was North Carolina. The state could be trendy, sleepy, southern, and charming all at the same time. At one point, she'd considered leaving since she'd assumed she couldn't successfully live in the same state as her ex-husband, but Tamika was in Charlotte. Her headquarters were based in Charlotte. And now, so was the man she...

"I'm in love with him."

She wasn't embarrassed or ashamed to be in love with O.B. She was embarrassed because of the situation she'd found herself in. This was exactly what Tamika had feared would happen putting her in the same room as a man like him.

Tamika sighed. "I know."

"You do?" Sam's head whipped around. "How?"

"Babe, I'm your best friend. There are two things I've figured out without you having to tell me, one of them being your feelings for O.B. The other is...he's broken that back hasn't he?"

She hesitated. "In half."

"That meddling a-hole can fuck, can't he?"

"Honestly, it was only one time, and we can't use my experience as a unit of measurement since I only have John to go off of."

"How many times since it happened have you thought about doing it again?"

Sam flicked her fingers, counting the instances in her head. "At least four-hundred, thirty-two thousand and sixteen times."

"That happened to me with Carson." Tamika looked off to the side as though prepared to bestow a great wisdom. "After the Christmas party, I found myself lying in bed, looking at the ceiling, wondering what the hell happened. I lost like four hours' worth of sleep unpacking all the inaccuracies I had about white boys. Even looked at some interracial porn. I won't lie."

Sam pressed her hand against her stomach, the muscles sore from laughing with Tamika all day. Things would change once she was married. They wouldn't be able to spend as much time together as they had in the past, but it didn't feel like loss. In fact, her relationship with Carson had made their relationship closer in many ways. She and Carson were already discussing children, and Sam had waited her entire adult life to be called, "Auntie."

The right side of Tamika's mouth pulled back. "I will say this. Carson and O.B. have been friends forever, so if Carson thinks O.B.'s fall—"

Knuckles sounded on the driver's side window, and Carson's baby blues appeared through the glass. "We tried to wait for you guys to get out, but we're hungry."

Tamika turned to get out of the car, but Sam grabbed her arm.

"What were you going to say? Carson thinks O.B.'s what?"

Carson pulled the driver's side door open, all but dragged Tamika out, and they wrapped their arms around each other like they hadn't woken up in the same bed that morning.

Sam took a moment to breathe before getting out on her side.

On one hand, she wanted Tamika to finish what she was about to say so her brain would stop finishing and then erasing the rest of the sentence. On the other hand, O.B. would look good. It was pretty much a guarantee, and she had to prepare herself for it.

She'd expected him to be across the parking lot closer to where Carson's car was parked, but he was in front of her when she got out, so close they bumped into each other. He had on a lightweight, gray sweater and a white, collared shirt underneath paired with black jeans and sneakers.

He was perfection.

They awkwardly separated, and it took Sam a moment to remember she had to close the passenger door. At the very same time she reached for it, so did O.B., and he pushed it closed before she could pull her fingers out of the way. The side of the door clipped the tip of her pinky, and her eyes instantly filled.

"Shit. Baby, I'm sorry." He grabbed her hand. "Did I get you? Of course, I did."

"It's fine, O.B."

It stung like hell, but in about an hour or two, the throbbing would go away. The fact that her body had responded to the pain with a flush of blood that warmed her face and brought tears to her eyes didn't help her case. It *did* look like she was crying.

He took her hand, raised it to his mouth, and sucked her pinky between his lips. His mouth was warm, almost hot, and he stared into her eyes as the pain waxed and waned against the heat of his tongue.

"That's not in any medical journal," Carson teased from behind them.

Sam glanced at him over her shoulder. "I think I read somewhere that sucking on a finger after you've jammed it does help with the pain."

Having O.B. Daniels suck on *her* finger after it got jammed sent signals to more than just the part of her body responsible for thinking. In fact, each flick of his tongue along the tip of her pinky rendered her brain more and more useless.

He slipped her finger from his mouth, kissed the tip, and kept her hand in his as he lowered it. "I really am sorry, Samantha. I didn't mean to hurt you."

"O.B., you wouldn't ever hurt me on purpose."

"No, I wouldn't." His tone firmed, like he needed her to understand that he wouldn't. Like she'd had doubts he needed to assuage.

"You two just about done?" Tamika asked. "Or should me and Carson go inside and give you some privacy in one of these cars or something?" Whatever Tamika read on their faces made her add, "Actually, let's go inside before you two take me up on that."

Right before they entered the restaurant, O.B. released her hand, and the heat of his body behind hers disappeared.

Heads turned and lifted, but no one approached them. People smiled and waved, and from the way their smiles grew, she knew O.B. had responded directly to them.

A young man came walking from the direction of the restrooms in the back, tall and broad-shouldered with close-cropped, dark brown hair. He wore a UNC jersey and had a certain swagger about him that screamed college football player.

He rounded the corner, raised his head from his phone screen, and searched the front dining area. When he spotted O.B., he froze and his jaw went slack, parting his lips. In situations like these, Sam wondered how she'd managed to go this long without knowing who O.B. was. Football was huge in North Carolina—huge in the South, really—but it never ceased to amaze her just how many people knew who he was. Tamika had tried to explain that it was like Tom Brady walking around Boston or Peyton Manning, Indianapolis. It had all been gibberish to her until she'd started watching O.B. videos like some kind of fiend, and she'd only learned who they were because either O.B. had played against them or with them in some capacity.

"Xander McMichaels, right?" O.B. asked.

The young man continued to stare.

"That Heisman race was close," O.B. added. "For what it's worth, though, I still see you being a Hall of Fame quarterback if you decide you do want to go to the league."

Carson and Tamika headed to the private dining space. Sam hung back, now so invested in the exchange, she felt obligated to see it through to the end.

"Xander McMichaels." The young man, late to the introduction, held out his hand. "It's n-nice to meet you, Mr. Daniels."

They shook, and Xander looked at his hand like O.B.'s had transferred a fourteen-karat gold bar.

"Same here," O.B. said. "You hanging out with the family before you have to head back to school?"

"My dad." Xander pointed to a man in the corner who waved with a broad smile on his face. "It's just me and him now. My folks split up a while back."

"I'm sorry to hear it, but I'm glad he's in your corner. I don't know if I'd have done as well as I did without my father."

Xander's face flushed. "Mr. Daniels, do you mind if I take a picture with you?"

"You can call me O.B., and not at all."

They stood close together, and Xander snapped a quick selfie.

O.B. held out his hand again, and Xander slapped his palm against it. "Good luck out there this season. It's been a while since y'all have been this high in the AP poll. You know 'Bama's coming for you, though, right?"

"I've got something for them." Xander, visibly more relaxed, grinned, and Sam knew this was a kid who would be one of those "devastatingly handsome" types in a few short years. "I know DeMarcus Loomey's about to be on my *ass,* though. Man had like sixteen sacks last season."

They chatted a few minutes longer, talking football. Sam got lost in the names and stats they tossed around like the people at her company tossed around C#, C++, Python, and Java.

"It was awesome meeting you," Xander said. He looked over at Sam and waved. "Hope you and O.B. have a good lunch, Samantha."

After another quick wave, he headed to his table.

O.B. tilted his chin toward the private dining room. "Come on. You know how Mika and Carson get when they're hungry."

"But how'd he know my n—"

His hand on the small of her back stole the rest of her words.

They found Tamika feeding Carson a strawberry, their chairs so close to each other they might as well have shared one.

O.B. pulled out Sam's chair. When he drew his back, he examined the space between theirs.

"Those two are way too close, right?" she asked. "How can they even eat like that?"

"So, you see it too." He sat, and his thigh brushed hers. "Weirdos."

Carson and Tamika pulled away from each other and started up a conversation about what they'd gotten done that day as far as wedding planning.

Sam stared at her menu, but none of the letters came together to form actual words. Did O.B. tell Xander what her name was? Most, if not all people, had no clue she was the brainchild behind some their favorite gaming hardware and software, so there was no chance in hell Xander had recognized her. If O.B. had told him her name, who'd he say she was? Was she looking too far into something that didn't mean anything?

Her phone buzzed.

Their server arrived, a young woman with a deep caramel complexion and blond highlights in her chocolate-colored hair. Her uniform pants fit snug to her body, showing off curvy hips, full thighs, and a heart-shaped behind. Each time she turned around, O.B.'s gaze tracked her curves, and Sam wished, instead of jeans, she'd worn a tight pair of leggings.

Or a bikini.

Orylin Brian: Are we really about to be in Scotland in December?

Sam: Yes. But, it's going to be lovely.

Their server left, and Sam checked to see if O.B. watched the other woman walk away, but she found his gaze on her. He didn't say anything. He never had to. He had that practiced look. That "you're always on my mind" look, and it was hard not to buy-in.

Orylin Brian: We're about to cast a shadow over Scotland with our black asses. Carson doesn't have enough family to balance us out.

She bit down on her bottom lip to avoid laughing out loud and calling extra attention to their table.

Orylin Brian: By the way, I know you won't believe me, but when you got out of the car earlier, a brother got some old school butterflies.

Their server returned with refills of sweet tea and water, and Sam noticed Carson's gaze tracking her as well. Carson and O.B. looked at each other, silently conveyed something, and went back to their menus, and it reminded her of a trip she and Tamika had taken to Costa Rica. They'd spent the entire night sending those looks to one another each time a tall, bearded, or loc'd muscular masterpiece walked through the door. She'd probably still do it now if they went back, but at the end of the day, she knew who she wanted to be with.

O.B. sent her a GIF of Tom from *Tom and Jerry* staring lovingly at a picture with hearts all around his head. She responded with one of a cartoon cat blowing a kiss.

Orylin Brian: That your way of telling me something?

Sam: Please don't.

Orylin Brian: That your pussy loves me?

Sam: Don't text me for the rest of lunch. You're in text jail.

He laughed, and the sound spread through her belly.

———

O.B. SILENCED THE THIRD PHONE CALL, IN A ROW, FROM Jerica. He'd told her he would be busy for the majority of the day helping Carson with his wedding planning. It was only a couple hours past noon, and she knew what the hell "a majority" meant.

They'd talked last night and, as expected, their conversation had segued into discussing Sam. He'd reiterated that she didn't have to worry about Sam, but he couldn't give her a straight answer about whether or not he had feelings for Sam. If he told Jerica he did, she would fly across the country, break into his house, and stab him in his sleep. If he told her he didn't, it would be a lie...because he did have feelings for Sam.

A whole truckload of them.

Carson knew. He knew the feelings had officially gone from, "Mika's friend, Sam, is fucking beautiful," to "I think the universe sent Sam to be my future wife, and who am I to argue with the universe?"

He'd told Carson it was fine not to change the song when "A Couple of Forevers" came on in the car on the way to lunch, one of the songs Tamika had requested as part of their wedding playlist. He'd found himself suggesting Ed Sheeran, Lionel Richie, Adele, and even Elvis damn Presley because "Can't Help Falling in Love" had been one of his parents' wedding songs.

The server had slipped him her phone number, and she was a cutie with a fat ass who he'd usually have twisted up and laid out before the week was out, but she'd told the table her name several times and he still had no clue what the hell it was. He'd been too busy pulling off his sweater to give it to Sam. A comfortable body temperature had become his primary focus the minute he caught her first shiver.

"You sure your parents are okay with coming to Scotland?" Carson asked, leaning back so their server—*Yolanda? Maria? Kristen?*—could place his order on the table.

"My mother would go to Antarctica for your wedding," O.B. answered. *Desiree?* put his food in front of him, her left breast grazing the ball of his right shoulder, and she apologized and caressed the spot like she'd spilled a drink all over him.

He covered her hand with his. "You're good. No harm done."

She nodded, set down Sam's food next, and walked off. He tried to catch Sam's eye, but she gave all her attention to her salad.

"Mom-Bridgette did say it's about time one of her 'kids' got married," Carson went on, eyes gleaming with mischief. "But I don't think she'll have to wait too long for another one."

O.B. shot him a look.

"Raina, of course," Carson clarified.

Tamika held back a smile, mouth working a bite of her turkey breast sandwich. Carson had to have said *something* to her, but O.B. prayed Tamika had the good sense not to take it back to Sam. He didn't want Sam knowing how he felt if he couldn't do a damn thing about it.

"Don't call my mother Mom-Bridgette," he snapped.

Carson shrugged. "You told me to stop calling her *Mom*. What about Mama?"

O.B. ignored him, all but inhaling his grilled chicken breast. For somebody hellbent on not going back to the league, he ate and trained like he still played. It would be easy to stay in extremely good shape even if he cut back a little, but a small part of him hoped for *something,* so he couldn't. Not yet.

Samantha: Think our server wants some O.B. Daniels 🥒.

O.B.: Good. At least one person at this table wants it. 💔

Samantha: Stop. You know I want you. God, do I want you.

He choked, and Tamika reached over to pat him on the back.

Gwendolyn? magically materialized with a pitcher of ice water, refilled his glass, then crouched next to his chair and spread her legs much wider than was needed for balance. "Are you okay, Mr. Daniels?" she asked. "Can I get you *anything* else?"

Back in the day, roughly a year ago before a fateful Christmas Eve party at his club, he would have followed her request with an innuendo considering the girl was coming at him hard. He would have let his gaze fall to those spread legs and said something along the lines of not needing a drink, but that he could use something to eat. He would have continued to tease her like that, throughout the week, until they met up and he fucked away that twitch she kept playing up as she walked. She might even be a cool girl, funny and cute, but then if he found himself wanting to see her again, he would have a small heart attack and ghost her.

"No, I'm fine with this." He tapped his glass. "Thanks."

"Let me know if there's *anything* else I can get you."

"Actually," he motioned to Sam, "you need anything, baby?"

It was Sam's turn to choke on her food. "Um, I'm good, Shea. Thank you."

His nose wrinkled.

Shea?

For the rest of their meal, there were no more accidental brushes by *Shea's* breasts, and she kept her legs closed. Still, her service was friendly and efficient, so they left her a decent tip.

The manager came over to ask them if everything had been to their liking, and O.B. was surprised to find that the man spent most of his time looking at Sam. It was refreshing to not be the center of attention for once, but couldn't he have picked Tamika? Just because his girl had juicy lips and a nice body didn't mean the man couldn't let his eyes fall elsewhere.

They finished the conversation and left.

O.B. kept his body behind Sam's as they walked to the door, and before they stepped through it, he glanced back. His eyes met the manager's, and the man quickly looked away.

"Samantha," he called. "Put that sweater around your waist for me, baby?"

———

CARSON AND TAMIKA WEREN'T READY TO GO HOME YET despite them having dragged their friends all over town all day. Instead, they wanted to go for a walk and take in the different sights, which was mostly all boutique shops, spas, and restaurants. He and Sam indulged them, giving them the "betrothed" special treatment that would be snatched away once they were married.

O.B.'s phone rang. Again, he silenced it. When he looked up, Sam was watching him.

Cute ass.

They fell into step next to each other, keeping their pace slow so they didn't run into or over Carson and Tamika stopping every few seconds to point something out like they both hadn't spent more than a decade in North Carolina.

"Had fun today?" he asked.

"I did." Sam inclined her head. "Apparently, our day isn't over."

Their fingers brushed.

"You go into the office this Friday coming up, right?"

She bumped his side, and he let his hand linger at her waist for all of two seconds. "I do. We've got a huge meeting coming up. The NFL recently terminated EA's exclusivity rights, which gave them the sole license to put out games for the last fifteen years. As you know, we've been itching to enter the football video game market, so now is the time and your girl has to be prepared. We also want to get something going with college sports, but we're holding off until a decision about pay-for-play is made. If we use students' likenesses, we're compensating them in some way."

There weren't that many people around, and those who were didn't look like they were the type to grab their smartphones at every turn.

So, he took her hand.

She slipped her fingers through his and squeezed.

Not even his feelings for Jerica had developed this quickly, and he'd been less cautious back then. These feelings for Sam also felt different. Right now, they were walking hand-in-hand, and he didn't feel an overwhelming need to pretend to be happy. Each time their eyes met, she closed one of hers, wrinkled her nose, and looked away. He smiled, heart beating harder than it had before his very first championship game.

He'd never been here. He'd been in the realm of hot sex, trips from coast to coast, spending sprees, and passionate fights, but he'd never been here at "I can't stop staring at her" or "My heart is going to give out."

Or, "I think this is more than infatuation."

They weren't even having sex.

Tamika suddenly gasped. "Sam, look! Just for fun? Please?"

It was a wedding dress boutique. Tamika already had a custom dress being made, but she still wanted to try on dresses? He would never understand.

"Guys, you can go ahead and go do whatever," Sam said. "Me and Mika are going inside."

"We can stay."

It wasn't until Carson looked at him that O.B. realized the words had come from his mouth.

"Or, I can," he corrected.

"I mean, as long as you're not getting your dress from here," Carson said. "I don't want to see you in it until the actual day."

A salesgirl greeted them, and Tamika did the introductions.

As she ushered Sam and Tamika to the back, he and Carson sank onto a velvety half-circle that was supposed to be some kind seating. It was a shade of purple he'd never seen before and had looked itchy at first glance, but it was comfortable, especially on his lower back. All those hits had left him with lower back tightness that came and went whenever it felt like it.

Carson cleared his throat.

"Say what you want to say, Carson."

"I don't have anything to say. Just noticed the handholding."

"And?"

"It's cute. Sam's sweet, and it's obvious she cares about you. As we both know, I'm a longstanding member of the 'Fuck Jerica Fan Club.' Let's just say, if I was walking down the street and saw her and Hitler getting mugged—"

O.B. burst out laughing. "That example keeps getting more and more dramatic."

"O.B., I know shit about your relationship with Jerica your own family doesn't know." Carson clasped his hands behind his head. "I haven't liked her beady-ass little eyes since I met her. Sam, I liked almost instantly, and she hasn't given me any reason to think I should feel otherwise. Plus, she looks at you differently. She looks at you like you mean something to her."

He'd noticed.

It did things to his stomach, his chest.

Sam looked at him as though she would be the reason his pain went away before she was ever the reason to cause it, and those looks were why the memories of his relationship with Jerica were coming back at a rate he could barely contain.

When the memories were front and center, vivid and distressing as they were, it became nearly impossible to sleep. He'd hole up in the house for days on end until Carson or Miguel came looking for him. They'd play, like scenes from a movie—heels flying next to his head, broken wine bottles, blood, tears. The tension from when they'd dated would manifest as though he was still in the relationship, and he'd get crass and turn into an asshole nobody wanted to be around.

Carson knew Jerica had once scratched his face during an argument. She'd done it before a Sunday Night game, and he'd had to give an on-the-field interview after their team's win. He'd pulled a beanie with the team's logo down over his forehead to cover the marks there and let his hair fall over his neck to cover the welts along the column of his throat. Fortunately, he'd had enough beard to mask the ones along his jaw. To Carson, he'd made it seem as if it was a singular event *and* his fault.

Although that incident had happened a few months after him putting his hand around Jerica's neck, to this day, he didn't know how she'd gotten him to stay *before* blackmailing him. If Carson and Miguel ever found out he'd endured Jerica's manipulation, for years, they probably wouldn't see him as the same man. His *father* wouldn't see him as the same man, or a man at all.

A group of women entered the shop, and the way they squealed over one in particular, it was painfully easy to tell who was the bride-to-be. It was an amazing feat to watch the shop salespeople corral groups and shuffle women wearing wedding dresses through and around each other.

"I like her," O.B. said. "Sam, I mean."

"You've already told me that."

"I mean, I like her enough that I want to be with her."

"Then, like I said, make it happen."

He groaned and scrubbed his fingers through his hair. "You

know I can't do that. I can't put Sam, of all people, in Jerica's crosshairs like that. I never thought I'd even get *here* with anybody never mind with a woman like Samantha fucking Norwood. Jerica can destroy me, yeah, but I want to make sure Sam steers clear of the nuclear explosion."

"What do you mean, 'destroy' you?" Carson leaned forward, elbows pressed into his thighs. "O.B., what's the real reason you can't 'walk away' from Jerica for good? You two have a secret baby or something?"

"You and I both know my mother would kill me, revive me, and kill me again if she found out she had a whole grandchild she knew nothing about."

"True, but that's not what I asked you."

Sam peered around the corner and waved to get their attention.

Carson waited for an answer.

O.B. didn't offer one.

The only sign that Carson was on edge about seeing Tamika in a wedding dress for the first time was the way he ran his palms over his slacks. Everything else—his face, poise, voice—was even and confident, but Carson had been rocking sweaty hands since eighth grade P.E. class.

Tamika appeared, and O.B.'s chest tightened to the point where he had to rub his knuckles over the spot to dislodge the nothing stuck there.

Carson headed to his bride-to-be, who stood on a round pedestal, and let his hands land on the beading on her waist. "Wow, baby. You look beautiful."

She did look beautiful. The dress sparkled almost as elegantly as the brown in her skin, and it flared into a big, lacy skirt at the waist. But, while it was beautiful, it wasn't Tamika.

"Is this close to the design for your actual dress?" O.B. asked, chest burning and tugging even tighter. "Because I think you'd look more 'Tamika' in something a little more snug."

"Something that shows off your...curves," Sam added.

"Ass," he clarified.

Sam nodded. "Yes."

"O.B., didn't I tell you last year to stop talking about my girl's ass?" Carson asked.

O.B. continued anyhow. "Mika, you need a dress that doesn't hide it. You have a nice body. A nice shape. Flaunt it. At least I'm being up front with y'all. You know other men are out here looking."

"Other men aren't my best man." Carson squinted. "Fuck. Best *friend*."

O.B. stood. "Nope, you already said it."

"Here we go."

Sam sent him a wink that, for whatever reason, made the discomfort in his chest grow. He'd already known he would be Carson's best man. There'd been *literally* no doubt, even as Carson had dragged his feet. In the meantime, he'd already started planning the bachelor party, so the confirmation should have made him happy. At the very least, it should have done something to stop the ball of whatever was putting pressure against his chest wall. If not that then Sam's wink and smile, but each time their eyes connected, it got worse.

"Oh, wait." Tamika hopped down from the pedestal. "Look at this. You guys wait here. Come on, Sam."

"Mika, I don't—"

"Come on. For me?"

They left.

O.B. searched the room, but the only exit he could clearly see were the doors behind them that hadn't stopped opening and shutting since they walked in. Exactly how many people got married every year in the city of Charlotte?

When Tamika reappeared, she'd changed back into her clothes, and O.B. took a few steps back, toward the door. The hairs on his arms raised and his breaths grew short. Whatever was coming, he wasn't ready for it.

"Now, it wasn't easy to get her to agree to do this, but y'all didn't see her wedding dress from way back when. You know those doilies our grandmothers used to keep on their plastic-covered couches? Even those were cuter." Tamika peered around the corner. "Come on, girl."

Sam walked out, hands covering her face. "I don't know how you convinced me to do this."

Tamika dragged them away, which revealed the deep flush that warmed Sam's brown skin.

O.B. took another step back.

Sam's dress wasn't "poufy." It was elegant, off-the-shoulder, lacy, and *form-fitting*. The back dipped into a V that stopped at the top of her ass. Lacy cups outlined her breasts with a cutout in the middle where a smooth, circle of skin peeked through. It was the perfect combination of sexy and sophisticated, which meant it couldn't have been made for anyone else.

"Sam..." Carson stepped forward. "You look amazing."

O.B.'s throat slowly closed. The boutique was suddenly too warm. Music filtered in from somewhere, classical but familiar. He saw Sam, but he heard Jerica:

"I'll destroy you."

"You'll never be able to let me go."

"Try to move on and see what happens."

"Doesn't matter where you go or who you see, you'll always come back to me."

"I'm sorry, but you know I only get this crazy because I love you."

Sam wasn't like that. Sam wasn't like *her*.

But the way she looked standing there, right now, his brain migrated and conflated. It merged Jerica's words with Sam's face and body in that dress, and if he didn't leave right now, he'd die standing up.

He couldn't do this. She was cute and the loveliest damn woman he'd ever had the pleasure of getting to know, but in no world could he actually do *this*. No matter how different *this* felt or how different *this* was.

"I have to step out." He pivoted, shoved the boutique door open, and walked with no intention of stopping until he was far away from this fucking shop of horrors.

CHAPTER 8

"It's not you," Carson reassured Sam, headed for the door. "It's...*fuck*. I'll be right back."

She'd never seen O.B. look that way, as if he'd finally understood the truth about what had happened to his childhood pet goldfish. She'd noticed he'd seemed uneasy when Tamika walked out, but she'd attributed it to him being a man cooped up in a wedding boutique with too strong smells, too much chatter, and way too many symbols of matrimony and commitment.

Her lips moved, but her brain theorized and calculated. Tried to figure out what happened.

"Mika...I need to go change."

"He didn't run off because you look bad," Tamika insisted. "You look amazing."

"That's not it." Sam hopped down from the pedestal and headed for the dressing rooms in the back, Tamika trailing her. Even if they did catch up to him and Carson, O.B. would never let her "be there" for him, but it wouldn't be because he didn't need somebody. It would be because he simply couldn't. She knew a panic attack when she saw one, but as a man, she'd quicker get him to agree to a root canal without any sort of anesthetic before she got him to agree that was what had happened to him.

She changed out of the dress back into her jeans and top. They grabbed their things, along with O.B.'s sweater, and left the boutique, headed in the direction they'd seen Carson turn. More people than before now littered the small, outdoor plaza, bumping into and stepping around them, their bags scratching Sam's arms and legs. Even with both men's heights, it would be impossible to spot them in a crowd this size.

"Do you think it might be Jerica-related?" Tamika asked.

Sam sidestepped a man walking by with a small child on his shoulders. "Why do you say that?"

"Because, according to Carson, O.B. wanted to marry her at some point."

She ignored her chest, heart, and stomach. "Let's go to the cars. Maybe they headed that way."

Sam: O.B., are you okay?

For all they knew, Carson and O.B. were already in the next county over—it had taken her forever to get out of that damn dress. She shouldn't have let Tamika talk her into trying it on, but for a woman who'd been married before, she'd never seen herself in a beautiful wedding dress. They'd been messing around, so she'd figured it couldn't hurt to slip into one while they were there.

Tamika's phone chirped. When she looked at the screen, her brows came together.

Sam peered over her shoulder. "What is it? Is it O.B.? Is he okay?"

Carson: Have Sam drive my car. Take it home. O.B.'s not okay.

Sam snatched the phone and texted back.

Sam: What do you mean he's not okay? What's wrong? Is he sick?

Carson: I've got him.

Sam: This is Sam.

Carson: I can tell.

Sam: Can you at least keep me updated?

Carson: I promise.

What could have gone wrong *that* quickly?

"Sam, I think I might know why O.B. seems to be stuck on Jerica," Tamika said. "I could be way off, but I feel like it has to do with what just happened."

"Did they secretly get married and she cheated on him?" she asked. "Did he propose to her on live TV and she rejected him?"

"No. It's nothing like that. I...look, Carson doesn't care for Jerica. He *hates* Jerica. The way he talks about her...maybe I'm bugging."

Sam sucked in a breath, closed her eyes, and did a quick three-count. "Mika, just tell me."

"He let it slip that once, Jerica got into a fight with O.B. and left marks and scratches all over his face. O.B. freaked out right before the game because he knew there was a possibility of him having to do a post-game interview or, even worse, an on-the-field one. Carson gave him pointers on how to hide them, but it never sat well with him because of how panicked O.B. had been. O.B. said the fight was his fault, but Carson knows O.B., so he knew it was a lie. O.B. never wanted to talk about it, and this was back when they were twenty-two. Sam, he stayed with Jerica for *three more years.*"

Sam cocked her head to the side. "She scratched his face?"

His beautiful, perfect face?

Who, the fuck, was this bitch, and where did she live?

Was that the real reason for O.B.'s inability to "walk away" from her? All anyone saw was the man he *wanted* them to see—smiling, sometimes crass, charismatic, unbothered. In his mind, since he was twice Jerica's size, he'd likely convinced himself there was no way he could have been anything close to "abused." It also didn't help that with his complexion, his height, his power, and his career choice, no one would ever believe it.

O.B. included.

He'd probably even blamed himself for her attacks. Justified them. However, Jerica had gotten into his head and used that heart of his he hid from everyone, the one Sam loved so much, against him.

"Sam?"

Most men would sit and starve on the island of denial before admitting a woman was abusing them. There'd been a man from their church, Isaac, who'd gone to her father looking for advice on whether he should leave his marriage. According to Isaac, his wife "changed" when she was upset, and there were times he'd "feared" for his life. Her father's advice had been that marriages were supposed to remain unbroken and, as the head of the household, it was Isaac's job to "control" her.

She'd worked after school as her father's assistant at the time, and she'd wanted to grab Isaac as he left to encourage him to think for himself, but there was no way he would have taken marriage advice from a fifteen-year-old.

Two months later, Isaac's job reported him missing, and detectives found his body in a freezer at his wife's grandmother's house, which had sat vacant for some time. The wife ended up with a life sentence, but there was no punishment that would ever bring Isaac back to his children, friends, and family. She wasn't about to lose O.B. the same way.

Tamika shook her shoulders. "Sam!"

Sam blinked her best friend into focus. "They weren't walls, Mika."

"What are you talking about?" Tamika gently cupped her jaw and brought their faces close together. "What weren't walls?"

"O.B. didn't push women away because he's afraid to fall in love. He pushed them away...because he's terrified to."

"Nope, not moving."

O.B. didn't have the energy to keep fighting. If Carson wanted to keep his ass planted on the floor next to him, so be it. He'd ducked into the first restaurant he could find, asked if they had any private rooms available, and he'd been immediately accommodated. Now, he was also on the floor of said dining room with his forearms on his knees, his head bent, his fingers dangling, and his pride shredded.

They'd let Carson enter the room with his approval, and Carson had proceeded to sit, tip his head back, and wait silently until he said something. Sometimes he fucking hated this man he loved like a brother. Carson didn't care about convention. He didn't stroll in and tell him to man up. Hell, he hadn't even asked him what was wrong. He just...sat down.

Carson's phone vibrated, and he moved his fingers over the screen before tipping his head back again.

"That Mika checking in to make sure this wasn't some kind of ruse to go meet up with pussy?" O.B. asked.

"Pussy?" Annoyance swept over Carson's face. "Okay."

"What?"

"You get crass when you're hurting bad."

Carson's phone buzzed again.

"I'm fine, Carson. Go be with your lady."

"It's not Mika. It's Sam."

"And what does Sam want?"

"To be put out of her misery."

"What?" The pressure in O.B.'s chest made a loop and built again, for a different reason. "Is she okay? Where the hell is Mika?"

"Sam just wants to know if you're okay, I mean."

"Oh." He rubbed his chest. "Tell her I'm fine."

"You want me to lie to your girl?"

"She's not my girl."

It pained him to say, but it was the truth. They weren't good for each other. He was better off worrying about three things—money, parties, and pussy. She'd feel bad for a moment and probably curse him out for leading her on and indulging in her feelings for him, but she'd be fine. She'd get over him. All of them did. A woman was a woman was a woman. It didn't matter that she was the one he wanted.

He looked up at Carson's silence. "What are you doing?"

"Texting Sam that you're fine and she shouldn't worry because she's not your girl."

"Don't text her that shit."

Carson put away his phone. "You about ready to tell me what happened?"

"Nope."

"I can sit here for a while, you know? There's a bathroom, food… I can wait, and you know I can wait. Took me years to approach Mika."

A snort of laughter helped to lessen the pressure in O.B.'s chest. "I hate you. You know that, right?"

"Yep. So, what happened?"

"I don't know."

"Did Sam do something?"

"Sam?" O.B. stared at the pattern on the opposite wall, white trim over dark paint in squares and rectangles. "Hell no. Sam could never. But, seeing her in that dress…"

She'd looked good. He could understand that, conceptualize it. What he didn't understand was why it bothered him so much.

"It made you think of Jerica, didn't it?"

"How…how'd you know?"

"Because I'm still waiting for the day you realize just how much damage she did. Do you even remember what you were like before her?"

It wasn't the first time someone asked the question. His older sister, Raina, had asked during a probe about how he'd really broken his fingers. She'd threatened to "jump" Jerica on several occasions. He towered over her, but their one-year age difference made her see "baby brother" whenever she looked at him.

"No, but I'm sure you're about to tell me."

Carson shook his head, and a smile pulled at the corner of his mouth. "Before Jerica, it made sense that we were close friends to people when they first met us. O.B., you've been there for me more times than I care to count. You were there for my father when he got injured and had to be out of work for almost a year. Orylin Sr. and Bridgette didn't raise a womanizing asshole. They raised a gentleman who *adores* his sisters and takes care of the people closest to him. After Jerica, instead of me seeing my best friend, I found myself having to constantly remind myself of who he used to be."

He did the same thing. It was a constant battle between trying to make his way back to the man he used to be and risk getting caught up in the same shit that broke him, or put up wall after wall so he was never tempted to and therefore never risked anyone getting hurt.

"O.B., did Jerica get 'physical' with you more than that one time before the game?"

"Carson, let's be real. Jerica's like half my weight."

"So, why is it so hard to walk away from *her*?" Carson asked. "You're trying to tell me it's not because you have no idea what she'll do if you let her know you're truly done with her?"

O.B., not wanting to continue this conversation in the event he came upon a weak moment, stood and headed for the exit.

"Me, Sam, and Mika are going out tonight," Carson called after him. "I suggest you show up. Sam, at least, deserves an apology."

O.B. stopped in the doorway. "Why'd you wait so long to ask me to be your best man when it would have been me and no one else?"

Carson shoved off the wall and onto his feet. "I could have asked Miguel."

"No, you couldn't have."

"To be honest, as best man, you'll have to walk down the aisle with the maid of honor."

"And?" O.B. mulled it over. "So, I'd have to walk down the aisle with Sam. What, you thought that would make me explode?"

"Nope." Carson made his way over, steps slow like his next words would cause O.B. to lunge at him. "I was afraid you'd try to take over my wedding. O.B., you are falling fast, and you're falling *hard*. You drool out of the corner of your mouth whenever she's around."

"And, as my best friend, I expect you to hand me a tissue."

Carson searched his pocket and pulled out a receipt. "The best I can do."

He did lunge for him, but Carson backed out of the way.

He could say Sam was absolutely gorgeous, cute, intelligent, driven, accomplished, had *body*, and her pussy was made of magic and rainbows—he hadn't so much as thought about another woman since their night together. He could also say Sam was open in a way that encouraged him to be less closed off. For him, she was a single phone call from the other side of the country that had been enough to erase a rough day; a bright smile and a cute wave at the airport; a woman unafraid to show she was excited to see him, bouncing on her toes so much he'd *had* to scoop her up and hold her as close as possible. She was lying in bed on the weekend with her feet in his lap, bringing him a level of comfort he'd never known.

Sam was peace.

"Show up," Carson reiterated. "You love her. It's not the end of the world, but if you keep hurting her and she walks away from you for good, I guarantee it'll feel like it."

CHAPTER 9

Jerica: Please talk to me.

O.B. tossed back his *nth* drink.

He had no idea how many he'd had at this point.

Carson had asked him to show up, so he'd shown up. It was always good publicity whenever he showed up to his own spot anyhow. Plus, it was a good night. The room swayed each time he turned his head, the music wasn't so loud that he felt like his eardrums would explode, and everywhere he looked, he saw pretty smiles, short dresses, perked up breasts, and nice asses. There was one in particular he'd been watching since she walked in, and it bothered him that she hadn't looked his way once.

Jerica: Are you mad at me? What did I do?

He tapped the bar top, and two more shots were immediately sent his way that he tossed back, one right after the other. If he made it through the night without alcohol poisoning, it would be a miracle.

Jerica: Please answer me?
    I'm sorry.
    I'm so sorry.
    I love you.

He went to tap again, but Carson stepped in and signaled to the bartender to cut him off.

"What the fuck, Carson? This is *my* spot. I own this club."

"Which is why I'm going to make sure you don't end up on the news passed out in the middle of it tomorrow," Carson said. "You're trying to replace the blood in your body with Hennessy."

"Because all brothers drink is Henn?"

"Because that's what *you're* drinking. Don't fuck with me."

Jerica: I love you.

O.B. scrubbed his hands over his face. "Shit, I'm fucked up. What's up with Sam, by the way? She won't look at me."

Carson grabbed his rum and coke and thanked the bartender. "I don't know. She's been extra quiet all night. Go ask her."

O.B. turned his head in the direction where Sam sat, and the room took several seconds to catch up. There was no way this night would end well. If he was this messed up already, and he could hold some liquor, he was going to have a month-long hangover starting tomorrow morning.

Jerica: Do you still love me?

"You sure she's okay?" he asked. "She doesn't look okay. Don't lie to me, Carson. Is Sam all right?"

Carson jutted his chin toward the door. "Miguel's here. Maybe he can ask her."

Miguel walked in, greeted them with a quick dap up and embrace, and made a beeline to where Sam and Tamika were seated. The minute he sat, Sam's entire demeanor changed. She smiled and grinned, like she was happy to see him. Like Miguel was her man or something.

"You talk to yourself now?" Carson asked, left brow raised. "And why do you care if Miguel's acting like her man? Didn't you say she wasn't your girl?"

The music selection changed.

Tamika and Sam stood.

Sam's hair was curly again, those bangs brushing her beautiful brows, and even in a black dress in the dark, he saw every outline of that body. Each curve was the perfect size for his hands, which wouldn't be possible if they hadn't been made for each other.

She took Miguel's hand when he asked for hers and let him lead her to the dance floor.

Carson drained his drink and slapped O.B.'s shoulder. "That's my cue."

He walked off.

O.B. tapped again.

The bartender looked at him. "Come on, Daniels."

"Disloyal ass."

The man laughed and turned back to the rest of the crowd.

Miguel now had his hand wrapped around Sam from behind, his head down near her ear. Not even air could pass between their bodies, and she was dancing with Miguel like she couldn't *see* he was watching them.

137

"Fuck this." He started toward them, the room spinning, but stopped when arms wrapped around his middle from the front.

"There you are."

O.B. looked down. "What?"

"I mean, I know it's your club and all."

His vision cleared and half the alcohol he'd consumed burned away in an instant. "Jerica?"

She took his hand and walked them over to where Miguel, Sam, Tamika, and Carson danced. Her entourage watched her with raised brows—he recognized only two faces since her friends changed so often—as she pressed her ass against his crotch and rolled her hips. He held her waist with one hand to keep her upright; she'd bent so low, if he hadn't, she would have fallen flat on her face.

He glanced over at Sam, who still wouldn't look at him. Tamika, on the other hand, shanked him with her gaze, sticking the shiv deeper with each blink.

Jerica wasn't one to fly to Charlotte, of all places, for no reason. Either she'd planned reconnaissance on him or some kind of confrontation with Sam, but if Jerica approached Sam with Tamika, Miguel, and Carson around, she wouldn't survive the meeting.

The fact that Sam paid them no mind only spurred Jerica on. A sane person would have seen Sam wasn't interested and let the issue drop. A sane person would have remembered he'd said Sam wasn't his girl and wouldn't be envisioning his grip around Miguel's neck if his friend didn't take his hands off his woman.

Maybe he and Jerica really did deserve each other.

Jerica bounced against his zipper while her entourage egged her on, and he studied the difference between a woman who lived to tear people down and another who'd created an entire legacy that would cement her place in history. Sam thought she was shy, but her fine ass didn't give a shit about Jerica, and that made him smile.

Wide.

His and Miguel's gazes collided. Miguel ticked his head behind him then down at Sam, and they left the dance floor, headed for the exit.

O.B. leaned down to Jerica's ear. "Baby, I'm going to the bathroom."

She nodded, forehead sprinkled with sweat. "Okay. Kiss-kiss."

He kissed her cheek, navigated through the crowd on the dance floor, and passed the bathroom, headed outside where Sam waited in front of a car at the curb.

Miguel grabbed him before he reached her. "Get your ass in that car before I forget who I am and how long we've known each other. Stop being a fucking asshole. You're better than this, man. Better. But, on God, if you do this shit again, know I'm going to *fuck the shit* out of Sam, get her pregnant, and leave you to babysit our Dominican and Black baby girl while we have sex all over Italy."

The words took a while to catch up to him. He couldn't look anywhere else but at, in, and through Sam's dark eyes. Fate was a crueler bitch than karma if it had dropped her into his life *now*. Did fate not know what he could have done with her had there been no Jerica Waters? Tamika and Carson weren't the only ones who could have a fancy, overseas wedding.

O.B. blinked, Miguel's words finally unscrambling in his head. "Wait, what?"

"You heard me." Miguel shoved him toward the car. "Now, go."

"That's very damn specific."

"I said what I said.

Sam climbed into the back of the car and left the door open. He slid in next to her, shut the door, and the driver pulled off.

It wasn't the hangover to end all hangovers, but the shit was still bad. It was even worse that he was at Sam's house, where'd they gone straight to after leaving the club, and he'd been out of commission for two days.

Served his ass right.

She left him only long enough to get food, Gatorade, and electrolyte powder. Then, she was right there with him, pampering him and dabbing his forehead and making him feel like royalty. Fluffing his pillow and making sure his covers weren't too warm. It felt like there was a shoe waiting to drop, however. Like, the minute he was better, she was going to chew his ass out.

He wasn't wrong.

"You think I'm some kind of game to you?"

O.B. drained the rest of his bottle of Gatorade and licked his lips. "No, I don't."

"You're lucky I..." She paused, exhaled, and held up the forefinger and thumb on her right hand. "I was close. *Close*, O.B. But then I knew the police would ask me why I let you choke on your own vomit."

He scratched the side of his head. "I threw up?"

"As soon as we walked through the door."

"Damn."

"You threw up in my foyer, my bathroom, all over my fucking arm."

She was cute when she cursed.

"Did you even eat anything before you tossed back all those drinks? You could have killed yourself, and maybe you would have if Carson hadn't stopped you."

"So, you're mad at me for drinking?"

"For going overboard." She tossed up her hands. "What the hell would I have told Raina? Your parents? O.B., what would I have said to Delilah, *your little sister*, if something had happened to you?"

He wanted to hold her.

"Do better." Her voice cracked. "You have people in your life who care about you. People who...love you. Consider them, at least, for a second. Please."

"Come here."

"No."

"Is that why you left with me? Because I was drinking too much?"

"Yes." She answered like it was the most obvious thing in the world. "What other reason is there?"

"I thought you wanted to—"

"Hell to the no."

"Or you wanted me to—"

"Didn't cross my mind." Her shoulders relaxed. "How do you feel?"

"Like I received five-star service."

He was a little bit hungry, but he wasn't sure mentioning it wouldn't make her bring him rat-poisoned laced cereal or something.

"Samantha, I'm sorry."

"Don't." She sat along the edge of the bed. "We have to talk."

"We do, but let me say I'm sorry first."

Tears spilled down her cheeks, and he took a chance on his life by dragging her over to him and onto his lap. It was his favorite way to hold her since he could get both arms around her. Pull up her against his heartbeat.

He kissed her hairline where curls peeked, the rest covered by a patterned headwrap, over and over until the quiet, frustrated sobs subsided.

"My ex-husband fractured my jaw."

It was the quickest rage had ever filled his body. "When?"

"Back when we were still married. Most of our relationship was him using the Bible as an excuse to demean and debase me. The more he pushed, the more I pulled away. I'd seen, firsthand, what guilt and obligatory subservience did to my mother, and I didn't want that. Then, one day, he caught himself trying to 'beat' me. He didn't expect me to fight back, but I did, and I left that same night. Never saw him again without a lawyer present."

O.B. searched his mind to see if he could remember the name of the man's church and where in the state it was located.

"He was my only," she crooked her fingers, "boyfriend. He was my only lover before you. He was a good-looking man, but I wouldn't call him a masterpiece."

He caught every other word, still plotting this man's murder. It was one of the quickest ways to enrage him, people using their power —size, strength, money, influence—over someone else. Especially when a man used his size against a woman. But, now that he'd done what he'd done, he wondered if he was allowed to feel the same way. If he truly was the monster he often felt like on the inside.

"You told me that for a reason," he said.

"I did."

"Did Tamika tell you?"

"She speculated." She brushed her fingers along the side of his face, and it felt like coming home after roaming, lost, for months on end. "O.B., what did that bitch do to you?"

"You are *adorable* when you think you can use curse words. You blink and tense and—"

"O.B., you can trust me."

A single sentence, and it stopped his heart.

"I promise you can trust me."

He took a moment to compose himself, his thoughts. They'd

been dormant so long, they were all jumbled pieces of a puzzle he hadn't tried putting together in a very long time.

"Jerica has a temper," he said, shoulders tight. "I guess you could say she's my first love or whatever. When we met, I hadn't even caught a pass in the league yet, and the ink was still drying on my contract. One of my old teammates who went through the draft a couple years before me invited me to this house party-slash-barbecue thing he was throwing. He'd said there would be a 'shitload of women in attendance.' Even when I was still in college I'd get pussy thrown at me left and right, and I was barely twenty when I got drafted. There was zero chance of me not going."

Sam eased off his lap and lay on her side next to him on the bed, but he needed to feel her. To hold her. To bridge the gap, he lay on his stomach and nudged her leg over his.

"The last thing I expected was to show up to this party and fall for some girl, you know?" he went on. "But, maybe an hour or so after I got there, Jerica showed up with some friends. She had a cousin who...let's just say, her cousin never met a ball player she didn't like. Jerica was nineteen and fresh-faced. Cute. I spent the rest of the night talking to her."

"Nineteen and at a party with a bunch of professional ball players?" Sam asked. "That had to be a little terrifying."

"She told me I made the experience much easier to handle."

He'd later learned it hadn't been her first party, as she'd claimed, but by then, he'd been so in love with her, he was surprised each time he inhaled he didn't suck debris from the field up into his wide-open nostrils.

"So, that's when you started dating?"

"Nah. I got her number, but I didn't call her until like six months later. Like I said, I was young and caught up in the life. That, very quickly, got old for me."

He'd craved stability. Falling asleep in a different pair of arms every night wasn't something he'd ever expected he'd get sick of. He'd seen other players, rookies and veterans, with different women every night, running trains, partying, popping pills. He'd assumed it was what he should have been doing. Pills wouldn't ever be his thing, and he'd only tried weed once, in a non-smokable form, because he'd needed his lungs in prime condition to beat some of the best corners and safeties in the league. But Patrón and pussy? It was like his birthday, every day.

"I'd see my boys and teammates going through women like tissue paper, and my ass was there wanting somebody to call after the games. Somebody to take on trips and get to know. I thought something was wrong with me. So, I called Jerica...and she didn't pick up. I kept calling her until she finally did, and she cursed me out about being treated like an option and whatnot. The whole time she cussed at me, I was like, 'I think I like this girl.'"

Sam exhaled with a low groan.

"Sam, do you really want to hear all this?"

"No." She licked those lips he loved so much and reached for his hand. "But...go ahead."

The memory came back as if he was sitting in a movie theater watching his life play out. His chest tightened at the same time Sam's grip did, as if she could tell what went on inside him. She shouldn't have been the one doing the consoling. It should have been the other way around, beginning with him finding her ex-husband's church.

"She started wailing on me with a metal bar one night, about a year into our relationship. It was after I told her I was breaking up with her because things were going downhill fast. The next thing I knew, she just started swinging." His chest tightened further. Sam squeezed. "And, I flew off the handle. I mean, not even my mother hit me like that."

"You grabbed her." Sam released his hand and smoothed his brow. It was the simplest gesture, but it soothed him like a drug. "And it left a mark."

"I wasn't even trying to hurt her, Samantha. I swear. I would never do that to you, and I don't want you be scared I'd ever—"

"There's nothing about you that makes me think you would."

There wasn't a day he didn't blame himself for not having better control over his temper.

"I still feel like shit for grabbing her. She called the police. Called her father. They took pictures. Her father's good with the police department, so they buried the whole thing, but those pictures still exist."

"And that's what she's threatening you with."

"Yeah."

She smoothed the other brow. "When did you two break up?"

"I stayed with her until I was twenty-five, tense and nervous the whole time because she could have decided to release the photos anyhow. I don't want people to see me that way, Sam, and I don't want my folks to know. I mean, I can already see my mother's face and..."

His mother would be ashamed of him if she found out what he'd done. That wasn't how she'd raised him. How she'd raised him to treat women. He'd failed her enough by fucking around and making it that even Carson had started seeing him as a dick. If he tossed this on top of the pile, none of them would ever look at him the same way again, and he loved them too much to stomach that.

"Anyway, when she left me and started seeing Landon, I thought I was in the clear, but things weren't the same for me after that. I couldn't get close to anybody, and I was afraid that if I did, she'd pull the shit she's trying to pull now."

Or worse, he'd unwittingly fall for another Jerica who would go one step further and take his life.

At one point, he'd convinced himself she'd been right to call the police. He *did* grab her; he'd never done anything like it in his life, so it had left him feeling like he didn't know himself. Like he truly was dangerous.

"She just kept..." He mimed the motion with his hand, the bar Jerica kept swinging. "And I'm taking these blows to my head, my neck, my shoulders, arms. Then, when she hit my fingers and I felt that *pain*, I just snapped."

"What pain?" Sam asked.

"These." He spread the fingers on his left hand. "She broke three of my fingers."

"Jerica *broke* your fingers?" She cycled through several deep breaths, eyes glossed over with rage she didn't so much as attempt to rein in. "Bet she apologized that night, didn't she?"

"All night."

"And you guys had sex."

"It was like a drug, I think. The way she'd get me keyed up was like a high. She'd do *things* I'd done before, in bed, but it was different because she was my girl. She'd then do something—break my fingers, throw wine bottles at me, fucking burn me—apologize, and fuck me into submission again. When I realized I couldn't keep forgiving her, my dumb ass went and grabbed her."

She gripped his shoulder tight, as though she wanted to be his warrior. "So, have you figured it out yet?" she asked.

"Figured what out?"

"Why you're a 'dog'?"

He laughed. "Samantha, I know how I love. I know how hard I love. I want what my folks have."

"That's *one* of the reasons you have those walls up." She stared at him. Stared through him. "I meant the other reason. How do you know something like that won't happen again?"

He didn't.

He didn't know it wouldn't, and he didn't know if he'd be able to see it coming to get out before it was too late.

"You're scared."

"Sam—"

"You're a man. A *Black* man. I know what society tells you you're supposed to do, how you're supposed to be. I know how society portrays you. Here, in this country especially, we do this thing where we put color and crime on the same spectrum so that at birth, you're already guilty in the eyes of the public if you happen to be born on the darker end. But you told me that your father explicitly told you to ignore it. To listen to him. That right there?" She pointed in a random direction, in the air. "That's called Intimate Partner Violence. She doesn't have to be stronger or bigger than you, she just has to have control over something you care about, whether it's your kids or, in your case, your future. *That's* why you left the league, isn't it?"

The assumption had been that, once he left, he'd be able to slink into the shadows. He'd used his money wisely, so finances hadn't been an issue. However, retirement had further catapulted his status. People started seeing him as noble and decent and mysterious, making him feel even more stuck than before because it made it a much higher fall from grace should it occur.

"Would you ever go back?" she asked. "To football, I mean."

"Now?" He drew her across the bedspread, closer. "I don't know. I still love the game, but...I don't know."

When she was silent for a while, he realized she'd drawn the same conclusion he had, and he almost choked getting the words out.

"Sam, I have feelings for you too. A shitload of feelings. I've had

147

them for a while, and I do a particularly terrible job of hiding them, so I know you can tell."

She closed her eyes, aware that his next words would be painful.

"But, I don't want you getting mixed up in this. I've felt like your protector for a long time now. I even got mad at Carson for not hooking up with Mika sooner so I'd be able to meet you sooner. I would have been there for you, every day and night. You would have never spent a single day alone during chemo. I would have even seen if I was a match for bone marrow donation."

"Don't..." She buried her face in his shirt, against his shoulder. "O.B., you can't tell me that and then tell me I can't have you."

"I want you, in every way. *God,* Samantha, I want you. I want to be with you more than you know. But all this drama? I don't want you in part of any of it. You lived a quiet life before me and my Jerica bullshit dropped into it. I'm not taking that away from you."

Her voice was strained. Tired. "It was a long shot anyhow."

"Yeah, it was. I mean, why the hell would a beautiful woman who's the CEO of an international, multimillion-dollar company with a nice ass and good pussy be interested in me?"

When he felt her tears collect on his shirt and heard her sobs instead of the laugh he'd been going for, it tore through him.

"I never wanted to hurt you," he whispered. "I never wanted to hurt *you.* Baby, I *never* want to hurt you..."

CHAPTER 10

"Your meeting with the NFL commissioner is coming up, and the Neerja Bhanot-inspired game finally moved out of story development. Also, NYU wants to make a bid to have exclusive rights to the simulation game. We let them know it's still a no because you want it widely-distributed for students to have access to."

Sam paced the room while her assistant, Layla, read off her schedule from her desk. She was too antsy to sit. It had been about a week since O.B.'s revelation, and she'd never wanted to scalp another human being as much as she wanted to peel Jerica's away from her skull.

They couldn't be together.

Fine.

It made her want to huddle in the corner, rocking with mascara stains on her cheek, until she fell asleep, but she *understood.* The risk to his livelihood was too great. If Jerica messed around and got really dirty, O.B. could end up in a worse situation than a lost career and endorsement deals. The last thing she wanted was for the other woman's lies to send the police to his door. She didn't want the police anywhere near his precious body.

"Lunch with Mr. Daniels is at noon, and then your afternoon is free."

"What?" Sam stopped and faced Layla. "Read that back again for me?"

"Um," Layla scanned her notes, "lunch with Mr. Daniels at noon, and th—"

"I don't remember scheduling lunch with O.B."

Layla smiled, her eyes taking on that dreamy, enamored effect that came whenever several dozen of the people working under her mentioned his name. "He called to set it up. Your schedule was free, so I figured it was okay? If not, I can—"

"No, it's okay."

"Miss Norwood, he's so fine." Layla giggled and covered her mouth. "Are you two dating?"

"Excuse me, Miss Norwood?"

Sam turned.

The woman who spoke, the one wearing the sleek pantsuit, was someone who worked in the building, but Sam couldn't recall her name right then. The other woman wearing the body-hugging black dress, Jimmy Choos on her feet, and had a Birkin bag tossed over her shoulder, she instantly recognized.

"Your name?" Sam asked the woman in the pantsuit.

"Kate, ma'am. I tried to tell her that you were busy—"

"It's okay, Kate. You can go back to your desk. Thank you for walking her up, however." She held out her hand. "What can I do for you, Miss...?"

Jerica's cheeks tinted. "You know who I am."

"Should I?" Sam ticked her head toward the door, and Layla grabbed her things and hurried out. "I didn't know Kate, and she works for me."

"My name is Jerica Waters."

"Ah. Nice to meet you, Miss Waters."

"Jerica's fine."

"And what I can do for you?" Lunch was in twenty minutes and O.B. had a habit of being punctual. She'd put money on the fact that he didn't know his ex was in the building.

Jerica held out her phone. On it was a picture of Xander and O.B.

"Xander McMichaels and O.B. Daniels," Sam said.

"No." Jerica turned the screen back to her, pinched to enlarge the photo, and stuck out the phone a second time. "That's you in the background, isn't it?"

Sam nodded. "Good. Yes, it's me."

"With O.B."

"Miss Waters...Jerica," Sam rubbed her forehead, "if you learn nothing else from this exchange today, I hope you remember that leading questions are pointless. So, kill the subterfuge and tell me, straight out, why you're standing in my office."

Jerica straightened her spine. "I keep asking O.B., but he's a natural born liar, so I came right to the source. Are you and O.B. seeing each other?"

Unfortunately not.

Because of you.

"No."

Jerica bristled. "You're not?"

"No."

"Are you fucking him, then?"

Sam dragged her tongue over her top row of teeth. "Jerica, let me explain something to you. You walked into *my* building, into *my* office. I'm a very busy woman, so I'm being nice by entertaining this conversation with you. You have five minutes. Use them wisely."

To her surprise, Jerica's mouth twitched. The corners tugged downward. A vat of tears sprung forth.

That mess doesn't work on me, Judas.

"Why are you crying?"

"Because all this time," Jerica swiped at her nose, "I thought he was in love with you. We went to my movie premiere together...I'm an actress, you see...and things started getting hot and heavy in the limo. Then your name came up."

"How?"

"It's not important."

"You are O.B.'s...what?"

"Fiancée." Jerica wiggled her fingers. "He doesn't listen and got the wrong size ring, so I'm having that fixed."

Fiancée? Next, are you going to tell me you're pregnant with his baby, Delilah?

"You have two minutes, Jerica."

"That's all I came here to get squared away." Her tears dried up faster than a droplet of water in the Arabian desert. "And, if you were even thinking about getting involved with him, I should probably tell you this." She lowered her voice. "He hits women."

"Sixty seconds, Miss Waters."

Jerica nodded and readjusted her purse strap. "Thank you for your time."

She headed toward the door, but Sam called out to her.

"You said you're an actress?"

Jerica spun around. "Yes."

"Do you know Michaela Davis?"

"Michaela Davis?" Her eyes grew wide. "Of course. She's one of the best directors in the game."

"We're good friends."

Jerica's lids pushed back even further. "Oh my God, Miss Norwood, it would mean so much to me if you could put in a good word."

"Do you have your bio? A resume?"

Jerica reached into her Birkin and pulled out a prepared folder. "Right here. I can get you a digital copy too if you need one."

"This is fine. It's always good to see women prepared when opportunity strikes. Michaela has some huge films planned and just one of those could catapult your career. If...that's what you want."

The girl was practically running in place. "That would be so amazing."

"All right. Expect a phone call."

She squealed and started forward like she was rushing in for a hug, but the look on Sam's face made her stop short.

She cleared her throat. "Thank you, Miss Norwood."

"You're welcome." Sam turned away, facing her desk. "Have a good rest of your day."

Once Jerica was out of sight, she flipped through the folder. She did have Michaela on speed dial. They'd both gone to the same university and pledged the same sorority, and she *would* go through with her promise and send Jerica's information over.

She hopped up on her desk, pulled out her phone, and scrolled through her contacts. Then, she set the folder down and leaned back on one hand.

"Hi, Deitra?" she answered. "It's Sam. Is there any way you can get me a face-to-face with Landon Johansson?"

Several minutes into her attorney's spiel, O.B.'s face appeared in the doorway to her office, and Sam's heart tumbled into her stomach. He was so damn beautiful. It was funny how simply seeing him could make her happy, all extra casual and sexy in a pair of jeans and sneakers with a jacket tossed over his hoodie.

She held up a finger to let him know she'd be right with him, and he busied himself by looking at the games she had on her wall. Every disc, their sizes shrinking as the years went by, was on display in its own individual case. There were also the gaming consoles they'd released throughout the years, those remaining around the same size just with more gigs, better RAM, lightning-speed processors, and constantly evolving graphics cards.

"Okay, thank you, Deitra. You too."

She hung up.

"You look good up on that desk," he said, walking over. "I like the way those skirts fit you and how you pair them with those tops and belts that show off your shape. Aren't those called pencil skirts?"

"Yep." She rubbed his sleeve between her thumb and index finger. "And you look nice all the time, especially today."

The air grew charged between them, the tension thick and delicious enough to lick, and she hated to have to break it, but she didn't want O.B. to hear from someone else that Jerica had popped in for a visit.

"So..." He stepped between her knees. "Ready to have lunch with me?"

"In a minute." She sighed, shoulders lowering. "Jerica stopped by today."

His expression went from horny to confused to pissed. "For what?"

"To ask me if I'm dating you or 'fucking' you."

"The fuck?"

"I told her I wasn't."

"You shouldn't have to tell her anything." He took a half step backward. "How long ago was this?"

"About fifteen minutes or so before you showed up."

He looked up at the ceiling, head shaking. "I don't want you in this shit."

"I'm not afraid of her, O.B. Plus, we're not together. Even if we were, now that I know what I know, I'll do what I can to protect you." She hopped from the desk, turned, and stretched across it to grab her purse. "It's not like I'd want her in our business any—*oh*."

He'd moved behind her, his fingers sinking into her hips. His warmth brought a sense of comfort, safety, and longing for his tongue in her mouth, between her legs, and him inside her body. Ever since that night where he'd essentially bared it all to her, they'd been wanting to jump each other's bones more so than usual.

"You ready to go eat something?" she asked.

He hugged her from behind. "I mean, I had lunch planned but you're looking a little bit better."

"Where are we eating?"

"On a boat. I figured that should give us a decent amount of privacy, right?"

Sam turned around. He didn't try to step back, which left her practically molded to him. Lord help her. It would be a task to end the day without ending up underneath or bent over in front of this man. Her brain told her that since she already loved him, there was no way sleeping with him could make her love him more. But then her heart smacked its lips, rolled its eyes, and chided her brain for making decisions based on territory about which they were both unfamiliar.

"Sam, Sam, Sam. We were doing so good before." He drew her even closer, anchoring her to his body. "What happened?"

They'd opened up to each other. He knew her fears and now, she knew his. There was one last frontier to intimacy their bodies wanted to venture through, and it was no longer hidden.

They heaved sighs at the same time and broke apart. He looked like he wanted to take her hand, and she was sure she looked like she wanted him to offer, but they headed for the elevators with what felt like miles between them even though it was only a couple of feet.

HE'D SAID BOAT.

It turned out to be a yacht.

It wouldn't be her first time on a yacht, but if he'd said yacht instead of boat, she would have known they'd definitely have access to a bed. She would have known that, after eating Bánh mì made with chicken breasts for her and the traditional way for him, after eating fruit and chocolate soufflé and drinking sparkling, alcohol-free brut while he sipped on an Old-Fashioned—or three, and after watching the sunset while he held her from behind, they would end up *here*.

In said bed.

Now, she stood in front of him while he sat on the edge of the mattress. His mouth and lips teased her red boyshorts, and every so often, he dragged his tongue along the curve of her behind. If it hadn't been for the hand he'd wrapped around her, she would have fallen to the floor a long time ago.

"I promise I didn't plan this," he said, breath warm against her skin.

"Even if you did, O.B., I wouldn't care."

He slipped his fingers into the waistband of the boy shorts, dragged them down over her legs, and tossed them where they'd discarded her skirt. She was surprised they'd made it to the bedroom; she'd all but attacked his mouth on the deck, and they'd maneuvered to the room as a pair of torsos with roving arms, stumbling legs, and no space between them for so much as an idea to pass through.

"Fuck." He gripped her hips. "So damn beautiful."

He nipped the curve of her bottom. Her hiss turned into a moan, unexpected pleasure coursing through her as he soothed his bite with a swirl of his tongue. He did the same to the other cheek and then eased back and smacked her with an open palm. This time, he didn't soothe the sting, but she found she didn't want him to.

"Damn, I can see that shit from here." He slid his fingers between her legs. "Is all this for me?"

"Yes."

He slipped two fingers past her entrance, and she wished she'd done this closer to something to hold onto.

"Sam, Sam, Sam! You are so damn sexy."

"Me?" She managed a strained, breathy laugh. "O.B., you are the sexiest, most beautiful man I've ever seen in my life."

He spun her around. "The first time I tasted you, I was drunk as shit."

She moaned through another laugh. "You both were."

"But I never forgot." He drew her closer. "I never for—"

His lips latched on to her lower ones, his tongue wasting no time jutting out to part her. The first swipe sent a rush up and through her body, turning her nipples into firm points.

He was good at this.

So good at this.

He eased off the bed, crouched in front of her, and tapped his left shoulder. "Put your leg up here for me."

"Just," she examined it, visually testing for strength, "on your shoulder?"

He didn't look at her. He didn't look at anything except between her legs, his lips glistening in a way she never expected to find so erotic.

"Yeah."

Then, his tongue was on her again, and when she lifted her leg onto his shoulder, it gave him access to go deeper. To lick the entire length of her sex, flicking and sucking, before he settled on the bud between them. His head bobbed as he worked her, and she alternated between looking down at him and letting her head tilt back, eyes closed.

"O.B., that's so good, baby."

He moaned and drew her even closer, covering her with his mouth. Each flick of his tongue begged for her nipples to be touched, so she unbuttoned her top, slid it off her arms, and unhooked her bra clasps. The bra fell to the floor, and she took her left breast, kneading it to match the motions of his tongue. She stuck her fingers in her mouth and stroked her nipple, and her other hand went to the back of his head. When he glanced up and spotted her playing with her nipple, he groaned and his eyes rolled behind his eyelids.

"Just like that." He spoke the words between each flick of his tongue. "Grab my head, baby. Put me where you need me."

She tilted her hips.

Every squeeze of her nipple, flick of his tongue, and harsh sound from his throat pulled her closer. And closer still. Then, he slipped two fingers inside.

"O.B.? Baby, I'm close."

His tongue flicked faster, and his fingers thrust harder.

Pleasure shot from her core to every part of her body. Her muscles quivered and clenched his fingers in waves. Moaning, he lapped and slurped at her until she shuddered and pulled away. When she did, he laughed, returned to the edge of the bed, and pulled her between his knees. Their lips met, and tasting herself on his mouth was always, surprisingly, one of the most erotic parts of the act for her.

He licked his way around her mouth. "We can stop here if you want."

"With you sitting there hard and unsatisfied?" She stepped back, held his face between her hands, and looked directly into his eyes. "O.B., I want you."

And I love you.

He couldn't hear the words she didn't say, and there was no guarantee he could see it in her eyes, but she hoped the message was still somehow conveyed. She didn't just want him tonight. She didn't just want him because he worked his tongue like some kind of Black warlock. She wanted him because he was easy to love. Although hidden, she'd still seen his heart. With him, she felt cared for and protected. He was sweet, and he made her feel beautiful without trying.

He searched her eyes, his grip tightening and releasing on her thighs. "I wish it was you."

"Wish it was me, what?"

"That I'd met seven years ago. I've been thinking that a lot lately."

She tangled her fingers in his locs. "How do you think things would be different?"

He lowered his forehead to her stomach, and she knew what came next was going to make her heart hurt without breaking it. It was going turn her stomach without making her feel sick.

"I don't know." His right shoulder lifted, lowered. "Maybe we'd be married."

"What about kids?" she asked. "I could see myself having a kid with your dimples. They'd be spoiled as hell, but cute."

He released a short, quick laugh. "And your eyes. I wouldn't want my daughter getting your mouth, though. Men, we think some sick shit when we see a pair of nice lips."

She tilted his face up and pressed her lips against his. "These lips?"

"*Mmm.*" He wrapped his arms around her. "Yes. Those lips."

She didn't know if it was the same for most other people, but her favorite part about kissing wasn't when she moved in to kiss some-one. It was the relief she felt when they kissed her back.

O.B. kissed her in a way that made her think he tasted her and realized he wanted to get drunk on her, his tongue darting in and out of her mouth. The hairs of his beard against her palm with each tilt of his head added an unexpected erotic sensation that carried all the way to the throbbing between her legs. He tasted like the Old Fash-ioned, sweet and bitter and citrusy, and he kissed her in a way that made her wonder if, possibly, maybe and hopefully, he was in love with her too.

They broke apart only long enough for her to tug and tear him from his clothes. Then she went back to him, their mouths hungrier, and he tipped them backward onto the bed and rolled so she was underneath him, the sheets cool and smooth against her back and legs.

"O.B.?"

He groaned and bit down, gently, on her bottom lip. "I love hearing you say my name."

"Please." She raised her hips, the wet and warm flesh of her sex meeting the flushed skin of his erection. "Please…"

He presented a packet, tore it open with his teeth, and leaned back to slide the condom down onto his length. It bobbed with each roll of the latex, and she was hit with an overwhelming desire to put it in her mouth. To suck until his toes curled. Right now, she wanted it inside her but, as far as she hoped, there would be a next time.

"How old is your father?" he asked, climbing over her.

It was an odd question to ask when they were both naked. "He had me older. He's seventy-nine. Why?"

"When God tells him what I'm doing to his 'innocent' daughter, I want to make sure I can take his old ass if he comes at me."

She laughed against his forearm.

The tip of his length met her entrance and he pushed his way inside, filling her. Allowing her to feel every solid ridge.

When he withdrew, she grabbed for him.

"I'm coming right back, baby." His groan stretched the length of his stroke. "You know I'd never get too far away from you."

And he kept his promise, pushing his way into her again, this time a little harder. Faster. She'd wanted him again for such a long time, dreaming of him and fantasizing, but she never thought it would actually happen.

"I'm yours, O.B." She couldn't help it. Couldn't keep it in. "All yours."

Their lips came together and he tilted his hips faster, but he kept a steady rhythm that she felt inside and out.

"You are?"

"I am."

Slow and steady went out the window.

Each thrust of his hips slid her along the sheets until she reached the headboard, and she pressed her palms against it over her head to keep herself in place. The movement opened up her breasts to him, bouncing with each thrust. He closed his eyes and a grimace covered his face.

Sam glanced down and even she started getting further turned on with the way her breasts leapt each time their pelvises connected, the brown areolas smooth and ripe for licking.

He opened his eyes, growled a low, "Fuck it," and lowered his head. Her left nipple firmed right before his mouth covered it, anticipating the warm play of his lips and tongue, but she didn't expect the sudden rush of pleasure between her legs, like a jolt of electricity.

When he raised his head and moved to the other nipple, the sensation hit her anew, and she cried out. Her hands collapsed, and he stopped only to prop pillows above her head against the headboard before driving into her again.

"Yes, O.B." He was as deep as she wanted. As thick as she needed. "Yes, yes, yes." She raised her hips to take him deeper and immediately regretted it when he found the horizon. "*Oh my God.*"

"Right?"

"I can't hold out any longer."

"Then don't."

She gasped and cried out, arching up toward him as her climax burst through her, every muscle in her body going slack except for the one squeezing him. He drove into her with a few more hard pumps and released while her skin blended with his and their sweat dripped and beaded.

Her heart gave an, "I told you so," tug. It *was* possible for her to fall even more in love.

"We'll be together, Samantha," he said, voice deeper than usual, rumbling near her ear. "I don't know how, but," he pushed up, onto his palms, "it'll happen."

"For now," she smoothed his sweaty brow, "we have this."

"But is that good enough?"

"It's with you, O.B. It's more than good enough."

They made love a few more times before exhaustion took over. When she finally fell asleep, it was on top of his chest while he caressed her back, her heart beating hard against his and confessing what she wasn't quite yet ready to say.

Right before she drifted off, she asked, "Do you think 'Black warlock' is a good concept for a video game?"

And, he laughed.

CHAPTER 11

Sam, Carson, Tamika, and O.B. stood in one corner of a large banquet hall where several tables had been set up along the stretch of the room, each with an assortment of dishes on top. On the table nearest them, Sam spotted salmon in a white sauce, a colorful salad, caviar—which Tamika hated so this would be interesting—several drink options, and a rack of lamb sitting on mashed potatoes. Each table appeared to be home to the different options for the courses that would be served at the Hollister-Boone wedding.

Jess appeared from a set of double doors on the other side of the room. Today, she wore a white collared shirt, gray pencil skirt, and a pastel blue tie around her neck that brought an unexpected touch of power and femininity to the outfit.

"Tamika, Sam." She embraced both women and air-kissed their cheeks. "Lovely to see you." She turned to Carson, hand extended. "You must be the lucky groom."

Carson shook her hand. "If you ask me, she's the lucky one."

Tamika nudged him in the side.

Jess spun, eyes landing on O.B. standing just behind Sam. "I know you."

"I've heard that before," he said.

"Sam," Jess shot her an accusatory look, "now, the entire time we've been meeting up, you haven't said one thing about having a beau, and definitely nothing about that beau being O.B. Daniels."

Sam, smiling, took a quick glance at O.B. "O.B.'s the best man."

"So much power in one room. Hmm." She studied O.B., fingers scrubbing underneath her chin. "Nice to meet you, in person, O.B. Daniels."

They shook hands. He flashed Jess a smile, and Sam playfully rolled her eyes. Just because he was beautiful, he thought he was cute.

Jess walked them to the first table, explaining what Sam had already guessed. Due to the shortened time frame, she'd simply had all the courses prepared at once for Carson and Tamika to sample. They weren't restricted to choices per table; if there was a main course on table seven they liked, they could pair it with the side dish on table two.

"On this first table," Jess gestured to the spread, "we have filet mignon, grilled rack of lamb, and herb-roasted chicken. Our side options are haricot verts in herbed butter, asparagus au gratin, and roasted summer vegetables. Bon appétit."

They stepped forward and picked up the tiny sampling plates and utensils stacked on each table.

The sides all tasted fine to Sam; the chicken could use something, maybe lemon. But while they were *fine*, these wouldn't exactly do for their guests. Tamika was throwing a fancy wedding for a bunch of down-home people. There wasn't enough sauce or cheese in sight.

"I like the lamb in this one the best," O.B. said. "What do you think, Samantha?"

Her lips parted to answer him, and he slipped his fork into her mouth. Then, he watched her with a smirk on his face, his eyes glimmering with mischief.

"Yeah, this is pretty good. I taste...peppers?" She chewed, avoiding his eyes, and something spread through her mouth with an underlying heat. It was just enough to flavor instead of overpower.

"I didn't taste any pepper."

Right.

Of course.

The food wasn't getting hot. *She* was.

First, it was her finger in his mouth and now his fork, and she wondered if he came up with these things on the fly or if he'd had these maneuvers in his "player" binder for quite some time.

They realized they were staring at each other when Tamika asked, "What's this over here?"

O.B. set his plate down, took Sam's plate and placed it next to his, and ushered her to the next table, so close behind her that it was impossible for him to take a step until she did.

The next table proved to be a little more familiar—lobster mac and cheese, shrimp and grits, pulled chicken, and green salad. While Tamika, Carson, and Jess chatted away, Sam tasted the grits. When the flavor hit her tongue, she moaned. O.B. stared at her, so she made sure to slowly drag the spoon from her mouth, her tongue flicking the inside.

He licked his lips and bent, mouth headed for hers.

"I think we should keep this mac and cheese," Carson said, reaching for another helping. "This shit is good."

O.B. stopped in the middle of his descent to kiss her and backed away.

"And the shrimp and grits," Tamika added.

Jess chirped with laughter. "Nobody'll be awake by the end of your reception."

"Right, Sam?"

Sam spun around. "Hmm?"

"Right?" Tamika appeared to be repeating.

"Right...what?"

"What about you, O.B.?" Carson asked. "What do you think?"

O.B. scratched the back of his head. "Uh...all of the above."

Tamika and Carson stared at them, unblinking, and they set down their dinnerware, contrite. They kept their flirtation to a minimum as they sampled seasoned trout, vegetable couscous, and fried chicken—which Tamika said was good but she didn't want fried chicken at her wedding.

"Now, on to desserts," Jess announced. "These desserts are going to pair perfectly with your choice of wedding cake, in my opinion. Then again, what doesn't go well with Red Velvet Cake?"

Tamika, Jess, and Carson laughed. Seconds later, so did O.B. and Sam, although they didn't know what the joke was.

Sam spotted a mini shot glass of chocolate mousse with whipped cream and reached toward it, but O.B. grabbed her wrist. She looked back at him, and he shook his head.

"The sugar?" she whispered. There were too many desserts around not to taste *some*.

He bent, lips brushing her ear. "Nothing creamy."

"Because of the sugar?"

"Because of the fact that I'm two seconds away from bending you over one of these tables, and whipped desserts will push me over the edge. I don't think our friends want to see that. Jess, maybe. She seems like a freak."

She nudged his hard stomach with her elbow, gestured to a platter of mini doughnuts, and he nodded. Sam snatched up one of the doughnuts, bit down, and was surprised by a mouthful of sweet, creamy vanilla filling.

Oh no.

"What was that?" O.B. suddenly asked no one in particular. "Oh, man."

Tamika and Carson looked their way.

"What happened?" Tamika asked. "What's wrong? Sam?"

"Samantha's feeling a little tired." O.B. rubbed a large hand along her back. "You maybe need to go sit down a minute? Maybe it's the lights and stuff." He looked up, searched the ceiling. "Or the vents. I can take you to my car for a few minutes. That okay with y'all?"

Tamika rushed over. "You sure you're okay?"

Sam released a heavy, theatrical sigh. "It's...it's just a little fatigue. I'll be fine."

"No." Tamika grabbed her shoulders and turned her around. "O.B., take her outside and have her sit for a minute. I've been self-ishly running you ragged with all this wedding planning and not thinking about how much it might be for you so soon. Go."

O.B. apologized "for the inconvenience," gently helped Sam out of the banquet hall, picked her up once they were out of sight, and all but tossed her in the back of his car. Shirts were raised and unbut-toned, zippers lowered, her skirt hiked, and they both sighed, mouths pressed together once he was sheathed and deep inside her as she straddled his lap.

"Since you don't like to listen," he thrust his hips up, and she held onto his shoulders for balance, "this is what you get."

"I didn't even know," she softly whined, the words barely making it out of her mouth. "I thought it was a regular doughnut."

He thrust up again, hands exploring every inch of her skin, his lips, teeth, and tongue marking her neck. It was a good thing she'd tossed extra foundation and concealer in her purse. Tamika, and most likely Carson now as well, knew what they'd come out here to do, but she didn't want to walk back in with the evidence splotched all over like some kind of freaky leopard.

She had little to no experience with riding, only having done it a handful of times with John. The last time they'd tried the position, he'd climaxed *hard*, moaning and whimpering. Then he'd claimed she'd acted "sexually immoral and impure," but they still had time to "receive inheritance in the kingdom of Christ and God" if they never did it again. Meanwhile, other married couples spouted that the marriage bed was undefiled and were *getting it in* with their spouses. How could it be immoral if her body had wanted it and his had enjoyed it?

"Sam, baby." O.B. graced her mouth with a kiss. "What could you possibly be thinking about when I'm this deep inside you?"

"This." She squeezed her inner muscles, and he groaned, sinking his fingers into her hips. "I haven't done it much, so how can I make it good for you?"

He drew her in for another kiss, open-mouthed, his tongue flicking the velvety flesh just inside her top lip. "Samantha, you're already making it good, but we can switch positions if you'd like."

"No, no. I've got this."

She raised her hips, every delicious inch of him stretching her tight, and didn't think it could get any better. Then, she lowered, and his hiss and lip bite was like a reward that made her want to do it again. And again. Over and over, she raised and lowered, the muscles in her thighs, cheeks, and abdomen flexing.

"Sam, Sam, Sam." He licked her chin, and she couldn't get enough of that tongue of his. "You were made for me, I swear."

This time, when she lowered, he met her with a pump of his hips upward that made her cry out and wrap her arms around his neck, which gave her a little more stability. Holding onto him, she isolated and pivoted her lower half in deep, tight, rocking motions.

"Oh my God, yes." He tossed back his head, Adam's apple bobbing, his fingers digging even deeper into her skin. "Do your thing, Samantha."

It was a single sentence that made her feel as strong, beautiful, and empowered as Laila Ali or Serena Williams. Maybe that would be her next venture, empowering Black women through reclaiming their sexuality.

She rocked and stroked him with her body, going to the tip before filling herself to the hilt again. She didn't think it could get any better still, but then he met her stroke for stroke. And didn't stop.

"*Oh...*"

"*I know,* baby," he said, his voice even deeper. "You think I'm playing. I would've had you bent over in that banquet hall, and nobody would have been able to stop me from fucking you."

She leaned forward and kissed his neck. "You feel so good, Orylin Brian Daniels."

He wrapped his arms around her and drove harder. "Only you could make that name sound sexy as shit."

She was torn—she wanted to stay like this a while longer, in his arms, while he filled her over and over, but she needed to climax. If she didn't, she'd pass out.

Suddenly, she was leaned back against the front seat and angled so that each time he sank inside her, he tapped right where she needed him. It also gave his hands access to explore her waist, hips, and breasts.

He leaned forward, tongue long and pink, teasing her nipple, and she squeaked out some kind of gasping, moaning sob. Her attention flicked between staring into his eyes, and watching how his mouth teased her when he pulled the orb into his mouth and gently suckled. It was the best way, in her mind, to describe it. He closed his mouth over the tip of her breast and worked it with his lips and tongue, so it wasn't just a *suck*.

He let her breast fall from his mouth, licked his lips, and pulled it back into his mouth again. The brief loss of contact made the shock of pleasure when he returned much greater, her moans and his groans creating a sensual duet.

"I'm close, baby," she said.

"You going to come for me, Samantha?"

She erupted.

He slapped a curse in the air and let go, going from hard to hardest, thick to thickest inside her, rocking them in a wave motion in time to the slowing of their breaths. Eons passed with them like that, joined and panting, muscles and bones liquified.

Somehow, they were able to get dressed.

They even managed to look decent as they reentered the banquet hall where Carson and Tamika sampled drinks and appetizers. However, if their friends didn't already know, they would have been able to guess what had gone down from the way they kept smiling at each other. The little touches O.B. gave her. At one point, he even stood behind her and rubbed her arms like he was warming her up, alternating kisses with his chin on top of her head.

Carson and Tamika ended up going with sliders, shrimp cocktail shooters, stuffed peppers, and bacon-wrapped jalapeños for their appetizers; the shrimp and grits, lobster mac and cheese, herb-roasted chicken, and chickpea curry for their main dishes; and the mini doughnuts, mini apple pies, chocolate mousse, and ice cream for dessert.

When they left the food sampling, they spent another few hours with Carson and Tamika before heading back to O.B.'s house where they made love in the foyer, took a semi-functional shower together, and she fell asleep in one of his shirts, in her new favorite position to fall asleep—her heart against his.

———

O.B. SLIPPED AWAY FROM SAM, PRESSED A KISS AGAINST her forehead, and took his phone out to the living room. It wasn't that late for them to already be in bed, but they'd worn each other out, so he couldn't blame her for being dead on her feet. They'd stopped at her house so she could grab her sleep scarf because, as she'd put it, she still didn't feel comfortable around him without it, which would change soon.

He hoped.

He flopped onto the sofa and lay back while the phone rang in his ear.

"O.B.? Hi, baby."

"Hi, Momma," he greeted. "How's it going?"

"Good, good."

"Pops, is he home or is he at Auntie Stef's and forgot his phone again?"

"He's here. Let me get him."

O.B. leaned against the cushion, waiting to hear his father's voice on the other line.

"Junior, is that you? Is that my baby boy?"

O.B. grinned. "What's up, young man? How you livin'? Momma taking good care of you?"

"Always, son. My woman is the love of my life."

As a child, he'd loved his father. He remembered putting on his father's shoes, his blazers, and his ties, emulating him. With the way he'd admired his father, he'd never considered their relationship could change. Could grow. When he became old enough to understand respect and reverence, he changed his tune.

"Now, since I'm your father, I'm picking up on something in your voice," Orylin Sr. said. "Usually, you only sound like this when there's a woman involved. I know you're rich and handsome, son. I mean, you got your looks from me. But you have got to leave these hoes alone."

O.B. saw, in his mind's eye, Sam sleeping in his bed. Where she belonged.

"This isn't a ho situation, Pops."

"Is it that Jerica again?"

"No, sir. I'm just checking in. Checking up on you."

"Junior, what's the girl's name?"

O.B. scrubbed his forehead. "Samantha."

"Carson's Samantha?"

"Don't say it like that. She's Carson's fiancée's Samantha."

"The cute one with them lips we met when we came up to see Tamika that first time?"

O.B. laughed all the way from his belly. "Yessir. That's the one."

"What'd you do to that girl?" Orylin Sr. asked. "Because she was a sweet little thing. Sweet, sweet girl. If anything happened, I know your bullheadedness played a role. You still out here trying to be a player from the Himalayas?"

O.B. released another deep, rich laugh. "No, sir."

His father's tone went from playful to serious. "Talk to me, Junior. What's the problem?"

How would the way his father saw him change if he told him what he'd let Jerica do to him during their relationship? Even if he felt ready, he wasn't sure he could. He didn't know why he'd even told Sam. Carson was the only person who knew even a small bit of it, and he'd ignored everything Carson had warned him about. Now,

Jerica was still interfering with his life, and he wasn't sure what would get her to stop. He wasn't sure she ever would.

"Let's just say I have some 'unresolved issues' with Jerica, and those unresolved issues are interfering with me making Sam my girl."

"How?"

"Jerica has some shit she can blackmail me with, basically."

He heard his father get up, heard a door close, and then the familiar sounds of the backyard he'd grown up in came through the phone. They'd moved into that house when he was seven after his father got his big promotion to Senior Aerodynamics Engineer. If football hadn't taken over as the number one career choice in his life, he would have been an engineer. Hopefully, he and Sam would have met anyhow.

"What kind of shit?" Orylin Sr. whispered. "The hell you been getting into, Junior? It's nothing illegal, is it?"

"Nothing like that, sir. Just some stuff she can lie about, and even if I can dig myself out of the ditch, my image and career might still take a hit."

His father clucked his tongue. "Hmm. Okay."

"If you were in my position, what would you do?"

The line went silent. O.B. leaned back, pressed his thumb against his temple, and stared at the ceiling. He smiled to himself, the feeling of Sam wrapped around him ghosting over his skin. Sam was a different kind of crazy. Her crazy made her take a chance on a man like him without caring what he thought of her feelings. It had blown his mind when she'd told him, straight up, that she had feelings for him.

Sam didn't know what she had, and he wasn't talking solely about what she had between her legs. She was a powerhouse. Yes, there were small bruises in her confidence, but she didn't let that stop her from doing what she thought was best for her, even if it was telling him there was something "clinically wrong" with him.

There were men who feared sharks and war, losing a family member or friend. There were men who feared the outcome of an uncertain illness. Yet, there he was, terrified because he was in love.

His father's voice broke the silence. "Junior, if you really want to be with Sam, if you truly want to be with a woman who I can hear makes you happy from all the way through the phone, at some point, you'll have to take the leap. If not, Jerica will be controlling you your whole life."

It was what he was afraid of.

If he put his desire to make something happen with Sam on a scale with his desire to appease Jerica, Sam's side would toss Jerica's across the room. That meant taking the risk, and Jerica wasn't of sound mind. But this thing with Sam, he couldn't do it anymore. She was his, plain and simple. He wanted to make that official.

"Thanks, Pops. That helps."

Orylin Sr. sighed. "Junior, I have a question for you now."

"Sir?"

"You know your family loves you, right? You know I love you, right?"

"Yes, sir. I do."

"Keep that in mind, then. We love you, and you can tell us... things. Even the things you think you can't."

O.B. swallowed, emotion tightening his throat. "I know."

"Did I ever tell you I stole your mother from another man?"

"Only about a dozen times."

Orylin Sr. burst out laughing. "Well, Sam's a good girl for you. I can hear your teeth through the phone, you're smiling so hard. That's always a good sign."

O.B. rolled his eyes, now self-conscious about the clown grin on his face. "Come on, Pops."

"You need to make sure you don't mess this up. Lord, them lips. Just like a Jolly Rancher."

"Pops..."

"She's not your girl yet."

"And on that note," his mother's voice cut in from the background, "I want to talk to my child."

He talked to his mother for about a half hour longer, catching up on everything at home. His youngest sister, Delilah, was at home visiting, and he chatted with her a while. Delilah was a bookworm, studious and hyper-focused on getting into medical school to eventually become an immunologist. She was also sheltered, and he'd had a lot to do with that. Because of how he'd found himself treating women, he'd wanted to make sure she never met anybody even close to being like him.

Now, as it turned out, he wasn't as bad as he'd once thought, which meant that at some point, he'd have to deal with his little sister dating. Plus, she liked men—she'd been in love with Carson since she was a kid—so he'd have to deal with his baby fucking sister getting plowed.

Nope.

Made him pissed and sick at the same time.

He'd convince her to join a nunnery or something.

After he hung up, he lay still for a moment. He didn't notice when it started raining, the white noise of the droplets on his windows and the ground outside a soundtrack to the peaceful night.

"O.B.?"

"I'll be right there, baby."

He left the sofa, headed back to his room, and slid into bed beside Sam.

"You okay?" she asked.

"Yeah." *More than okay.* "How about you? You still feeling me so far?"

"Definitely." She kissed the ball of his shoulder. "You're even better than I imagined."

Then she had the nerve to turn away from him after saying something like that.

"Samantha?"

"Hmm?"

He drew her back against him and sunk his way home. At this point, a condom subscription was looking like it would have to happen.

She gripped the sheets. "I...shouldn't...tell you nice things."

"Oh, yes." He thrust up, over and over, finding the steady pace she liked. "You should."

CHAPTER 12

Sam blinked until the car's interior came into focus, not sure when she'd fallen asleep. She remembered O.B. putting her things in his car, climbing into the passenger seat, and then getting about a mile from her house. Despite having had, essentially, a full night's rest, she was still tired all the way to her bones. It probably didn't help that she'd started going to Miguel's football games with Carson and Mika —O.B. couldn't bring himself to so much as glimpse the stadium. She was also assisting full-time with Tamika's wedding planning, and she now spent the majority of her nights with O.B. inside her.

She started to turn in her seat until she recognized the music playing throughout the cabin.

Is this the Hamilton soundtrack?

Not only that, he sang and rapped the different parts of *The Schuyler Sisters,* word for word, beat for beat.

She stretched.

The music selection suddenly changed.

"What was that you were listening to?" she asked, facing him.

The seat had also been reclined, and that she definitely didn't remember doing.

"Hmm?" He pressed his lips together, which caused his right dimple to pop out. "What's that now?"

"How many times did you go see it?"

"See what?"

Sam yawned. "Okay. If that's the game you want to play, I'll pretend I don't know you're a Hamilstan."

"It's actually called a Hamil*fan*."

"Oh, I know."

He snuck a glance at her. "A few times on Broadway. Once in DC and Atlanta. Once in London for Carson's birthday. We went with my parents who wanted to celebrate their 'good' son's birthday with him. They tell people he's biologically theirs, just light-skinned."

She laughed and absently reached over to pull a piece of lint from his sleeve. He'd paired a cream-colored oversized sweater with black jeans. The temperature during the day was lovely but fell at night, so she'd chosen lightly lined leggings, a light sweater, and she had a scarf and knitted wrap she could toss on when the sun went down. Her wig was simple—straight, black, with a part down the middle—but lately, she'd been playing with the idea of going without one.

"Anyhow, I told them I hadn't seen it yet, but then I got a little too caught up in the songs and my cover was blown."

It was adorable, but she was afraid telling him that would make him stop at the side of the road, and she was still worn out from the night before...and that morning...and three hours ago. Since the sampling with Carson and Mika, they'd spent every day together. Some days, she fell asleep in his bed. Others, him in hers. Fridays at the office now felt longer than an entire week because she'd spend her time watching the clock, waiting until she was done with meetings and updates from the different departments, to see him again.

She returned the seat to its normal position and got a full view of where they were, high up in the mountains. Trees thinned out by the approaching winter lined the sides of the road, and between their small gaps, she made out the mountain ridge outline in the distance.

When she'd woken up that morning, at her place, he'd brought her breakfast and told her to pack her bags because they were going away for the weekend for her birthday. His bag had already been tucked away in the trunk of his car, and he'd had Carson break it to Tamika that this was the first birthday Tamika wouldn't be spending with her since they'd met.

They'd lazed around for much of the morning and afternoon before heading out.

"Are we in Asheville?" she asked.

"Yeah, actually," he said. "Good guess. How'd you know?"

"A memory from long ago."

Her father had been out of town for a church-related conference that would cause him to miss Christmas at home, so her mother had suggested a road trip. She remembered being awed by the way the earth had transformed with it being her first time out of Charlotte. The snow was heavy, flakes whipping around the car like lightning bugs.

They'd met up with Aaron Winston, a deacon from their church who she'd already been familiar with. He'd treated her to all the hot chocolate she'd wanted and taught her how to ski...a little. Her mother had introduced him as a friend, and it never crossed her mind to wonder why they were spending time with him. After all, it was what friends did.

She never once saw her mother and Aaron kiss or even so much as hold hands, but looking back on the time they'd spent with him, she could recall a certain intimacy she'd never seen her mother share, not even with her father.

They'd assumed her father was controlling, but when he found out about her mother's affair, they understood just how controlling he could get. It was why she only spoke to him a few times a year. She used to speak to her mother more often, but her mother's depression made that a rare occurrence now as well. Sometimes, she wondered how different things would have been if they'd simply *tried* to love one another as people rather than the vessels society had urged them to become. The good times she could remember had been more than good, and those times had made clear what had drawn them to one another in the first place. But, for reasons she'd never learn in this lifetime, those moments had dried up as quickly as they appeared.

O.B. spent the rest of the drive telling her all about Carson's birthday trip to London.

A log cabin appeared up ahead, nestled on a slight rise and watched over by skinny pine trees. There were a few more in the distance as far as she could see, and a sign on the right side of the road welcomed them to the Blue-Ashe Cabins.

He turned left onto a smaller road and headed toward the third cabin in the spaced out row. The days were shorter, so it was only around five but already dusky outside. Twinkling waterfall lights lit up the roof and a porch that appeared to go all the way around the property. The cabin was decked out for the holidays, despite Christmas being several weeks away. Then again, she'd seen Santa Claus displays in stores back in September.

The car stopped in front of the cabin and O.B. sat, fingers gripping the steering wheel, staring at it.

"This is what you planned for my birthday?" she asked.

He licked his lips. "Apparently."

"I...don't understand."

"I didn't then, either, but I think I do now."

He turned off the ignition, stepped out, and went to the trunk.

She offered to help with the bags, but he waved her off, grabbed them both, and headed inside. She slung her purse over her shoulder and followed him.

The first thing she noticed when she walked inside was the vaulted ceiling, and the west-facing windows that made up one wall. The wood accents were a delicate mix of modern and traditional. A stone fireplace was the centerpiece of the room, and it was already lit, giving the room a comfortable, sleepy kind of warmth. Outside wasn't as cold as she'd remembered Asheville being when she'd visited as a child, but the temperature certainly lent itself to fireplace-cuddling.

O.B. said he'd planned this months ago, before they started fooling around, yet everything about the cabin screamed "romantic."

"How many bedrooms?" she asked.

He studied her with a heavy dose of intensity. "Just one."

"And you planned this months ago."

"Apparently."

She walked over to the wall of windows and peered out over a large back deck. Trees spanned the yard as far as her eyes could see, and there was nothing discomforting about being in the mountains, in the middle of virtually nowhere, surrounded by trees, with this man.

When she turned around, he was still watching her.

"How do you like the cabin?" he asked.

"It's absolutely beautiful, O.B. Thank you. This is wonderful."

"We just got here. Don't thank me yet."

"Was this supposed to be a trip for Carson and Mika?"

He broke his stare, glancing behind her. "No. I planned it specifically for us."

"Months ago."

"You keep saying that."

"We weren't doing *this* months ago." She stepped away from the window. "Does this place have any food, by the way?"

He glanced at his watch. "We got here a little ahead of schedule. I had an early dinner arranged that should show up in the next half hour. After that, we're...going apple picking."

"Apple picking?"

His head fell. "Please don't make me repeat it. I'm not entirely sure what's happening to me."

She took a few steps closer to him. "Anything after that?"

"I planned for us to go downtown to walk around and explore together." Their gazes met again. "But if you don't want to do that—"

"I do."

He further closed the gap between them. "That's just tonight. We're here until late Sunday, and I plan to use every single minute to make sure you enjoy your time with me."

She asked the question weighing second heaviest on her mind. "Why a cabin?"

"Would you have expected this?"

"No, but I wouldn't have expected anything from you for my birthday."

"And that's my fault. But, if I'm being honest, I've wanted to do a weekend in a cabin for a while now. You're just the first person I've wanted to do it with."

Not even Jerica?

"You know, when you wrinkle your nose like that," he circled the space right in front of her face, "I can tell what you're thinking. And no, not even Jerica. There are a lot of things I didn't so much as consider doing with her that I want to do with you, which makes me think I didn't lo—" He coughed into his elbow. "You can check out the rest of the cabin if you want to."

She squeezed his left bicep and walked past him to their room to set her purse down. When she finished checking out the bedroom—there was a fireplace, glass doors, and a massive bed sprinkled with flower petals—she walked around the rest of the cabin. There wasn't much more to see. It had a smaller footprint, but the high ceilings made it appear larger. It was perfect, and she preferred the close quarters to something that would have forced them to be in different wings for most of the trip.

Stairs led up to a loft, which she figured would have been a second bedroom if she'd agreed to come on the trip but their relationship hadn't been as close as it currently was. The kitchen opened up to the great room, and there were books in the built-ins on either side of the fireplace. She skimmed them and spotted a few releases from Boone.

In front of the fireplace, there was a soft area rug, and she couldn't wait to get him down on top of it. She could already picture them, bodies slick with sweat, her straddling his waist while she rode him like the expert she was becoming, and that look of pleasure that came over his face whenever she sank deep.

Had he said he'd made the preparations for the trip days ago, she wouldn't have been surprised. Romantic O.B., the one Carson had told her about, had reared its head. He brought her flowers and sent flowers to her office. He made them candlelight dinners, rubbed her feet, kissed her long and hard, and made love to her slowly. It was even romantic when he found a way to touch her, in some way, on their wedding planning "dates" with Carson and Tamika.

A couple of days ago, he'd accompanied her to her follow-up with her oncologist and asked a boatload of questions, the main one being, "How likely is it that this will come back?" Then, he'd wanted to know how he could support her and if, just in case, he could do whatever tests necessary in the event she needed blood or something else.

She wrote him cute notes that she left in his things whenever he had to go handle his own businesses. So the people at his office or nightclub didn't gossip, she took some of his favorite foods with Carson and Tamika or Miguel, and they'd have lunch as a group.

She found out that when she kissed places like his chest, the back of his hand, his shoulder, and his cheekbone, it made him smile. Big.

She loved him, and she wanted him to love her.

If he already did, she wanted him to say it first.

They were acting like they were together which, in some ways, they'd tacitly agreed they were, just in private. It *was* enough for her, for now, like she'd told him, but she saw the moments when he didn't feel satisfied with the arrangement.

"Sam?" He poked his head through the bedroom doorway. "Food's almost here."

He'd changed into a pullover and a pair of joggers, and everything about his solid frame and the way he filled out the pullover screamed "snuggle with me."

After dinner, they hopped back in the car. This time, he openly played his Hamilton soundtrack, but he didn't sing along. Still, it was cute to know about this "hidden" side of him. He spent so much time putting up walls, she wondered if he realized that oftentimes, a wall was all people saw. He treated vulnerability like a terminal illness, and she couldn't imagine how much it had to have hurt for Jerica to do what she'd done when all he'd wanted was to love someone.

"I can feel you burning a hole in the side of my face."

She faced the front windshield, unaware she'd been staring. "Sorry."

"Something on your mind?"

"Nope. Just looking at my beautiful man."

"You finally said it." He kept licking and biting his lips, but every time each action ended, the smile he tried to hide started up again.

"Said what?"

"You called me your man."

They pulled up to a relatively packed orchard, and he made a few loops around the property before they found a parking spot. When they got out, he offered his hand.

"Don't ask me if I'm sure," he said. "Come on."

The place was filled with families. More than once, they had to bend or twist to move out of the way of a child running away from a parent or chasing another child. Sam studied a few of the families, ranging from those with small children to those with teens. There were some couples who looked like newlyweds.

"Should we get one bag or two?" O.B. asked.

She tore her gaze away from a baby gumming an apple slice. "One bag. We'll just fill it all the way up."

"Hey, isn't that O.B. Daniels?"

The person whispered it, but Sam heard. People had glanced their way as they walked into the orchard, obvious recognition on their faces, but they'd kept a respectful distance.

"Think he'll take a pic with me?"

"Honey, he's here picking apples with his girlfriend. Leave him be."

"I'll never get another chance!"

"Then, fine. Go ask him."

O.B. smiled, cheek cresting, when he picked up on the conversation.

Sam released his hand and stepped off to the side to watch him interact with the fan. The woman, who sported a round belly underneath a long, floral dress and coat with riding boots on her feet, could barely hold herself upright.

"Excuse me, do you mind if I get a photo with you, Mr. Daniels?" she asked. "I've been a fan since I was at Duke. My name's Trinity, and I've been watching football since I was like two. You are one of my top five favorite players of all time."

"I feel like an old man," O.B. teased. "Hope I don't look like one too."

"Oh God, not at all. You look great. Amazing, really. My husband even let me keep the copy of the Bod issue with you on the cover."

O.B.'s gaze flicked over Trinity's head to where her husband stood, and the man shrugged.

"I just graduated earlier this year from the education program," Trinity added.

"I'd love to take a picture," O.B. said. "Samantha, what do you think would make the best backdrop?"

Sam startled, hearing her name. "Um...how about in front of those two large apple decorations on that wall?"

He nodded and directed Trinity over.

It took a moment for Trinity to compose herself, and she was so gracious afterward, her face flushed more crimson than the apples in the orchard.

"Can you do me a favor, real quick, Trinity?" O.B. reached into his pocket and pulled out his phone. "Can you take one of me and my girl?"

The woman's head nearly bobbled off her neck. "Of course."

He motioned Sam over and she stood next to him, leaving a gap between their bodies. He groaned, stretched his arm out, and pulled her up against his side to smother the gap. She took the opportunity to snuggle against his warmth.

Despite all the "intimate" predicaments they'd found themselves in, this was definitely the best way to hold him. This close, she could appreciate the contrast of his hard body against the soft cotton of his pullover and the deep, earthy and spicy notes of his cologne.

Trinity snapped several pictures, examining each one. Somewhere in between the dozens of camera clicks, Sam had let her head fall against O.B.'s chest.

"This one is definitely the cutest!" Trinity squealed and held out the phone. "Look. See?"

He took his phone and stared at the screen, a wistful smile on his face. "You do good work."

"It's easy when you have great subjects to work with."

"Think this is Insta-worthy?"

"Definitely."

"What's your username? I'll tag you."

Trinity's mouth fell open, and it took her a few seconds to collect herself and rattle off her information. O.B. looked up her profile, confirmed it was hers, and clicked to add her as a friend.

"A good portion of my students are football fans," she said. "This is going to blow their minds."

Behind her, her husband cleared his throat.

"Right." Trinity extended her hand. "Nice meeting you, Mr. Daniels. And you, Samantha."

O.B. and Trinity's husband shook hands and the couple walked off, Trinity's husband cradling her lower back while she gushed over the photo. O.B. watched them walk away then turned to Sam and held up the bag.

"Ready?"

"Your girl?" she asked.

"If I'm your man, like *you* said earlier, who else would you be?" Grinning, he held out his hand. "Come on. Let's go."

A sign let them know the first row they came upon would be an orchard of Arkansas Black apples. Sam approached the first tree, plucked one of the dark, round fruits from a branch, polished it, and sank her teeth into the skin. A flush of sweet and tart filled her mouth, and she smacked her lips and pressed two fingers against the side of her neck.

"Tart?" O.B. asked.

"And somehow sweet." When the spasm in her neck subsided, she took another bite. "These would make good pies."

"Will you bake one for me?"

"Sure."

He bent forward. "Let me taste."

She held up the apple.

"I was just going to get some of that juice off your lips, but this works too." He sank his teeth into the apple and immediately drew back, squinting. "Samantha, that is not tart. That's sour."

"It's like a Granny Smith."

"Which is sour."

She held up her left index finger and took a second bite. "Tart."

The rest of the rows promised Golden Delicious apples, Fuji, Pink Lady, Ambrosia, Gala, and one called Candy Crisp she'd never heard of before. The perfectly ripe Golden Delicious turned out to be her favorite while O.B. favored the Gala. After a couple of hours, they had a bag full of assorted fruit, and they headed back to the farm's large, main barn to pay for them.

There were more whispers and looks, but no one else approached them. She spotted camera phones being discreetly held up while O.B. sampled an apple doughnut from a platter, and he made sure she didn't get too far away from him by keeping a hand on her lower back or taking her hand and pulling her along.

To their assortment of apples, they added apple jelly, a slice of pie, apple cider, and apple bread.

Once they'd paid for everything, they headed toward where the car was parked, but Sam was several steps ahead of O.B. before she realized he'd stopped. She looked back and he crooked his head toward an empty picnic table, sat their stuff down, and pulled out the slice of pie, forks, and the two small Ball jars of cider.

She sat across from him.

"Sit next to me," he insisted.

"Our elbows are going to crash."

"Then sit on my right side." He held his fork between the fingers on his left hand. "Problem solved."

She obliged him and accepted the fork he handed over. When she dug her fork into the pie and slipped a piece between her lips, she moaned.

"Makes sense, right?" he asked.

"Definitely." She took another piece. "It would have been a travesty not to eat this warm."

They ate in silence, his large frame blocking the majority of the winds whipping around them and slowly transitioning the evening from cool to cold. The temperatures were lower than normal during this time, at least from what the woman who'd brought their food at the cabin had told them, but it made for a very romantic weekend... which the woman had also said.

Sam twirled her fork in the air. "I have questions, O.B."

"Naturally."

"But I won't ask them right now."

"Not even one?"

She licked pie filling from her lip. "You're not really going to post that picture, are you?"

"Yep."

"And what, pray tell, will your caption say?"

"Hmm." He tilted his head up, jaw moving in the longest bite and swallow in modern history. "How about, 'Haven't done this since I was a kid. Great memories then, even better memories now. Beautiful company.' My hashtags would be something generic like #applepicking, #perfectevening, #mylady, #blacklove. Nothing too extensive."

She elbowed him in the side.

"You have a problem with my hashtags?"

She scooped up the last of the pie and gave him the same treatment, slow chewing and thinking while his gaze in her direction created a hole in the atmosphere.

"I...don't, actually." She lowered her fork. "And I'm starting to realize just how perfect this birthday weekend really is."

He didn't look away.

For a while.

She opened one of the jars and popped a straw into her cider.

"So, you're just going to say that to me then suck on something?"

Sam nearly choked on her sip.

"I mean," he shrugged, "I'm just saying."

They finished up and headed to the car.

She fell asleep on the drive, again, and when she woke up, they were idling in the driveway next to the cabin's front porch.

"You always sleep this much?" he asked.

Sam yawned, stretching her arms above her head. "Not in recent months, no. Why?"

"Do you feel okay?"

"How do you mean?"

"Do you feel...sick?"

Between the lines, she read that he wanted to know if she thought *Lou* could be back. And fatigue *was* the first symptom she'd noticed. Then the bruises. She'd assumed she'd been bumping into things and forgetting until they became deeper in color and more extensive. By the time she went to see her doctor, she'd already had a pretty good idea what was going on with her, but the confirmation had shocked her to her core.

"I don't feel sick," she reassured him. "And you came with me to my last physical. Everything was fine."

"Mika said you've been working a lot."

"There are a couple projects that I have to be hands on for, but once those are over, I'll go back to handing everything off until I'm ready for full retirement."

He shut off the car. "Come on. Let's go inside."

There was still a while before their apparent trip to explore downtown, so when O.B. sank down onto the sofa in front of the fireplace and reached for her, she automatically went to him.

"What did your folks do when you told them about your diagnosis?" he asked.

"My father came up a few times to pray for me before I started chemo." As well as to try to convince her to reconsider her choice of treatment, but he'd never understood the inner-workings of his data-driven youngest child. He never could quite understand how she could love both science and her faith. "My mother doesn't leave the house anymore, not really, and he'd wanted to come alone."

"The whole preacher's wife bit?"

"She had an affair when I was younger with a man from our church. I guess, to make up for it, she does any and everything he asks."

O.B. slowly moved his palm along her left arm. "An affair? You know I want to know your family's business."

"Well, my father has this austere way about him," she explained. "He's into interpreting the Bible as close to verbatim as possible. He was different when he was younger, resulting in his three boys with three different women, so his aim was to live a virtually ascetic life once he got saved."

"Minus the abstaining from sex part, if you're here."

"Right. Well, my mother, she didn't mind being his wife, at first, but he eventually started treating her like his prisoner. In our living room, there used to be this huge, framed print of *1 Corinthians 7:4*."

O.B. looked up at the ceiling. "It's been a while, but isn't that the one about the wife not having authority over her body?"

"Look at you."

"I still remember a little something, now."

"Yes, you're right." She snuggled closer and wrapped both arms around his middle. "After he found out about my mother's affair, he switched it to *Proverbs 12:4*: 'A virtuous woman is a crown to her husband, but she that maketh ashamed is as rottenness in his bones.'"

"Damn. How'd he find out?" Realization dawned on him. "The trip you took to Asheville."

It wasn't logical to blame herself for what her parents' relationship had become because she'd been too young to know better, but that hadn't stopped her from doing so for years.

"Daddy was out of town for the holiday, so I thought it would be a girls' trip type of thing. I'd just turned six, and when I saw the mountains as we drove up earlier today, it reminded me of my first time seeing that view but with snow covering the ground. We stayed at a hotel instead of a cabin, and the man's name was Aaron Winston. He was a deacon."

"I don't think I'd believe this story if he wasn't."

She used every ounce of willpower she had to avoid kissing him, already tasting the sweetness from his slice of pie and jar of cider on her lips.

"Did you tell your father you and your mother met up with his friend?" he asked.

"Yes. One day, in his church office. I let it slip that we lit candles while on vacation with Mr. Aaron. He then asked me what else we did, and I told him we went skiing, had hot chocolate, and ate together. He asked me if me and Momma shared a room or if it was Momma and Mr. Aaron, so I said she stayed with Mr. Aaron. He wanted to know if they shared a bed or had separate beds, and I told him they shared a bed so Mr. Aaron could give Momma massages with their clothes off."

O.B.'s brows popped up. "You walked in on them?"

"Once. Mr. Aaron was straddling my mother and his hands were on either side of her, down near her lower back."

"Good position for deep penetration. A classic dick-down. Mr. Aaron knew what he was doing."

"O.B., please. I've already unsuccessfully tried burning the image from my memory."

His laugh was as warm as his body. "Did you tell your father the straddling part?"

"As best as I could explain it as a newly-minted six-year-old."

Things had changed in their household almost overnight. There was yelling, her mother's incessant tears. The new wall print went up. Her father's sermons turned scathing and cynical. People at church looked at her with concern and cradled her wrist or tipped her chin whenever she walked around with the collection plate. Her father's control exploded, eventually extending to her, and she'd done whatever she could to make things better for the three of them.

"I was already quiet and introverted and shy before that, but I almost became mute for a few years," she said. "Daddy's control was like...you know when a room is past the point of being cozy and the heat gets suffocating? Like that. It was *just* like that."

"You still have a lot of that in you," O.B. pointed out.

"It gets worse around men I'm either attracted to or there's a romantic component to our relationship."

"Because your father continuously told you to submit, so

195

speaking up around men wasn't something that came naturally. Delilah, she's like that. She'll curse me out for drinking her coconut water, but you can barely hear her when Carson's around."

"Awww." Sam flattened her palm against his chest. "Delilah has a crush on Carson?"

"Damn near obsession. Can't wait until she grows out of it."

"Isn't she like twenty-one?"

"She'll grow out of it."

Sam choked out a laugh. "What about Raina?"

"Raina?" He scoffed. "You could release that girl naked in a room full of dicks and she'd still come out unfucked."

Sam laughed until it brought on a mini coughing fit.

"I'm serious. Raina took every last drop of that fighter DNA, which is probably why Delilah's so shy. And, honestly, I used to worry about it. I still worry about her with these fuck-boys pretending to be men, but now that I've gotten to know you...I'm less worried."

She backed out of his hold and tucked one leg under her. "Why's that?"

"Look at what you've accomplished. You have men like Steve Jobs and Bill Gates who got credit for being introverted and reclusive. If a woman's successful, she's automatically expected to be more like Raina. Even I would tell Lilah she has to be louder and more outspoken to be successful, but really, that girl is fucking brilliant. She can become a Samantha Norwood one day. Matter of fact, I hope she does."

Sam felt her eyes fill, and she looked away from him and blinked until the tears went back to where they'd come from.

"Thanks, O.B."

He smiled. "Anytime."

"By the way, I never got to see that picture of us."

He pulled out his phone, unlocked it, and handed it to her. She navigated to his Photos app, and it was the first picture that popped up.

Thank God.

She half-expected to come up on one of Jerica, naked and spread-eagle.

"You're doing that thing with your face again," he said. "I don't have naked pictures of women on my phone, courtesy of my little cousin who's better at navigating a smartphone than I'd anticipated, and definitely not any of *her*."

"This is cute." She tilted her head left and right. "We're cute together."

"We *are* together."

She handed the phone back to him. "Explain? Please?"

"I don't want this with anybody else, Sam. I found you, and I wasn't even looking."

There were words she wanted to say, but they hadn't arrived yet. That admission, said with his voice, while looking at his face, had her brain all scrambled like those D.A.R.E. public service announcements they used to show at her elementary school.

She pulled her sweater over her head. "How important is that walk downtown?"

"Not at all important." He stripped out of his pullover. "Unless you want to do that instead."

She shoved off her leggings, panties, tossed her bra, and walked over to the area rug in front of the fireplace where she lowered onto her knees to watch him finish getting undressed. Once he was naked in all his glory, she beckoned him with a finger.

"Stay right there," she instructed when he was about a foot away. "Just like that."

She leaned forward, flicked her tongue over the tip of his length jutting out to greet her, and the resounding hiss he released was exactly what she'd been waiting for—her little reward. At this point, she was conditioned to do nasty things for him just for that hiss.

"This, I don't have much experience with, either." She flicked a second time and followed it with a quick suck that made the muscles in his thighs tighten. "But, I've been practicing."

"And just how—*fuck.*"

She sucked again, this time longer and harder.

"Just how exactly have you been practicing?"

"On Miguel."

"Sam—"

"Kidding, kidding. I like seeing you get all jealous and primitive-like."

"You're lucky, because I was about to take you *and* him out... right after you were done."

She laughed, reached for his base, and wrapped her fingers around him as best as she could. When she went in for another suck on the head, she took a little more of him into her mouth, and the muscles in his thighs contracted again. Like the hiss, that thigh pull was quickly becoming her second reward reaction.

"I love your body, O.B." She licked all the way down to his sac and back up. "I love everything about it, so tight and brown and hard."

She bobbed her head, swallowing more of him with each pass until she'd taken him as far as her throat allowed. What she couldn't swallow, she gripped and moved her mouth and hands in tandem, coating him with the moisture from her cheeks and throat.

"Damn, Samantha. You don't know how long..."

"How long you've wanted this?" She looked up at him, and he stared down at her, glassy-eyed. "Why didn't you tell me?"

"I wanted you to get here in your own time."

"What is it about it?" She took him to the back of her throat and applied pressure along his length as she withdrew. "What do you think about?"

"Your lips on my dick."

"My lips?"

"Those *lips*."

This was even more empowering than riding him until his eyes rolled back in his head.

She didn't try to suck him neatly, and she didn't worry about making too much of a mess. In fact, the more of a mess she made, the harder he seemed to get. She slurped and stroked, and when his hand graced the back of her head, she almost climaxed.

He thrust his hips.

She hummed and moaned and pumped him with her hands while sucking the soft crown. Whatever moisture she found there, she lapped at while holding eye-contact.

"Samantha, as much as I'd love to come down your throat, you know what I want."

She nodded, pulled away, and lay on her side.

He tossed a roll of condoms within arm's reach, rolled one on, and lay behind her.

"Is this how you want me?" He impaled her in a single, deep motion. "You sure about that, Samantha?"

She'd thought so...until that first stroke. Until the sensation of him, thick and hard, moving inside her wet sensitive flesh. She felt *every single thrust,* going in and when he pulled out only to surge again.

He held her against him and pounded into her until she could no longer moan, reduced to tight whimpers. Her breasts bounced with each slap of his pelvis against the curve of her behind. He raised one of her legs and brought it back over his hip, giving his fingers access to between her thighs. Him touching, rubbing, and stroking her was a different sensation than her own hands. So when she cried out, climax punching into her like a fist, she felt how much of a mess she'd made on the condom, her thighs, and on him.

He flipped her onto her belly, the urgency of his strokes increasing until he cursed and groaned, drawing out the deep, breathy sound like her body had given him more than just pleasure.

"So, how committed are you to those plans this weekend?" she asked.

CHAPTER 13

O.B. fucked Sam so hard, they popped three condoms, and it took him less than ten seconds to slip on another one and sink back into her body. He fucked her against two walls. After giving her a small break, he fucked her on the kitchen counter, bent over the mattress in the bedroom, and again in front of the fireplace. He'd had plans for them to drive the Blue Ridge Parkway to see the fall leaves because he knew she would have *loved* it, for them to go to a cooking class, hit up a gaming spot, and then relax in the hot springs.

He'd *tried* to leave her body.

She'd tried to let him.

He was now almost waist deep inside her and had the nerve to ask, "Are you sore?"

He'd, essentially, been inside her since last night.

"In so many places, but don't stop," she said, voice airy and filled to the brim with pleasure. "Please, don't stop."

Palms planted on the floor on either side of her, he pivoted his waist and pummeled her, mesmerized by her dark nipples and bouncing breasts. Every stroke was as good as the first. Every inch of her gripped him, no matter how deep he went or how far he pulled out, and her arches, moans, and gasps drove him crazy.

The only reason he pulled out was because he was about to break apart, and he wasn't ready. Not until she had another one, which didn't take long after he pushed her legs to either side and licked the entire length of her slit.

He rotated through impaling her, pulling out, licking and then impaling her again. Hard. So hard. He was pissed at her for brushing aside every wall he'd erected like they'd been made of foam. She didn't care about telling him she loved being with him, didn't care about wrapping her arms around him when she felt like it. She'd told him, straight up, she had feelings for him even back when he'd pretended he didn't feel the same way. Hell, she called him beautiful. She called him a good person. She called him her man.

"O.B.? O...*baby.*" Her body bowed, and she went hot all over. *All over.*

When he came, blind white-hot passion sparked behind his eyelids. It was a whole-body experience, an out-of-body experience, and so powerful that the only thing he could do was lower his chest to her breasts.

She wrapped her arms around him and kissed whatever skin she could reach. "This was perfect. Thank you."

"You're thanking me for making love to you?"

"Yes."

"Samantha, what do you usually do for Thanksgiving?" he asked.

She lazily stroked his back. "Usually, I go to Mika's, but she's spending it with Carson's family. I was just going to make some turkey legs and watch movies."

"Come home with me."

"You mean *home*, home? In Chapel Hill?"

He pushed up and looked down into her face. "Yes."

"I'd love to."

He kissed her. And kissed her.

The only reason he stopped kissing her was to pull out, toss the condom, and ready another one.

"I can slow down if you're sore," he reminded her.

She responded by pulling him down and, with her lips fused to his, she rolled him onto his back. As she rode him, looking down into his eyes, he realized that this woman was going to play a significant role in his future.

THEY HAD BREAKFAST AROUND LUNCHTIME.

While Samantha showered, he set out the eggs, chicken sausages, toast, and fruit they'd ordered. Next to her plate, he set down her birthday gift. He usually didn't like staying around to watch people open his presents. Not even his sisters. For reasons he never learned, it embarrassed him. When he got Raina the car she'd wanted forever, it was his mother who told him she'd cried. He'd sent Delilah to an elite summer microbiology program in Washington D.C. after she graduated from high school. Apparently, she'd bawled.

Sam waved as she walked toward him from the bedroom, fresh out of the shower and wearing one of his pullovers, her legs bare. Black frames perched on her nose, and she was so cute with her little glasses on. Cute enough to bend over the side of the bed and fuck until his spine separated. He wanted to pull off that sweater, smack her ass, and tunnel his way to South America in her pussy.

The woman is sore, O.B.

"I love that about you." He pulled out her chair. "That little wave you do."

She sat and examined her breakfast first and then her eyes landed on the gift.

"Happy Birthday, Samantha."

He took his seat and preoccupied himself with his food, unable to look at her. The wrapping paper crinkled, there was a tear, and then he heard a small "pop" as the box opened.

"Oh...O.B., this is beautiful."

He looked up just as she clasped the bracelet around her wrist. He'd known she would look good in sapphires and diamonds. The way it sparkled against her skin, he wanted to get her matching earrings. He *should* have gotten her matching earrings.

"Thank you." She hopped up, stepped around the table, and dropped a kiss on his mouth. "Thank you so much."

"You're welcome, baby."

She reclaimed her seat and started on her meal. "Were you serious about me going home with you?"

"Of course."

"What do I tell your folks?"

"You don't have to tell them anything." He washed sausage and eggs down with a sip of coffee. "I already told them me and my girl are coming down for the holiday."

A flushed spread over her face. "Okay."

"Jerica's never gone home with me." Why he chose just then to offer up that information, he didn't know. "She's met my parents, but it was when they flew out for one of my games."

"Did they like her?"

It was more like tolerated. His father had commented on the fact that she was pretty, and her mother had lauded her for pursuing an acting career, but each interaction was stiff. They'd met her one more time after her "transformation," and those interactions had been even more rigid.

"They tolerated her," he replied.

"Oh."

"But they'll love you."

"What makes you say that?"

He stared at his plate. "Because I do."

Silence.

He didn't hear any excited, or disappointed noises, and it forced him to look up to make sure she was okay.

Tears glistened like jewels against her brown skin and streaked down her face, dripping from her chin onto the pullover.

"I probably should say that while looking at you." Anxiety and vulnerability coiled around each other and stretched from his chest to his navel. "Sam, I had no idea being with somebody could feel like this. You make me feel like a king, like I mean something to you and it's important to you that I'm in this world. You support me, care about me, and care *for* me. You fight *for* me, not *with* me. I love you, Samantha."

Her bottom lip trembled, and her nose turned red.

"Mika's about to get married, and you know that'll change some things," he went on. "She's been your main source of love and support. I mean, not even your own Pops is there for you, but everybody needs at least one person to fight for them. I'm not going to leave you alone in this world for the next thing to come along, and maybe Mika can't be there for you because of Carson's needs or if they have a child. So, although I know you can fight your own battles, now that I'm your man, expect me to fight some of them for you."

Her lips parted. "I...you..."

"Samantha, it's okay." He left his chair and kneeled next to hers. "Tell me later."

"I..." She frowned and shook her head. "I've wanted to hear that for longer than you know. I...I can't believe...O.B., I love you too. I love, love, love you too."

He pulled her down onto his outstretched thigh. "After we get back from my folks' place, I need to know if you'll be okay with people knowing what you mean to me. I didn't come into your life to rip through your privacy and take advantage of your personality, but I don't feel comfortable telling you I love you only to hide you from the world." He met her eyes. "Are you with me?"

She nodded. "Yes."

"Some shit might go down, Sam."

"O.B., I'm with you."

He kissed her and wrapped her in his arms, his tongue exploring her mouth.

The woman is sore, *O.B.*

"Let's finish up and head back," he said, lips brushing hers. "Did you enjoy your birthday?"

"I enjoyed it very much."

"I've already got some stuff planned for next year."

"As long as you're there." She kissed him. "As long as you're there..."

CHAPTER 14

Landon Johansson's twenty-three-year-old blond head was currently bowed toward the floor, his right leg bouncing. She was surprised he'd shown up. Deitra had let him know they were thinking about going into business with Jerica, and that they were essentially building a character profile to get a sense of Jerica's moral compass. He'd asked if there was any way he could speak to the head of Two-Twelve, privately, and Sam had agreed to meet up with him as quickly as she could.

"Landon, I didn't know," she said. "I'm very sorry that happened."

"I don't even know why I told you." He raised his head. "You have to understand, Miss Norwood, I...she...I'm a man. A big man. Bigger than most. And Jerica, she's a paperweight, really."

"From what you're telling me, her preference isn't physical fights."

His leg bounced harder. "It didn't even start out that way. She was so sweet. We had a whole handshake that we'd do at the start of my games. She looked good on my arm. I mean, I knew she and O.B. Daniels had a past, but when we started getting serious, she told me he used to beat her up."

"He hit her?"

"That's what she said, and I believed her, at the time."

Sam swallowed her first response. "What happened then?"

"I went caveman and wanted to protect her. We got closer. She was *still* sweet. And then, she found out…" The bulb in the column of his throat bobbed. "Miss Norwood, this can't get out."

"Landon, whatever you tell me here today is between you and me. If it makes you feel better, I can tell you something secret about me."

"O…okay. Yeah."

"I recently started a relationship with O.B. Daniels."

Landon's eyes rounded. "I know what I just said, about him hitting women and stuff like that, but let me tell you the rest first. Let me tell you the rest and then you can decide if you believe he's really like that."

Sam agreed.

"Jerica changed when I asked her to…when I asked her for a threesome."

Sam studied his face. "But not with two girls."

"No."

"You're bi."

"Yes. I know I want to be with a woman long-term but, you know…" He shrugged and let his head fall back. "She changed almost overnight. It was like I gave her power by telling her. She started giving me the cold shoulder, threatening to tell the world that one of the best point guards in the game…"

He didn't finish, but he didn't have to. Sam filled in the blanks on her own.

"See this right here?" He craned his neck to show off a scar. "She cut me. With a kitchen knife. When I saw the blood, I freaked the fuck out. I thought she hit a vein or something. Then, it continued. It got worse. Miss Norwood, I married her. I married *that*."

"Because that's what she wanted?"

He nodded. "Yes."

"Landon, why did she end up leaving you?"

"She said she saw her ex with some new woman and realized she didn't love me. I didn't argue. I just got the fuck out of there." He shivered. "I feel for O.B."

"Why do you say that?"

"Because I know Jerica behind closed doors." He held up three fingers on his right hand. "O.B. got three rings before the age of thirty. I know, without having to talk to him, that he loves the game of football just like I do basketball. After Jerica started acting crazy, I went back and watched some of his games. I remember them saying he broke his fingers in a freak accident, and I knew that was a lie. She nearly broke mine. If you ask me, I think she's the real reason he left. And, it's a damn shame because that man is a beast on the field."

"I agree." She smiled at him. "I've watched some old games."

"I know you just started seeing him, but Jerica isn't who she claims to be. I don't think O.B. beat her up. From the way she treated me, I feel like she probably had something over him too."

"So far, he's been nothing but kind and a gentleman to me," she said. "And you seem wonderful yourself."

A bright smile lit up his youthful face. "Thanks, Miss Norwood. When your lawyer told me that you guys wanted to offer Jerica some kind of deal, I knew I had to talk to you. Don't give that woman any money, power, and I hope no man ever gives her a baby. Something's not right with her."

He rose and Sam stood with him, Landon dwarfing her with his nearly seven-foot height. To her surprise, he leaned down and wrapped her up in a hug, and she could only imagine the strength it had taken for him to tell her his secret.

He squeezed and released her, and she walked him to the door.

"One last thing," he said. "I know it probably doesn't mean much, but I didn't know you were behind Two-Twelve. When I was a kid, my grandfather bought me one of your consoles and some games to keep me company while I was in the hospital. I had leukemia when I was a kid."

"I...I'm less than a year in remission. Same diagnosis."

He gave her another hug, this one tighter. "I spent a lot of time in the hospital and, it sounds stupid, but your games got me through. It gave me a chance to think about something other than needles and medicine or seeing my parents cry, so I'm more than honored to meet you."

"That's not stupid at all." A tight lump weighed down the muscles in her throat. "I'm honored to be able to have done that for you."

"I used to live in Louisiana then and a hurricane hit, so we lost all our stuff, but your games are still a good memory for me."

"If you need anything, you call me," she said. "And, if exclusive licensing for NBA games disappears, I might need you to come in for a consult."

His smile was like an extra light in the room. "Will do. I'll see you around, Miss Norwood."

She waved and Layla showed him the rest of the way out.

Sam mentally crossed talking to Landon off her checklist, went back to her desk, and added another task to Layla's duties for the day —have a console and games sent to Landon Johansson.

A half hour later, the love of her life showed up.

"You ready to go?" He walked to the edge of her desk. "You look beautiful today."

"And you look sexy." She stood, collected her things, and ran her fingers through her curls. "Yes. I'm ready to go."

CHAPTER 15

Delilah Daniels, who was slightly taller than Sam had expected, launched herself into her brother's arms the minute he stepped out of the car. She was more on the lean side with a large pair of breasts O.B. likely had no idea existed. Men were hitting on her; there was no doubt in Sam's mind. Delilah simply didn't appear to be interested in anything not under a microscope...yet.

Watching Delilah interact with him, she saw what O.B. had referred to. Their similarities. As Delilah got older, that innocence would wane, but there was nothing wrong with her being more academic than social, not really into groups, and soft-spoken in some situations. It wasn't about who she was. It was about what she could do.

"O.B., I have so much to tell you," Delilah said.

He squeezed her, rocked her side to side. "Is it about a boyfriend?"

"No."

"Thank God. Girlfriend?"

Sam, smiling, shook her head. He really didn't want his sister to get plowed, but it happened to the best of them. She wouldn't be surprised if Delilah eventually got bent in half by something thick with a slight curve, like she was on a regular basis. She wouldn't be surprised if Delilah already was. It wasn't exactly something she'd share with her brother.

"No. It's about molecular biology, specifically about B-cell tumors." Delilah stepped back, grinning up at O.B. like she was looking at her idol. "It's the continuation of a project I started at the biology camp."

If Sam had seen this interaction before meeting him, she would have known there was more to him than even she had given him credit for in the very beginning.

Raina, who was a fitness model and it showed, was shorter and closer to her height. She stepped up and wrapped her arms around O.B., whispered something in his ear that made him chuckle, and glanced at the car. She sent a little wave that Sam returned. Then she asked O.B. something he answered with a nod, released him, and came around to the passenger side door to pull it open.

Raina extended a hand.

Sam wrapped her fingers around Raina's.

"I'll grab the bags," O.B. announced. "Raina, Lilah, you mind introducing Samantha to everybody? Make sure she stays away from Uncle Charles?"

Delilah walked ahead of them toward the house. "By the way, Sam, Daddy made the mistake of showing Uncle Charles your picture, and he...well..."

"He wants you to be his next 'baby mama,'" Raina finished. "It's a wonder how he and Daddy are related. Truly."

Sam paced her breathing.

They stepped inside the house, and she was introduced to uncles, cousins, and aunts. The house was full and bustling with energy, and she knew it was going to take a lot of mental work to get through the number of people who were around. She'd do it for O.B., though.

Raina and Delilah directed her to the kitchen.

"Momma," Delilah called. "O.B.'s girlfriend is here."

As she thought back on it, Sam realized she'd never been a "girl-friend" before. Boys had been off limits in high school, and her father had handpicked her husband. She never got into anything serious after her divorce and, having spent so much time under a man's thumb, she'd wanted to relish in a bit of freedom. O.B. was her first for a lot of things.

O.B.'s mother turned away from fiddling with something on the kitchen counter, and when her eyes landed on Sam, a smile spread across her face. Bridgette Daniels was an adorable woman who didn't look at all like she had children close to the age of thirty. Curly locs fell to her shoulders and glasses that matched Delilah's sat low on her nose. Her skin was a smooth, almost soothing brown only a few shades deeper than her son's. He did, however, get her dimples.

"Shh." Bridgette touched her index finger to her lips. "I'm drinking Merlot back here and I don't want anybody to know. Come here, baby."

Laughing, Sam stepped into her arms, and an unexpected memory of her lying in bed next to her mother while her mother made up silly stories washed over her.

"It's lovely to meet you, Mrs. Daniels."

"Bridgette. Wine?"

"Oh, no thank you."

"Lilah, get Sam some of that lemonade, will you?" Bridgette flicked her hand toward the fridge. "I forgot O.B. said you don't drink. I'm sorry, baby."

"Did he say why?"

Bridgette twirled a curl that hung over Sam's forehead and another memory, this time of her mother waking her up with tickles, flashed through her mind. She'd always known her mother had changed, but she hadn't realized just how much. The last time she'd seen her mother happy, it was with Aaron.

She'd needed this more than she realized.

A mother's touch.

A mother's embrace.

"He did," Bridgette answered. "But I won't talk about it if you don't want to, baby."

"It's okay. I don't mind talking about it. I'm just not a fan of the C word."

"Oh, sweetheart." Bridgette pulled her in for another hug, this one longer. "You are so beautiful. Did you do this cute style yourself?"

"Yes, ma'am."

Bridgette stepped back and examined the curly cut with the off-center part. "Can you do my hair for Christmas? You have skill. I'll be the hottest woman on the block."

Sam swiped the air. "I'm sure you already are."

"That's what I keep telling her," Raina chimed in. "Momma, you have got it going on."

Bridgette spun in a circle, did a little dance, and grabbed her glass of wine. "I do, don't I?"

Sam felt O.B. before he spoke. Smelled him. Being there with him, after all the warnings and the push and pull of their "relationship," it felt like she'd finally stepped off a wobbling balance beam onto solid ground.

"Hey, Momma," he greeted. "Miss me?"

Bridgette pulled him down for a tight hug and kiss on his cheek. "I always miss my baby boy."

"I'm the youngest," Delilah argued. "But you'd never guess it because O.B.'s a spoiled brat."

"I am not." He pretended to pout. "Momma, tell them I'm not spoiled."

"You're spoiled, baby." Bridgette patted his arm. "But it's okay. I'm allowed to fawn over my children. After all, I made ya'll. Your father's taking a nap, sweetheart, but he'll be so happy to see you."

Raina leaned against the refrigerator. "He'll be happy to see Sam. He said she has lips like Jolly Ranchers, and I see what he means."

O.B. drew Sam up against him, kissed the top of her head, and placed his mouth near her ear. "You okay?"

She nodded.

"You need a break?"

"Small one."

"Which room is Samantha's?" he asked. "I'll walk her up."

Bridgette pointed. "The last one upstairs on the right. I gave her the good guest room with the queen bed."

When they were away from the chatter of the front room, Sam released a breath. It was only in moments like these that she realized her father hadn't done her any favors by keeping her locked up in the house as though punishing her for her mother's actions. Like him, she'd already been born introverted. Isolation, control, and introversion was like the Dark Triad of extreme shyness.

O.B. took her hand and held her bag in the other. It wasn't heavy, considering they were staying only four days, but she loved the way the veins in his forearms bulged as he gripped the handle.

"This is the room my grandfather died in," he said, reaching for the knob.

Sam grabbed his wrist. "What?"

"My grandfather, Amadou. Momma's father. He was sick for a

while, so he came to live with her from Senegal. Died right here in his sleep."

Then he grinned.

"Don't do that, O.B." She clutched her chest. "You had me thinking I'd have an old man looking down at me while I touched myself in the middle of the night."

He stopped short of opening the door. "Come again?"

"Yes, that's just what he would say."

His grin grew wider, and released a laugh that made his eyes sparkle and glimmer.

The room was quaint, simple, and cozier than the bedroom she'd had growing up. The carpet was soft and fluffy, the paint was a calm green, and the modern dresser and nightstands matched the wooden headboard above the bed.

"You like?" He set the bag in a corner. "It's comfortable, isn't it?"

"It is. I'll feel right at home."

"Good. That's what I want." He pointed with his chin. "And that's a queen bed."

"I see that."

"Queen beds can fit two people, especially if one of those people is six-foot-four, handsome, and sneaking in in the middle of the night."

"If it's okay with you, out of respect for your—"

She went sailing through the air and landed on the bed with a huff. The huff tossed her backward, gently knocking her head against the headboard, but she decided to play it up.

"Ouch. Is that mahogany or something? That really hurt, O.B."

He climbed onto the bed. "Damn, I'm sorry. Where does it hurt?"

"Right here."

"Right there?" He kissed the back of her head. "I'm really sorry, baby."

"I can hear you laughing."

He touched another kiss to her injury. "It's funny, but I really am sorry."

"Now that I think about it, you, Miguel, and Carson grew up here," she said. "Does Miguel have a Thanksgiving game this year?"

He rolled onto his back. "No. It'll be only a matter of time before they show up. My cousins and uncles still hold a grudge from last year when me, Carson, and Guel beat them at our annual game of backyard ball."

"I don't think I ever learned how you three officially met." She propped up on her elbow. "You and Carson have known each other just about your whole lives, right?"

"Since elementary school. We were...round."

"Chubby?"

"Understatement."

"Aww. That's cute. Those dimples of yours make more sense now."

He tapped the side of his face, and she leaned forward to kiss one.

"Guel came to our school in the second grade. At first, he thought he was too good for me and Carson. We looked like that one kid from *Charlie and the Chocolate Factory*. You know the one that turned blue and they had to roll her out?"

"Stop."

"I kid you not." He stared at her to convey the accuracy of the statement. "But we were fat and Miguel's teeth were fucked up, so he had no choice but to be our friend."

Sam choked on a laugh and touched her forehead to his collarbone. "I don't know what I'm going to do with you."

"I actually thought you were feeling him for a while."

"I was," she answered. "A little. He's really sweet, O.B. I mean, he's sweet, Carson's a sweetheart, so I was completely confused as to why the heck they were friends with you."

He snorted. "You don't think I'm a 'sweetheart'?"

"You have your moments."

He rolled, pinning her beneath his body. "I send flowers to your office every week. We made s'mores that one time in the fire pit in my backyard. I go down on you, all the time, like a fiend. I'm a sweetheart."

"I didn't realize those were the requirements. I'll have to alert the women of the world."

"So, what happened?" He kissed the tip of her nose. "Why me and not him?"

"It was always going to be you, O.B."

He kissed her again, this time on her mouth.

"I do have one question, though."

He pushed away, off the bed. "No."

"You wouldn't even consider it now?"

"Do you know how drunk I would have to be to watch Miguel put his dick in you and not want to kill him?" He shook his head. "At that point, I'd be so wasted my dick wouldn't work anymore, so I'm not about to be drunk, soft, and watch Guel fuck my girl. Not happening."

She pressed her lips together, swallowed...anything to stop herself from grinning. "What if—"

"Samantha."

"Okay, what if he doesn't put anything *in me*, in me? Just in my mou—"

She gasped, cried out, and rolled out of the way, off the bed, seconds before he would have grabbed her. She stole a pillow from the mattress, held it in front of her like a shield, and stood with the backs of her knees pressed against the nightstand. It was hard to keep upright considering how hard she laughed. He was so cute when he was fake mad.

"O.B.?" a quiet voice called from the door.

He didn't look back. "Yeah, Lilah?"

"You have a guest."

"Let them know I'm helping Sam get settled in."

Delilah fully poked her head into the room. Her eyes were dreamy and glossed over, and her brown cheeks were flushed with color. Right now, she looked like a lovestruck teen instead of a college junior.

"I think Carson's here," Sam said.

SAM SAT SANDWICHED BETWEEN DELILAH AND RAINA while they showed her pictures of the Daniels siblings when they were younger.

Miguel had showed up with Carson.

Tamika was in the kitchen with O.B.'s mother, and the guys were on the back patio arguing about some football game that half of O.B.'s family thought had been "stolen by the refs."

"That's O.B. when he was seven," Raina said. Then she met Sam's eyes, a smirk on her face.

"Oh. Oh, wow." Sam leaned closer the photo. "He didn't lie about his, uh, *fluffiness*. Is that Carson next to him?"

"Mm-hmm," Delilah answered. "Momma said they were that round because their bodies had to stretch later. Daddy said they were that round because his job used to give out free vouchers for McDonald's."

221

They kept turning, and it did something to her heart when Sam saw how many pictures of O.B. included Carson, or Carson and Miguel. She and Tamika didn't meet until college, and they hadn't even pledged the same sorority, but she knew it would have been like this if they'd met earlier.

"Is this them in high school?" she asked.

"Mm-hmm." It was Delilah again. "High school is when Carson started getting hot. Tamika is *so* freakin' lucky. I had it written down in my diary to go after him when I turn twenty-two."

"O.B. would have just loved that," Raina teased. "One of his best friends smashing his baby sister."

"*Loved*," Sam echoed.

O.B. wasn't going to have any locs left after Delilah got her first boyfriend. And that was if she didn't have one already with those globes sitting full, round, and high on her chest.

Raina stared at her sister, and Sam got the sense that Raina and O.B. feared the same thing for Delilah. At some point during the trip, she wanted to get some one-on-one time with them, especially Delilah. The girl had a lifetime of defending her personality and pursuits ahead of her, but hopefully it was a bit easier now that people were finally beginning to understand that Black girls were as diverse in color, interests, and abilities as any other social group. Maybe even more so.

Delilah pointed to a picture and sighed. "This is them senior year. See what I mean about Carson's hotness?"

O.B. was definitely one of those boys in high school whose name she would have doodled on her notebook. He'd gone from adorable and cute to *gorgeous*.

She admired the stories the girls told and wondered what her life would have been like if her father had claimed his sons. The majority of their congregation didn't know the older boys existed, but she imagined it would have been difficult for her father to claim them and shirk his past life at the same time. From what she understood, all three boys rocked to the beat of their own drum. One was a cable installer, one a boys basketball coach, and one a real estate developer.

Raina had played basketball in middle and high school, and there were a multitude of pictures of her in her uniform, pictures of O.B. with different trophies and awards, and shots of Delilah grinning in front of blue ribbons and science experiments.

"What were you like in high school, Sam?" Raina asked. "Think O.B. would have noticed you?"

She thought about Kelce Majors.

"I'm...fairly certain he wouldn't have. I ate lunch with my math teachers."

"I did too!" Delilah's eyes lit up. "Well, my biology teachers, but Mr. Harrington was awesome. He explained cell biology to me using my Caesar salad."

"My math teacher, Mrs. White, explained the Triangle Inequality Theorem using a slice of pizza."

Delilah giggled.

"We like you, Sam," Raina said. "And, don't get me wrong, we did try to like Jerica in the beginning, but that shit lasted three-point-five-seconds."

"I never warmed up to her either," Delilah chimed in, wiggling her nose as though it itched. "I think there are things she did O.B. never told us."

"Like what?"

Delilah shrugged. "I don't know. Maybe cheat on him with his teammates. O.B., he's kind of soft-hearted. He's like Raina on the outside but me on the inside. No matter what people say."

And Sam was more than happy she'd learned that was the case.

223

When she realized Raina was quiet, she nudged Raina's shoulder. "You think something different."

"I do." Raina stared at a picture of the trio when they were much younger. In it, Delilah was a newborn, so Raina and O.B. were still in elementary school. "O.B. is my little brother no matter how big he gets. So, I wanted to rock Jerica's shit when he came home during bye week and there was just something...sad about him. This was the same year he got his first ring, so I told myself it couldn't have been anything major if it didn't affect his game, but..." She released a shaky sigh. "I think Jerica broke his fingers. Each time we asked, his story kept changing."

Delilah's mouth fell open. "Me too! Remember when he had that," she flailed her hands at her neck, "one cut here? I mean, O.B.'s been playing football nearly his whole life so why, all of a sudden, was he getting banged up like that?"

"Do you think something like that would happen and he wouldn't mention it?" Sam asked.

Raina snorted nearly exactly the same way O.B. had earlier. "Of course. Momma raised us a certain way. For O.B., she didn't want him to be ignorant about women, so she taught him about periods the same time she taught me. I mean, it took him years to stop peeking in on me and Momma because he was *convinced* we'd bleed to death, but he eventually got it."

Sam snickered a laugh. "That's adorable."

"I can see O.B. being the type to make excuses if a woman did shit like that to him," Raina went on. "But I also see him being the type to have a breaking point, so I have to be wrong if he stayed with Jerica's ass for four years, three of those *after* the broken fingers."

Sam swallowed, wishing she could tell them, but it wasn't her information to share. She hoped he did tell them, someday. He was afraid they'd be ashamed of him or see him in a different light, but not when they loved him like this. If anything, Jerica would have to go into the Witness Protection Program.

Raina held Sam's gaze. "You stand up for O.B., and you make sacrifices for him. I mean, you've endured our loud-ass family, and he told me that you're more like Lilah. It's our family, and even she needs a break."

Sam laughed. "I'm okay. It makes him happy."

"So do you."

Delilah nodded. "You really do. I want him to marry you."

Raina swatted at her sister. "Slow down, Disney princess."

"*Samantha the Jolly Rancher.*"

All three heads whipped around. Raina smothered her face in her palm, and Delilah's head rocked slowly from side to side as she stared at her father in disbelief.

"Mr. Daniels." Sam left her seat and went to him. "It's nice to see you again."

He grabbed her up in a tight hug. "Same here, sweetheart. Lord have mercy, the Black woman is a thing of beauty."

"Pops, you wake up and go straight to my girl without coming to see me first?" O.B. called from the French doors that opened up to the back patio. "That's cold."

"Oh, your girl? For the first time in your life, you listened to your old man?"

"I always listen to you."

Orylin Sr. yelled in the direction of the kitchen. "You hear that, baby? Apparently, Samantha is O.B.'s 'girl' now, so does that mean she can't be my second wife anymore?"

"You have to take that up with O.B., babe," Bridgette called back. "Lord knows I need another set of hands to deal with you."

Orylin Sr. gave Sam another tight squeeze and then went to embrace his son, letting him know he loved him and that he'd missed him. After he released O.B., he gave Carson and Miguel hugs and slaps on the back.

"My boys." He flicked his thumb at the men who, together, looked like a gang of sequoias. "I practically raised these three. Does it show?"

"I think so," Sam said.

Orylin Sr. rubbed his palms together. "I heard ya'll talking about playing some ball. Did I hear right? You trying to settle the score from the last scrimmage?"

"I am if they are," O.B. said, pointing a thumb behind him. "Is it still me, Carson, and Guel against *everybody else*?"

"Your cousin Calvin can be running back," Orylin Sr. suggested.

Miguel asked, "Do you really think we *need* a running back? Especially Calvin, who's breaking ankles at Clemson?"

"My house, my rules. Come on, Sam." Orylin Sr. extended his hand, and she stepped forward to grab it. "You ever seen O.B. play?"

"No, sir. Not in person."

"Well, wait until you see this."

———

SAM TOOK THE WRAP O.B.'S MOTHER HANDED TO HER AND tossed it around her shoulders. The temperature outside was quickly dropping, but the men in the backyard stood around like it was the middle of July. They'd gotten O.B.'s cousins and younger uncles together with a few of the men who lived on their street, none of them wanting to miss the chance to play football with O.B. and Miguel. Before they started, naturally, the men had wanted pictures.

They broke off into two teams—Carson, O.B., Miguel, and Calvin...against the world. Four against nine seemed like a major disadvantage, especially since the other team had extra men for substitutions, but no one on O.B.'s team looked nervous about it.

Tamika and Bridgette sat behind her, Raina and Delilah next to her on her left, and Orylin Sr. sat on her right side. The rest of the family crowded around them.

"Wait, did Carson play football?" Sam asked. He looked too comfortable and too poised tossing the football over his head and letting it land in his hands with a soft thud.

Orylin Sr. nodded. "Yep. Even played a couple years in college."

"I didn't know that," Tamika piped up. "Why didn't he ever say anything?"

"He never wanted to go pro. His heart wasn't in it."

"But he could have," Delilah slipped in, eyelashes like butterfly wings. "Carson's really good, but he wanted to write, and he's really good at that too. He's, like, good at everything."

After the release of his book, while people were interested in his writing, Carson's first media appearance had, apparently, caused a stir. Magazines and websites that had virtually nothing to do with writers coveted him to grace their covers and home pages. His social media profiles were littered with thirsty comments.

The other team won the coin toss and chose to start on offense. O.B.'s Uncle Kassé, on his mother's side, had played quarterback in college at Jackson State, so he stepped in as quarterback for the other team. Carson was quarterback for the guys' team.

Sam felt keyed up watching O.B. slip gloves onto his hands. Only O.B. could make wearing gloves look sexy and erotic, and he'd worn gloves from time to time when he was in the league. There was a look on his face she'd seen before, focused and detached at the same time. It was the look he got before every game. Headphones over his ears and his head bobbing, he'd tune everything out until the first snap.

Everyone said it, that her man was a beast, and now she was about to witness it firsthand.

Her man.

The thought gave her goosebumps all over.

"You want some fruit, baby?" Bridgette asked.

Sam stared at O.B.'s mother's face until her thoughts returned to wholesome. "Hmm? Oh, yes. Thank you."

She took a glass bowl of grapes, cantaloupe, pineapples, and watermelon balls.

The other team was good. Kassé had a bullet of an arm, but O.B.'s team played good defense.

There was no score, and they turned the ball over.

Carson tossed the football in the air with one hand while he and the three other men huddled. Behind Sam, Tamika whimpered and sighed.

"You really didn't know Carson played?" Sam whispered.

"No." Tamika stroked the column of her throat and slowly shook her head. "I did not."

The first snap went to Calvin who stepped through, around, and over the other men like they weren't actively trying to take him down. When they finally did, he'd covered nearly half of the "field."

Calvin tossed the ball to Carson, and they reset.

If Kassé had a bullet, Carson's arm was a rocket. He dropped back and let the ball sail with little to no effort, and it landed dead smack in Miguel's palm.

And Miguel was good.

Really good.

She'd gone to some of his games, so she'd seen him play, but it was still a thing of beauty to watch. His hand-eye coordination was impeccable. The way he snatched the ball out of the air, it was like he could see exactly where it would land in his mind's eye.

Within a few minutes, the guys' team was up by a score.

Orylin Sr. leaned over near Sam's ear. "What do you think about my boys so far?"

"They're amazing."

"Wait until you see this."

Sam shifted in her chair and popped a couple of grapes.

The other team took their turn, this time scoring as well. They taunted a little, all in good-natured fun, but O.B. and the rest of the guys didn't seem the least bit *shook*. She could actually feel how calm and relaxed O.B. was from where she sat on the back deck.

He looked up at her, smiled, and winked.

The team lined up, yelled something, and snapped the ball.

O.B., Calvin, and Miguel went into motion.

Carson dropped back. *All* the way back.

When he released the ball, O.B. was somehow already at the other side of the large backyard, hugging the left side. He raised his left hand, turning at the last moment like he had a Jedi, midichlorian-generated force-type sense for the ball, hopped into the air, and snatched it down. It took roughly sixty-seconds, and their team had scored again.

"Whoo!" Orylin Sr. hopped up. "*That's* my boy! That's *my* boy!"

The rest of whatever he said came through muffled as Sam watched on with rapt attention. O.B. caught the football like a magnet to metal. Like there was Velcro in his gloves. And he was so damn confident with it. Football obviously made him happy, so for him to leave it behind...it had to have hurt.

The game ended with the guys' team winning by three scores.

Sam rose when O.B. neared, and he wrapped an arm around her waist and dropped a kiss on her mouth.

"How'd I do?"

She could barely contain herself. "You...were...*amazing*. It's different from watching you on the internet and ESPN reruns. It's like you have magnets in your gloves or something. And how do you track the ball so well? Is it a natural thing or did you practice? How do you know exactly where it's going to land? I've wondered that for a minute now."

He kissed her again. "You are good for a brother's ego, Samantha, I swear."

"Is this your first time playing since you retired?"

"It was." His brows came together. "Didn't realize that until just now."

"How'd it feel?"

"Felt good to show out in front of my girl." He gave her a third, longer kiss. "I'm going to get cleaned up. I'll see you in a bit."

Sam squeezed his hand. "No problem. You were so good, baby."

"*Mmm.* Thank you." He walked off, doubled-back, and kissed her one last time. "Cute ass."

Then, he disappeared inside the house.

When Sam turned, she realized O.B.'s parents had been staring in their direction. There was a soft look in his mother's eyes and his father smiled wide. Delilah held up her left hand and tapped her ring finger, and Sam's face got so hot, she feared her nose would burn right off.

———

"Who's *Ms. Trinity's Classroom*?"

Jerica's head popped up. "I don't know."

"O.B. added her as a friend not too long ago, and then she posted a picture with him."

Jerica studied the outstretched phone, checked the username, and pulled up the woman's profile on hers. "Trinity" was some sort of schoolteacher in Asheville, and it looked like she was pregnant. But O.B. didn't have a baby on the way. They'd seen each other at the premiere only a few months ago. He would have mentioned it to her.

"Tasha, she has a husband," Jerica said. "Look, he's in her fourth picture. She's probably just a fan."

The woman she'd called her best friend and rock these past two months rolled her eyes. "Read the caption, Jer."

It was sooo awesome meeting one of my top five favorite football players. Pics or it didn't happen! My students are going to be so stoked. It was amazing meeting you @OBD84. Hubby and I still can't believe it! I hope you and your girlfriend, Samantha had a great time at the farm picking apples. Your picture came out so cute. You guys are a beautiful couple. What do you guys think? I'm having a boy. Maybe O.B. isn't such a bad name, hmm?

"Samantha?" Rage nearly made Jerica drop her phone. "Samantha who? Not Samantha-fucking-Norwood who told me, to my face, that she wasn't fucking my man? Not that old ass bitch. She thinks just because she has Rihanna money, she can do whatever the fuck she wants?"

"Old?" Tasha asked.

"She's thirty-something." She pulled up Sam's page. "This is her."

Tasha pulled the phone closer. "Jer, she looks our age."

"She's damn near forty, I think."

"And Black. There's a difference. Black forty is like twenty-five. Look at my Auntie Stacy."

It was too bad she hated this bitch. If she didn't, she would have been impressed. *Sam* Norwood had pictures with Oprah, Michelle Obama, Beyoncé, Rihanna, Ava Duvernay. A slew of actresses and businesswomen. Apparently, she even had her own woman-run investment firm? What did a woman like that want with a man like O.B., of all people?

"It *is* her." Jerica tapped on a picture of an apple orchard and enlarged it with her fingers. "Why would she be in Asheville picking apples at the same time as O.B. if it's not her? That's his shadow in the background."

"How can you—"

"Bitch, don't try to tell me I don't know my man's shadow."

Tasha held up a hand in defense. "I'm just saying, Jer. O.B.'s moved on. You were with Landon for two whole years, and he didn't bother you. Maybe leave him alone."

"No. He doesn't get to fucking do this. I own that motherfucker, do you understand me?" Jerica leapt to her feet. "I'm so damn mad right now. This hurts, Tasha. *Hurts.* I let him fuck whoever he wants, but he should know that I'm the only woman he's allowed to love."

"Didn't Samantha Norwood get you that meeting with Michaela Davis?"

"And? Look, Sam did it because she was trying to bribe me because she knew she was fucking O.B. behind my back."

"But you and O.B.—" Tasha ducked a heavy, glass face cream jar that would have busted her nose if she hadn't. "Jer, really? I told you that if we're going to be friends, you can't do shit like that!"

"He betrayed me."

Tasha stood, collecting her things. "Bitch, you need help."

"Whatever. Leave. I don't need any of you hoes anyway."

The minute the door shut, the pain seeped in.

O.B. didn't get to do this. It was fine if he wanted to see women casually, fuck whoever, but apple-picking? He never did anything like that with her. Was he in love with this bitch? What was wrong with her that he didn't want to be with her anymore?

"Jerica?"

She didn't remember picking up her phone or calling her father. "Daddy..."

"Jer? Are you crying?"

"Daddy, I can't do this anymore." She sank to the floor. "It's O.B."

"What did O.B. do, Jer? What did that bastard do?"

CHAPTER 16

It was a perfect holiday weekend, and Sam couldn't wait to go back. She appreciated the warmth with which the Danielses had greeted her and how they'd openly welcomed her into their family.

Delilah had shared with her about the project she was working on and her dream to go to medical school to eventually work in immunology. She'd also shared that she was self-conscious about her personality and feared it would cause her to be alone for the rest of her life. Sam had reassured her that she had a lot of life left and plenty of time to meet people who would want nothing more than to be part of it. One of the games they'd released dealt with a post-apoca-lyptic, vector-borne disease, so she promised Delilah that she'd come get her when the sequel was in development so she could meet some of the scientists they worked with.

Raina told Sam that she understood struggling with body changes, and they'd done a few Pilates-type workouts together. It was O.B. who'd gotten his sister to go to therapy to deal with her body image issues after she'd confessed to bingeing and purging, and it was

O.B. who'd returned to Chapel Hill each free moment he'd had to check up on her and sit in on a few sessions with her. Now, Raina was "kind of seeing, but not really" someone she met in New York she'd met when O.B. took her with him for a media appearance. She only kept it from her family because she wasn't sure what she "wanted to do" with the man yet.

Sam promised to keep her lips sealed.

Now, she and O.B. were at his place.

They'd made love several times to make up for the days of it they'd missed at his parents' house.

Carson and Tamika had come over, and they four of them ate leftover food and pie. They'd started out watching a Hulu series O.B. had been the one to recommend, but he'd fallen asleep on the sofa, his head on her stomach, in under ten minutes.

She liked him there, on her stomach. It gave her access to play in his hair, smooth his eyebrows, and he had her wrapped up, long arms on either side of her body. There was no warmth like O.B.'s warmth.

Four hard knocks on the door startled her as well as Tamika and Carson who were cuddled up on the loveseat.

She and Tamika exchanged glances.

Sam's heart raced. "That sounds like—"

"Yeah," Tamika cut in. "Carson, you have access to O.B.'s cameras, right?"

Carson pulled out his phone. "It's the police."

Sam's stomach wound into a ball of knots. "Carson, can you get the door? Does anybody know O.B.'s lawyer's phone number? Never mind. I'll just call mine."

"What's going on?" Tamika asked.

Carson hopped up and headed for the front door.

"They're here for O.B."

"How do you know?"

"Do you have a warrant?" they heard Carson ask.

"We do. So, he can either come out here or we can come in to get him."

Sam, sniffing and trying to swallow with a quivering throat, stroked O.B.'s shoulder. "Baby? Baby, wake up."

O.B. raised his head, his sleepy eyes beautiful, and slowly blinked at her. "Hmm?"

His expression changed once comprehension set in that something was *very* wrong.

"It's the police," she said.

They stared at each other.

"It'll be fine," he reassured. "I'll go with them. I'll leave my phone with you. Call my lawyer—David Browne. There are cameras all around my property. My passcode is Lilah's birthday."

"Okay."

"Sam." He cradled her face. "I'll be okay."

"What if they—"

"Do you remember Delilah's birthday?"

"Yes."

"Call my lawyer."

"I'm following them," Carson said, his eyes dark and his face marred by a level of rage Sam had never seen. She'd never seen Carson anything but smiling and easygoing.

"I'll be okay." O.B. leaned forward, kissed her. "I'll be okay. I love you."

She watched him go, his phone at her ear, and walked as far as she could before a uniformed officer asked her to stay back.

"Samantha," O.B. called, a warning. A reminder.

She stepped back.

They left, Carson following close behind.

She called O.B.'s lawyer and, for good measure, her personal legal team. When Tamika's hand landed on her shoulder, she nearly leapt out of her skin.

"We should go too," Tamika said. "Carson told me why they were here. What the charge is."

Sam closed her eyes. "Felony?"

"Yes."

"What's the charge?"

Tamika hesitated, and Sam knew.

CHAPTER 17

"What kind of probable cause could they have possibly had in order to arrest him?" Sam asked. "Don't they need probable cause, especially for a potential felony charge?"

Two days.

O.B. had been gone for two days because that was the soonest his arraignment could be held. It was two days where she didn't know what was happening to him, two days where he didn't know what would happen to him, and two days of her pacing Carson and Tamika's place at all hours of the night because she couldn't sleep.

Two hours after his arrest, the story broke. In less than a day, sponsors started revoking their contracts. All the information wasn't out yet, and O.B. was already being vilified based on Jerica's rape allegation.

She would have understood the ire if it was true, but the fact that she knew it wasn't, that she knew how much O.B. had already suffered at the hands of that woman, made the pain so much worse. Then the pictures of Jerica's neck "leaked," and Sam had asked herself, several times over the course of the last couple of days, who she would have believed if she hadn't known him personally.

In the court of public opinion, O.B. was a monster. Her O.B. The man she'd gotten to know. Never mind that up until this point, he'd been lauded for his upstanding character. He didn't even have instances of getting into it with other players on the field. If anything, his teammates had said *he'd* kept *them* level-headed.

They'd been waiting for hours—her, Carson, Miguel, Tamika, and O.B.'s parents. Orylin Sr. had remained silent the entire time, tears had clouded Bridgette's eyes nonstop for the past two days, Raina wanted Jerica's head on a stake, and Delilah was inconsolable. It was the reason she and Raina weren't there at the courthouse; Raina had stayed back to keep an eye on her. She'd screamed when she found out.

David Browne had a legal team of his own, but his and Deitra's team had agreed to work together with David as primary. Sam knew O.B. had it, but she was ready with the bail money, no matter what it was set to.

As long as they gave him the chance to go home.

She leaned forward, hands clasped. Bridgette had helped her down onto the bench next to her when she'd started swaying on her feet. Across from them on another bench were Carson, Miguel, and Tamika. Someone had given her a protein bar and water.

She'd done her best to be a rock for the past two days, crying only when she was alone in the bathroom or guest room. She'd tried avoiding the news and the internet, but curiosity had gotten the best of her. O.B. wasn't who everyone thought he was, but he was big and Black and Jerica was tiny and pale-skinned.

Sam shook her head to clear the deadliest of her thoughts. "What all do you guys know?"

Carson didn't answer.

Tamika had told her she'd never seen him like this, furious, cold, and distant. Between the arrest and now, he'd only spoken a few sentences, all of them to Sam as though trying to keep her propped up when all she wanted to do was collapse.

It was Miguel who answered.

"Jerica's allegation is that when O.B. went with her to the movie premiere, when they left the after-party, he assaulted her in their limo. The limo driver and someone at the hotel are, allegedly, corroborating the story. Apparently, O.B. left LA the same night, even though his flight had been scheduled for the next day, so they're saying he was," Miguel crooked his fingers, "'fleeing.'"

He'd left to come see her. If she'd told him to stay, would this have happened?

"Don't hotels have cameras?" she asked.

O.B. said he didn't sleep with Jerica.

She believed him.

But if they got the footage from the hotel and it showed him so much as going into Jerica's room, for any reason, the odds of him being believed by anyone outside of the six of them and his sisters would drop significantly.

"David's working on that," Carson said, but it didn't sound at all like his voice. There was too much scratch, too much strain. "He doesn't want you to tie yourself to this, Sam. As of right now, nobody knows you're together, and he doesn't want his mess affecting your business."

"That's for me to decide."

She and O.B. had texted while he was in LA. They'd FaceTimed. She'd have to check her text history to see if any of it overlapped with when Jerica claimed he'd assaulted her. If the limo driver corroborated the story, a story she knew was false, it was only a matter of time before he or she slipped up. The driver and the "hotel witness" could both slip up.

Her stomach lurched.

Two people. Two people could be paid to lie, right?

Sam, stop.

He didn't do this. He didn't do this.

Her faith in him couldn't be shaken if she expected to be strong for him. O.B. had given her no reason to think he was violent in any way, and Landon had independently echoed O.B.'s agony about his tumultuous relationship with Jerica. If anyone's character was in question, it was hers.

"Is Jerica's name out?" she asked. "Do people know she's the... victim or whatever?"

"She outed herself," Miguel said. "She said she didn't want to hide from it because she wanted to be strong for the women going through the same thing."

Sam retched.

It took God-like strength to keep the protein bar down.

"Carson, O.B. can't travel internationally." She met Carson's eyes as the realization weighed in. "As long as this is going on, he can't leave the country."

Carson shook his head. "I'm not getting married without my best friend."

Tamika rubbed his back. "Damn straight."

Outside was a circus. They'd had to navigate through yelling, shouting, flashing lights, and people firing rapid questions and nearly shoving them down. It was the only reason she was afraid for O.B. to be released instead of remanded. She didn't want him to have to walk through that. See that.

"He's not a criminal, damn it!" She stomped her foot. "She

doesn't get to hurt him for their whole relationship then turn around and do *this*."

All eyes landed on her.

"Hurt him *how*?" Carson asked. "I swear to God...I was right, wasn't I? Sam, was I right?"

She'd slipped up. It wasn't her story to tell, but they weren't going to turn away. They weren't going to rest. She just hoped he would forgive her for it in the long run.

"Jerica's the one who broke his fingers," she replied. "Those scratches you helped him hide, Carson? It wasn't a one-time thing. You were right. It happened for most their relationship. She's hit him, cut him, burned him—"

Orylin Sr. launched from his seat. *"What?"*

"The same night she broke his fingers, he grabbed her. He left marks, and she used those pictures to threaten his career if he left her."

"So..." Bridgette's fingers went to her chest, clutching invisible pearls. "Those pictures were real?"

"Yes, but please understand that he snapped. She was beating on him with a piece of metal. When he felt the fingers fracture, the pain made him grab her. He wanted her to stop. It's a normal human response."

"I know my baby," Bridgette said. "And if he got to *that* point, then that girl did something that hurt him bad. I know my baby."

She burst into tears.

Orylin Sr. soothed her with soft words near her ear while pressing his cheek against hers.

"Why didn't he tell us?" Miguel asked, the svelte quality he usually had to his voice, gone.

"He was embarrassed," Sam said. "He knew if he told you about what Jerica did, he'd have to tell you why he stayed. And he thought if you found out that he grabbed her, you would see him differently. He sees himself differently because of it."

"He thought we'd throw him away for one thing?" Carson asked, his voice one that could cut metal. "I've known him my whole life! Yeah, everybody on the outside saw that *dog* shit, but how many of those people tried to get to know him for who he really was? Now I know why he changed in the first fucking place."

Tamika tried to console him, but he pulled away, the rims of his eyes red and droplets on his lashes.

"Fuck that, Mika. They're saying this shit about the man who paid my father's motherfucking medical bills after his accident. His mortgage. For a *year*. He kept my family afloat when I couldn't do that shit myself. So, everybody just decides he's, what? The big, bad Black man? Fuck that."

Tamika lay her head on his shoulder and continued to rub his back. "I'm sorry, baby."

"I knew something was up," Orylin Sr. said. "I can't believe I didn't know my son was suffering like that. My baby boy."

Bridgette cried harder.

Sam continued to hold it together. It was a struggle, but strength now meant strength for O.B. later.

Just because Jerica was small and a woman didn't mean she didn't follow the pattern of abuse to a T. She'd lured both O.B. and Landon in by portraying herself as one way, and then she showed her true self once they fell for her. She made O.B. blame himself, made him feel like he was the one who'd done something wrong. She'd taken him on those highs and lows, reeling him in like a drug with her cycle of abuse and apologies.

Sam knew the pattern. She'd lived that pattern.

Both she and O.B. had the same capacity for being manipulated. John had used her faith; Jerica used O.B.'s future.

Carson's phone rang. "Let's go," he said, motioning to her. "It's David. They're going to issue the release order the minute bail is posted."

They sprinted.

Sam didn't hear how much his bail was, didn't care. As soon as she paid it, she searched for him.

It took longer than she thought was necessary to release him.

They had *everything* they needed.

Before she saw him, she heard his voice. "Where's Samantha? Is she here? Did she come?"

O.B. saw Carson first, and they embraced. Miguel followed Carson. They both said something to O.B. that made him nod and tear up, but she didn't hear what it was.

Tamika hugged him next. Then, his parents. When Orylin Sr. embraced his son, tears spilled from the older man's eyes, and O.B. reassured him that everything would be fine although none of them knew if that was actually true. Sam had stayed up reading articles starting from Brian Banks all the way back to Rubin Carter, Iowa State...which she probably shouldn't have done. All they'd done was give her nightmares.

As long as there was breath in her body, O.B. wasn't going to see a day in court, and when it was all said and done, Jerica had better steer clear of them. If Jerica so much as blinked in her direction, she was going to beat the brakes off the manipulative, abusive snake. It would only be the second time in her life where she'd felt the need to fight, but like with John, she'd make sure it counted. Some people understood with words. Others needed the message brought across in a more...salient fashion.

"Carson, is Sam here?" O.B. continued to ask. "Did Samantha co —" His eyes landed on her, and he wrapped her up, squeezing her so tight it made her ribs ache.

"Are you okay?" she asked. "They didn't hurt you?"

"I'm fine. I'm okay."

"How do you feel?"

"Thank you for being here." He hugged her even tighter, lifting her feet off the floor. "Thank you for not giving up on me. I didn't do this. I swear to God, I didn't rape Jerica."

"I know."

"I mean it, Sam. I wouldn't do something like this. I wouldn't. I grabbed her, yes, and I'm pissed at myself for losing control like that back then, but I didn't do this."

She kissed his temple. "I know, baby. I know. I believe you. We knew something would happen. We didn't anticipate this, but I'm not going anywhere."

David and Deitra flagged them down.

David ticked his head. "We'll go out this way. I don't want you walking into that circus, O.B. Come on."

O.B. might have been spared the circus, but as Carson looped around to the front of the building, he got a glimpse of the ruckus anyhow. She saw the emotion on his face and couldn't begin to imagine what he was going through.

"What are people saying about me?" he asked.

She slipped her fingers through his. "It doesn't matter."

They'd called him all sorts of names. Some had recorded themselves burning his jersey.

Those had hurt the most.

She wanted them to see what she saw. See the O.B. she knew. She'd looked up article after article, read page after page of men who'd come forward with their stories of being abused by their girlfriends and wives. Many of them had been victims of coercive control like O.B. and Landon. Some of the stories had come from parents, friends, and siblings because the man had taken his own life, fearing no other way out and not wanting to come forward because he figured no one would believe him.

Even worse, she wasn't sure how likely it was *she* would have believed O.B.'s side of the story if she hadn't known what she now knew. She'd never once stopped to consider that something like this happened and happened regularly.

Jerica was a narcissist Sam had no pity or empathy for. She didn't care about Jerica's childhood, her upbringing, or her past. None of it. The woman could have grown up in the middle of an active war situation and she still wouldn't give a damn. All that would do was explain her ways. It wouldn't do a thing to excuse them. Past pains and traumas weren't walls or fences. They were obstacles to climb over, to overcome, not hide behind.

O.B. didn't want to go home, so they agreed to stay at Carson and Tamika's. Sam had volunteered to go to O.B.'s house to get him whatever he'd need to hang out at Carson's for a while, but he'd asked her not to leave him.

Tamika and Carson went.

After he'd showered and changed, they'd silently eaten takeout together. When Delilah woke up, she'd wrapped her limbs around her brother, bawling, and O.B. had finally let the tears he'd held in all day shed when he witnessed his youngest sister's agony.

He'd reiterated that he didn't do it and that he didn't want them to look at him a certain way or think he would do anything to hurt them. They'd, continuously, reassured him that they knew that already.

David and Deitra's teams were already preparing for the case. O.B. had pled not guilty, and the issue would be brought before the grand jury before the week was out. David had reassured them that even if the grand jury went through with an indictment, it didn't mean it couldn't all still get tossed out. All it meant was they'd be headed to trial, but they were certain that once they got their hands on the prosecution's evidence, it wouldn't get that far.

Everyone turned in for the night before it was even seven o'clock and Sam was sure, just like she and O.B., no one slept.

O.B. lay on his back on the bed in the guest room Tamika and Carson had fixed up, last minute, for them. O.B.'s parents were in the other room that had already been prepared while Raina and Delilah slept down in the living room on the pullout. Sam appreciated that O.B. had so many people supporting and surrounding him at a time like this. His confidence had taken a significant hit.

"Why do you believe me?" he asked, all of a sudden.

"Because I know you, O.B." She faced him, on her side. "Don't let what everyone else is saying get to you."

"But *they* don't know me. Why would they believe me? I mean, I look—"

"O.B., baby, don't do that." She laid her head on his chest and he wrapped her up, never letting her get too far. "Don't let their opinions of you start changing the way you see yourself."

"I'll probably get indicted."

"Remember what David said?"

"Two people came forward and were willing to lie to say I hurt Jerica," he said. "Two people's lies were believed over me simply saying I'm innocent. No one's going to look at me and believe a thing I say."

"That's not true, O.B. Trust David and Deitra."

Trust me.

"Samantha," his voice broke, "can I tell you how much this shit hurts? So fucking much."

She remained quiet, giving him the space to vent.

"I worked my whole life to maintain a certain image. I didn't want people to see me as the angry Black man or the overly arrogant football star. My father raised me a certain way, and *that* was what I wanted people to see. I wanted them to see how good of a job he's done as my father." He sucked in a breath and released a shaky sigh. "I was worried about Jerica turning me into a woman beater in the public eye. Yes, I slept with some women and didn't pursue anything further, but Sam, I *wish* I could have told just one of them how much drama I was saving them by being a fucking asshole. This is worse. This is...so much fucking worse."

She wrapped her arms around him as best as she could.

"Can you imagine what people see when they look at me now? Can you imagine how I look when they picture me...*hurting* Jerica? Companies don't want to work with me, people are already distancing themselves from me. I feel like I woke up that morning, before all this shit happened, as a man, and then I went to sleep that night as a monster."

Her tears dripped onto his shirt.

"I don't want you mixed up in all of this, baby." He stroked her back, and she knew it was more for his comfort than hers. "I don't want you tied to me and have your image suffer for it."

"That's for me to decide," she reiterated.

"Sam, you don't like a lot of attention. You prefer your life quiet. Behind the scenes."

"O.B., I'm not your girlfriend only when it's convenient."

"I didn't see shit going like this in my head. I thought, 'Okay, she's my girl now. I finally decided to man up and stop pretending I don't love her.' Then, I wanted to buy you things, take you on those trips you want to go on. Make you happy and keep it that way. Sam, you don't know how much I love being with you. How much peace you bring to my world. My life."

Sam pushed up onto her hands and looked down into his face.

"I wouldn't blame you for being even the slightest bit disappointed in or disgusted with me. I feel like all I do is apologize to you."

"O.B., listen to me." She stared into his eyes. He needed to hear *and* see this. "I've never been happier, in my life, than I am when I'm with you. Hear that. Absorb it. Understand it. Number two, I believe you. I don't see you as a monster. I don't see you as dangerous because you reacted, like any other human or animal would do, when being violently attacked. Number three, as long as there is breath in my body, I *will not* let Jerica get away with this. What was it they used to say? Put that on everything?"

He smiled, eyes glistening. It was his first one of the day. Probably of the last three days.

"Sam, my little warrior. But this isn't your battle to fight."

"O.B., everybody needs at least one person to fight for them. So I promise you that, although I know you can fight your own battles, now that I'm your girl, expect me to fight some of them for you."

He raised his lips to hers, and she got the feeling he'd been wanting to do that for the last few days.

"I love you," he said.

"I love you too, O.B."

CHAPTER 18

Three weeks had passed since the indictment, which had crushed O.B. so badly, he didn't speak for days. But David and Deitra had already been preparing for it. As it stood, the prosecutors wanted the case tried in LA County. Currently, everything was still in Charlotte.

O.B. didn't feel like leaving Tamika and Carson's.

Nobody made him.

Delilah was excused from school until the end of winter break as long as she finished some of her assignments virtually. The only person who got her to so much as try was O.B., and he sat with her and pretended he understood her assignments just to get her to complete them.

Sam didn't want to go back to work.

O.B. assured her it was okay. That he would be fine. It was only one day out of the week, and he would be there when she got back. He *wanted* her to go back to running things and promised her that, when all of this was over, if she wanted to retire and have them travel the world together, they would do that.

Carson and Tamika had halted their wedding plans, but O.B. asked them not to. To continue. If he could only be there virtually, he would even wear his tux. It hadn't sat well with Carson, who'd clammed up even further.

Although Sam didn't want to go back to work, for O.B.'s sake and sanity, she had.

"Miss Norwood?"

She heard a voice from far off, but she wasn't sure where it came from.

"Miss Norwood?"

"Oh, Layla." She briefly squeezed her eyes shut. "I'm sorry."

"It's okay. I just wanted to let you know Landon Johansson is here to see you. Can I send him in?"

"Yes. He can come on in."

Landon, long and lean, came through the door, the top of his head nearly grazing the frame. She walked over expecting a handshake, but he pulled her into a tight hug that took her feet off the floor.

"Hey, Miss Norwood."

She squeezed him. "Sam. I think you can call me Sam at this point."

"Can I sit?"

"Sure."

He released her, and they sat across from each other in the lounge area in her office.

"First of all, thanks again for the gaming system," he began. "How've you been holding up?"

She sighed, too tired to hide the defeat she knew was plain as day on her face. "Barely."

"What about O.B.? Is he doing all right?"

"He's putting on a good face." During the day he wore a mask.

At night, he peeled it off. Each time he did, it took skin. "We're getting through it."

"Oh, man." Landon slid to the edge of his chair. "Sam, O.B. didn't do anything with Jerica that night. *I* had sex with Jerica that night."

Every cell in Sam's body froze. "What?"

"She called me. I asked her what happened to O.B. because I knew they were supposed to be doing the premiere thing, and she said he went back to his hotel."

"Landon, she...why...what made you go?"

"My secret."

Of course.

His secret.

She would never ask him to reveal it, but if he chose to testify on O.B.'s behalf, there was a nearly one-hundred percent chance it would get out. That meant there was very little chance they'd be able to use his testimony. The videos from the hotel had also been tossed out as inadmissible because they hadn't been acquired legally due to a "handling mishap" within the LAPD.

"I still have the texts she sent me." Landon pulled out his phone. "I keep all of Jerica's texts, actually. I've been hoping to get something *I* can hold over *her* to get myself out of this mess."

He left his seat to sit next to her.

Jer: Hey, you around?

Landon: Yeah

Jer: I'm wet.

Landon: That right

Jer: Come over?

Landon: Thought you had that movie premiere tonight. Didn't you go with your ex?

Jer: He's being a pussy. He walked me ALLLLLL the way to my door but then went back to his hotel talking about he's hungry and tired.
    He turned me down.
    Me!
    Hi-fucking-larious.
    Probably watching porn, fisting his dick, wishing it was my pussy.

Landon: Maybe he really was hungry and tired.

Jer: Are you coming or not?

Landon: I don't know. I have shit to do.

Jer: Is this one of those nights when you prefer dick?

Landon: Fine, Jer. I'll be there.

Sam gripped the edge of the cushion to stop herself from bouncing in her seat. "Landon, why are you showing me these?"

He stared at the messages, silent for a moment. "I didn't know who else to go to. I mean, I have a lawyer, but I thought it would be more helpful if I came directly to you because you're O.B.'s girlfriend. You are still his girlfriend, right?"

"I am. One hundred percent. But...what do you expect me to do with these? Present them as evidence?"

"Yeah. What, we can't?"

She cradled his wrist. "Landon, what if...what if your secret comes out?"

"Sam, if Jerica can do this to O.B., what's to stop her from coming at me with something worse? I'd rather be a bi basketball player than have her frame me for murder or something. I'm telling you, she's not right in the head, and I couldn't live with myself if I knew I had these and let O.B. go to prison over something he didn't do. I didn't hear the details about *when* she said this happened until two days ago, but I flew out as quickly as I could."

She could kiss him.

And, she was beginning to sense Jerica had a pattern when it came to choosing her victims. On the outside, they were portrayed one way —big, athletic, tough. On the inside, they had hearts so huge and lovely, no one would believe it without knowing them. It was so sad it was almost comical there existed people who benefited from the damage of stereotypes and stigma. People who lived to reap those benefits.

"Actually," Sam cocked her head to the side, "I'm not so sure it'll get out. This completely discredits Jerica's allegation so, after this, no matter what she says, no one will believe her. Has she tried to contact you? Does she remember she sent these to you?"

"No, and I don't know." Landon searched her face. "So, can this help, at all?"

"Yes. Let's call O.B.'s lawyer, right now."

"If you hadn't met up with me, I don't know if I'd be able to do this," he said. "You made me feel comfortable telling you...you know. Even after I left your office, I didn't sit on pins and needles expecting for it to come out. Let O.B. know that you had a lot to do with this, and he should buy you the most expensive piece of jewelry he can afford."

He was just a kid. Looking into his face, hearing his words and his fear...he was just a kid. Hopefully, this gave him the peace he'd been robbed of by getting caught in Jerica's web.

"Sam? Are you okay?"

"Am I crying?" she asked.

His smile was soft. Boyish. "Yes."

"I'm just so happy. And I'm grateful for you, Landon. So grateful for you."

She pulled out her phone and dialed.

O.B. TURNED OFF THE GAS STOVE AND PILED SPAGHETTI onto two plates. He didn't have a ton of recipes in his memory bank, but he was a boss at spaghetti, and he wanted to have something prepared for Sam when came back.

He'd finish out the rest of the weekend at Carson and Tamika's and then go home, but he wanted her to go home with him. For good. If she didn't like his place because of the marble and the baby grand piano, they could "go home" to her place. He didn't know how many more normal days he had, days outside of a cell, so he wanted to spend as many of them with her as possible.

He removed a saucepan from the stovetop and poured his made-from-scratch marinara over the noodles.

"O.B.?" Delilah called, entering the kitchen. "Here. Your phone was ringing. It's David Browne."

She looked so much meeker than she had before. She cried every day. It killed him that this hurt her so much.

"Thanks, Lilah," he said, and raised the phone to his ear. "What's up, David?"

Delilah running up to grab the pan was how he realized he'd nearly dropped it. It was only about a minute of conversation, although David promised he'd call back a little later after everything was finalized, but when O.B. hung up, he could barely move.

"O.B.?" Delilah stepped in front of him. "What happened? What did he say?"

Somehow, his mouth worked. "He, uh...he said that new evidence has been brought to light that exonerates me completely, and he's going to request that the DA's office dismiss the charges."

Delilah's eyes grew larger than he'd ever seen them. Then, she screamed, screamed some more, and tossed her arms around him. The noise brought Raina into the kitchen.

"What happened?" she asked, looking around and poised as though ready for a physical confrontation. "Did something happen?"

Delilah repeated the news to Raina, and then again when their parents, Carson, and Tamika entered the kitchen.

"Did he tell you what the evidence was?" Carson asked, shaking his hands.

O.B. shook his head. "No, but it's apparently conclusive."

"I'll call Miguel," Carson said, leaving the kitchen phone in hand.

The front door chimed to indicate someone had entered. Everyone else was spoken for, so O.B. knew it could only be one person.

He stepped through his family and friends and met Sam in the foyer. She looked up at him, beautiful with those curls falling over her forehead. It was her. He felt it all the way down to his bones that she was responsible.

"Sam, David called and said he's getting my charges dismissed," he said. Then, he waited for her response.

She didn't scream and jump into his arms, which meant she already knew.

"So...Landon Johansson," she said, hanging up her coat. "When you told me about what Jerica did, that very first time, I decided I wanted to approach this from multiple angles. On one hand, I wanted to see if I could get Landon to talk to me to find out if she did the same thing during their relationship. She did. She got information about him she could hold over his head, and then she made his life a living hell. That angle was character assassination, and I was ready to lie if need be. Fight fire with fire. She paid people to lie, but she has no idea what my kind of money can do. I can buy and sell Jerica, and I wanted her to know that, especially since she tried to hurt my man."

Samantha, I love you.

"Approach number two was to get her a sit-down with Michaela Davis. Me and Michaela go way back, and she has major clout in the movie industry. She could make or break Jerica's career with the snap of a finger, which meant *I* could make or break Jerica's career with the snap of a finger. This was the quid pro quo angle. If she threatened to expose you, I would snap that bitch out of a career like my motherfucking name was Thanos." She held up a hand. "Excuse my language, Mr. Daniels. Bridgette."

They waved her off.

The smile that spread across O.B's face felt like it came all the way from the soles of his feet. She was so cute when she thought she could curse.

Samantha Norwood, I love you.

Sam slipped off her heels and let them hang from the fingertips on her right hand. "But then Landon came to see me today to let me know that he slept with Jerica the night in question, and she texted him to come over. In her text, she specifically stated that you turned her down and went back to your hotel, and Landon keeps all of Jerica's texts because he's been waiting on bated breath for her to give him something to hold over her. He saved her texts for his freedom. When he showed me the texts, we sent them to David."

She took a step forward.

"O.B., I love you, okay? I love you so much, it's hard to breathe sometimes. You are a good person. You are a good man. You aren't..." She paused to gather herself. "You aren't what everybody out there is trying to make you out to be. You're not dangerous, you're not a brute, and you're not a rapist, and I wasn't going to let Jerica put that on you. So when I found out what she did, from the *very first time* you told me, that's when I decided I was going to do whatever I could to take her down. No one, no matter your color or creed, deserves to be subject to abuse. I might be small, but I wield a mighty checkbook."

He laughed, tears in his eyes. "God, Samantha. Marry me."

"W-what?"

"You're right." He massaged his forehead. "I need a ring."

"No, you don't!" Sam, Tamika, Delilah, Raina, and Bridgette yelled, at the same time.

"No...you don't," Sam repeated. "Ask me again."

"Samantha Candace Norwood," he lowered to one knee and took her left hand, "you are the most incredible, beautiful, and wonderful woman I have ever met in my life. I love you, baby, and I will love you forever. I told you—I found you when I wasn't looking. When I wasn't even expecting you. And now, here you are, the love of my life, and the most amazing person I have ever met. Will you be my wife?"

"Of course I will, O.B," she said, choking back tears.

Behind him, their family and friends cheered. He picked her up and kissed her until they were both breathless.

"O.B.?"

"Yeah, baby?"

"Is that your marinara sauce I smell?"

CHAPTER 19

In sixteen hours, Sam would be leaving for Tamika and Carson's wedding in Scotland. Once she left, she would be out of the office for the next ten days. She'd been on her way out the door, waiting for O.B. to come down from her office, but the Good Lord had seen fit to bring this blessing to her doorstep, right before her departure.

She'd prayed for this.

Literally.

She told Tony Maiava, Two-Twelve's head of security, to let the woman through, and then glanced up at O.B. who was on the second floor open area of the building and making his way down.

"Miss Waters, what business do you have here today?" she asked, hands clasped behind her back.

Jerica, who'd gone into hiding after O.B.'s charges were dismissed and her lies were brought to light for all the public to see, strode across the lobby, purse slung over her shoulder.

"I need to speak to you," she said, voice comically gentle and sweet-like.

"About?"

"You destroying my life."

"I won't take credit for that." Sam held out her hands. "I believe you did an amazing job of that yourself."

Jerica needed anger. She thrived on anger. She'd come there hoping to play the innocent victim, all soft-spoken and quiet to get big, bad Samantha Norwood to do *something* so she could then say she'd been the wronged one all along. No one could fight for men like O.B. and Landon. Not against a woman.

Jerica's attention caught the rock on Sam's left hand, and the sweetness got swept out of the window. "You have got to be fucking kidding me."

Sam lowered her voice. "Please calm down, Miss Waters."

"Calm down? Bitch, who the fuck do you think you are? I know you put Landon up to fabricating those messages with his bitch-boy ass. Were you fucking him too? You're fucking a fag and a rapist?"

It had been verified that the messages had come from her phone.

Jerica knew that.

"You think you're better than me just because you have more money?"

Sam shook her head. "Bless your heart, you think money's the reason I'm better than you? Maybe it's because I'm not a predator. It could even be because I don't put my hands on people, though I could be convinced to lay hands on the right person."

Jerica dropped her purse.

Sam watched it cascade to the floor.

Tony took a step toward them, but Sam put up her hand to stop him. "Don't worry, Tony. We'll work this out. Miss Waters is just a little riled up."

"You might be able to control them." Jerica pointed around the room and the small gathering of onlookers. "But you can't do shit to me. At the end of the day, I'll still get O.B. He might be toying with you, but once he's done, he'll come back to my pussy."

"Obviously, your pussy wasn't enough if I'm the one with the engagement ring. Maybe you should have, I don't know," Sam shrugged, "offered something more substantial."

"Fucking bitch."

Jerica raised her hand and swiped it across Sam's face.

Tony started forward again and, behind her, Sam felt O.B.'s presence. She motioned for them both to take a step back, slipped out of her shoes, stretched the muscles in her neck, and bounced on the balls of her feet. Smiling, she rubbed the tender spot on her cheek. It stung a little, and it would probably leave a mark for a few hours, but that was fine.

"Tony?"

"Yes, Miss Norwood?"

"Who swung first?"

"That would be Miss Waters."

"Good."

She didn't hit Jerica with an open palm.

She hit her with a fist.

Before Jerica had a chance to recuperate from the blow, she grabbed her hair, tugged her head back, and bent to speak directly into her ear. "O.B. and Landon might not be able to fight you, but I can. *And I've been waiting for you.*"

Jerica tried to scratch her face, but Sam tugged harder.

"You think you can walk around and do whatever you want to good people? How many people have you hurt, Jerica? I know it's not just O.B. and Landon. Do you hate this? Do you hate what I'm doing to you, putting my hands on you like you put your hands on others? Is this the only way you'll understand what it feels like?" She leaned closer. *"God, please strengthen me just once more, and let me with one blow get revenge on the Philistines for my two eyes.'"*

She released Jerica's hair, and Jerica stumbled backward.

Jerica advanced again, and Sam slapped her with her left hand, punched her with her right, and would have wrapped her hands around her neck for an actual choke-out—since she wanted the world to think O.B. choked her, she might as well give the woman the real experience—but O.B. hooked her around the waist, lifted her off her feet, and pulled her back.

She made sure Jerica was looking at her and mouthed the, "Gotcha, bitch," she'd sent O.B. before Tony dragged Jerica away— for good measure. She knew Jerica had sent O.B. the added sentiment for the sole purpose of decimating his already tortured soul.

Sometimes God's wrath took too long.

This, Sam would consider a filler.

"Where are you taking me?" Jerica demanded, twisting in Tony's grip.

"Miss Waters, you just assaulted my boss. You're leaving here in the back of a police car."

O.B. carried Sam to the elevators, pressed the button for the top floor, and didn't set her on her feet. When he stepped out, he stopped in front of Layla's desk.

"Layla, make sure not-a-damn-body comes up here for the next two hours, understand?"

Layla's head bobbed. "Yes, sir."

"You might want to leave yourself." He walked toward Sam's office. "And if it sounds like a woman's getting hurt...don't come save her."

He set Sam down in the office and locked the door behind him. She backed up against her desk, the first time she'd ever seen that look in his eyes, and it made her nipples so hard, they ached.

"Girl..." He pulled off his belt, shrugged off his blazer, and pulled his shirt off over his head as he stalked toward her. "Sam, Sam, Sam. My dick's so hard right now, I might fuck you unconscious. You need to be scared."

Sam's chest pushed high in her top, the middle of her panties damp. "We're supposed to be going out for dinner. We fly out tomorrow, remember?"

"Ask me about some damn dinner when I'm bottoming out in your pussy."

He tore her top down the middle, popped off her bra with the flick of his wrist, tore off her panties, and spun her around. Her skirt went up around her waist, and he gently eased her face to the desktop and then pushed his way inside her.

One motion.

One stroke.

"Now, I know you can handle some dick, baby," he groaned, slamming into her. "That's what my girl does. She handles shit, even for her man. So, you can take this dick. Am I wrong?"

Sam scrambled for a grip somewhere on the desktop.

"Samantha."

"N-no. Y-you're r-right."

He tilted her hips and made good on his promise to *bottom out.*

"Samantha, are you the future Mrs. Daniels?"

Apparently, she answered.

"Then take this dick, and tell me you love this dick with your beautiful, sexy..." He groaned, yanked her up, took them to the floor, and urged her forehead to the soft area rug that extended from beneath her desk.

"O.B., please..."

"Please, what?" He drove into her, holding her hips in place so she felt the depth of each stroke. "No, no. Don't you go a-damn-where. You just told me you could take this dick, so guess what you're about to do?"

"T-take t-this d-dick?"

"That's right."

Sam gripped whatever fibers in the rug she could find. A climax pulled tight inside her, and she had no control over when or how hard it came.

The dam broke.

Her inner muscles swallowed and suctioned him.

He pumped his hips faster and released deep inside her body.

Sam's legs gave out and she collapsed onto her belly. O.B. hovered over her, his sweat dripping onto her back and neck. She tried to turn over, but he held her in place.

"I'm not done with you yet. We're not done until I have you climbing the walls, understand?"

"Y-yes."

"Yes, who?"

"Y-yes, O.B."

He eased down into a push-up and kissed the back of her neck. "Samantha...thank you for believing in me. Thank you for loving me when I forgot how to love myself. I love you, and I can't wait to make you my wife."

"I...luh...you...too."

CHAPTER 20

Tamika and Carson said their vows, and their four-month-planned, Scotland wedding went off without a hitch.

Due to all the stress leading up to the wedding, Carson's bachelor party had consisted of O.B., Miguel, and a few more of their friends taking Carson to all his favorite spots in Chapel Hill from when they were growing up. There were no strippers, for either the bachelor or bachelorette party, and nobody got slapped in the face by a penis.

Tamika's party consisted of a mini yoga retreat followed by a spa day with their closest friends and line sisters.

The wedding was as fairy tale as Tamika and Carson had hoped, the reception magical. Now, Sam watched with stars in her eyes as her future husband finished his best man speech.

"Carson is the kind of friend who gives," O.B. said, microphone in his left-hand, tuxedo jacket gone. "He gave a shy, chubby elementary school kid one of the cookies from his lunch box and had no idea how that simple gesture would change that kid's life. And by the time I'd reached a certain point in my career and in my life, I'd assumed

Carson couldn't possibly give me anything else. His friendship for the last couple of decades had done more for me than I would ever be able to repay him for. Then, he met Tamika Boone and I thought, 'there he goes again, bringing this woman into our lives' that I now love like my third sister. Who I love because of how she loves him. There's absolutely nothing else he can bring me *now*, I thought. Give me. My best friend's happy and has somebody who truly loves him. There's nothing else I need."

He looked at Sam.

"I was wrong. So wrong. He brought me my baby. As Tamika says, my 'Footprints in the *Sam*.'"

Laughter moved throughout the room.

"My best friend had somehow managed to bring me the love of my life." He cleared his throat. "That's how I know all of this is meant to be. That, on that faithful day, I'd shared a cookie with the man who was predestined to become my brother. He believes in me when I don't believe in myself. He pushes me when I want to give up. He's always there for me, without a complaint, and he never gives up on me, even when I ask him to."

He turned to the bride and groom.

"Carson, Tamika, I love you. I love you with everything in me, and I pray this union brings you strength, purpose, and a life neither of you could have imagined had it not been for the other. I plan to follow you down the aisle not too long from now, and I want to make sure I stand here, look you in the eyes, and say, 'thank you for your love, thank you for saving my life, and most of all, thank you for introducing me to the woman who I can't wait to make my wife.'"

Carson wiped at his eyes and stepped forward to hug his best friend.

The festivities continued for the remainder of the week, culminating in a beautiful Christmas morning where they exchanged gifts and shared stories with their families and closest friends.

When the bride and groom left for their honeymoon in Greece, the guests and wedding party went home.

Things slowly transitioned back to normal.

There was no mention of Landon's personal information.

All the sponsorships that had initially been dropped were returned to O.B., with apology, and he even picked up a few more. He and Landon decided to break their silence about what had truly gone on during their relationships with Jerica. Former assistants, Jerica's boyfriend from high school, a friend of Jerica's named Tasha, and even one of Jerica's siblings joined them, sharing their own stories of terror. Currently, there were charges pending against her for aggravated battery. She'd tried to turn O.B. and Landon, because of their sizes, athleticism, and backgrounds into "big bad, dangerous, abusive monsters." Now, that was how the world saw her.

The front door alarm chimed, alerting Sam that O.B. was home. She was in the master bedroom watching a football game. She'd come to enjoy the sport after having watched so many of his games, and it was even more enjoyable now that she knew formations and could even call a few plays herself.

"Hey, beautiful," he greeted, standing in the bedroom doorway. "You look good in my shirt."

"Hi, love of my life," she said. "I feel good in your shirt."

He pulled a folder from behind his back. "I have something to show you."

She took the folder, opened it, and scanned the documents. "Really?"

"Yeah."

"O.B.!" She hopped up and launched herself into his arms. "I'm so proud of you! I'm so happy for you."

"It's just a few more years."

She leaned back and looked down into his face. "Is this what you want?"

"Yes. So now, I have everything I want. I have my life back, my sanity back, my career back, and I have the best damn woman in the world."

"You are so sweet."

"So are you." He licked his lips. "And I'm *feenin'* for a taste."

Smiling, she lowered her mouth to his, and he lowered her onto the bed.

EPILOGUE

It had gone on for a minute already.

O.B. looked around the stadium, a massive knot in his throat, while seventy-five thousand people clapped, cheered, and chanted his name, on their feet. He'd assumed what he'd gone through would have made him weak in the eyes of many, but in the months since telling the truth about his relationship with Jerica, he'd become an inspiration.

Sports news outlets replayed the old interviews he'd revealed he'd given while hiding some sort of injury. Sports anchors got pissed, on air, when talking about his broken fingers and how they wished they'd known how it had really happened. Even former teammates had come forward and said they wished they'd asked more questions so they could have been there for him.

He'd even come clean about grabbing her, but people didn't see him as a monster like he'd feared. They'd seen him as a human being lashing out against a violent attack. A human being who'd simply wanted the assault to stop.

Just like Sam had said.

He found her in the crowd, clapping the hardest, that rock on her finger catching the light. Last night, they learned they would soon have something else to celebrate. The oncologist had given her the all-clear months ago, and they weren't sure whether it would actually happen, but faith had been on their side since the beginning. They wouldn't have met if that wasn't the case.

His baby was going to have his baby.

The crowd noise died down when the refs and team captains headed to center field for the coin toss. The away team won the toss and deferred to receive at halftime.

O.B. strapped on his helmet and, before he ran onto the field, took one more look back at Sam. She blew him a kiss and waved. He smiled and waved back.

Cute ass.

Thank you for reading.

xoxo,
Alex

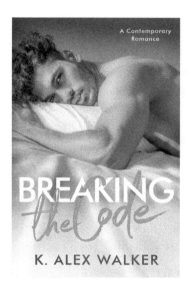

Even when she turned away to receive another round of well wishes, and he pretended to be fully invested in something someone near him said, it was only a matter of seconds before their eyes were on each other again.

He winked and mouthed, "You still love me, don't you?"

Which made her roll her eyes.

And smile.

Miguel didn't know how no one else noticed, especially Delilah's family. Especially Delilah's brother, O.B., his best friend. He didn't know how no one noticed him staring at any and everyone who approached her, keeping a raw count in his head of how many seconds too long they held on with each embrace. All he needed was a few minutes alone with her. Right now, he wasn't sure what he would do with those minutes, but they were too precious to spend doing one single thing.

O.B. walked up and slapped him on the back. "What's up, Guel? You've been more quiet than usual. Everything good?"

Miguel skirted a hand over the loose curls on top of his head. "Yeah. Just ready to get on up out of here."

"It *is* a lot of fucking people." O.B. looked back over his shoulder. "And Samantha said she's hungry. With how much my wife eats, I'm wondering if my kid might be too much like me. He's already playing football in her uterus and giving her heartburn and headaches. If he comes out and his cries sound anything, at all, like the word 'fuck,' I'm putting him back in."

Miguel laughed and glanced Delilah's way.

She turned her head.

Their eyes connected for less than a second.

"Are you coming to the house for the little graduation thing?" O.B. asked. "I know things have been off with you, so you don't have to show up. We'll do something another time. Smaller. For close family and friends only."

Delilah laughed with a group of graduates, gowns creating a cloud of black.

Their eyes met.

And his entire system rocked.

All that time he'd wasted searching for the one person who would prove there was more to this fuckery called life than eat, sleep, and die. Of course, she would be in the last place he would have ever thought to look. Most people never noticed the love right underneath their noses, no matter how sweet it smelled.

"I'll wait for the smaller get-together," he said. "Thanks, man."

It had been him, O.B. Daniels, and Carson Hollister ever since elementary school. Although college had forced their trio to split up, keeping in touch had taken little effort. Without him uttering a word, both Carson and O.B. had noticed that something was "off" with him, but he never offered more information than that. Not when *he* barely knew what was "off" with him.

After a quick hug, O.B. rejoined Sam, who was standing with O.B.'s parents, Bridgette and Orylin Sr., Carson, and Carson's wife, Tamika. Raina, the oldest of the Daniels siblings, had hurried out after the ceremony, late for a speaking engagement in Greece.

Miguel took one last glance at Delilah before heading to the parking lot. It should have been someone else. Something should have intervened and stopped them from falling as hard and as quickly as they had. For the last three months, he'd tried to convince himself that she was better off without him.

Because she was.

Yet, he didn't leave.

Delilah emerged not long after, phone to her ear and head down as she walked toward her graduation present from her parents—a sparkling white Mercedes four-door coupe. Flowers were tucked under her right arm with three helium balloons knocking against each other above her head, all whose messages sported some variation of "Congratulations on Your Graduation!" Her heels, silk press, manicure, pedicure, and outfit had all been gifts from him, and it hadn't been easy getting her to accept each offer. She'd expected him to ask for something in return, but asking for a second chance at her heart in exchange for a couple thousand dollars didn't seem like a fair tradeoff.

She opened the coupe's back driver's side door and fiddled with the seatbelt until the flowers were strapped in like a toddler in a car seat. Then she closed the door, ended her call, and looked around.

"You know my lovesick ass is still here, Lilah," Miguel mumbled to himself, walking over.

She waited until he was directly in front of her before looking up into his eyes, her irises polished with a hint of gold from the evening sun's rays. Anxiety beat in his chest, open palms on hollowed out drums covered in burlap.

"Hey there, Delilah," he sang.

The song by the Plain White Ts was one of her mother's favorites. Mrs. Daniels blasted everything from Nat King Cole to Post Malone on the weekends when she cleaned. She'd done so since they were kids, and he, O.B., and Carson would let out the longest groans known to humankind whenever she woke them up to Back-street Boys or Freda Payne on Saturday mornings. Yet, they wound up throwing miniature concerts with brooms, dusting wands, and plungers until they heard her coming up the stairs to check whether the bathrooms were "no longer a crime scene investigator's dream."

"Miguel," Delilah said, her voice taking on a tone that alluded to the question that would follow, "O.B. said you were bringing a date to my graduation."

"For no other reason than to make you jealous," he openly admitted. "But let's be honest. That was never going to happen."

"Me being jealous or you bringing a date? Because one of those would have definitely happened." She squeezed her forehead, eyes briefly shutting. "Actually, what am I saying? You have every right to date someone. We're not together anymore."

"No, I don't. You must've forgotten what I told you. It's me and you. It'll always be me and you. If I tell you I slept with a super-model, how do you respond?"

"That it's none of my business."

"No, you say, 'Last night was amazing, my king. My next shoot is in New Zealand, my stallion. I'll see you there. I love you.'"

A smile broke free on her face, like sunlight breaking through a forest canopy.

He'd grown up as an extension of the Daniels family, which meant Delilah had grown up like a little sister to him.

Like a little sister.

She wasn't anything close to being the real thing.

Now, a gorgeous, brown-skinned, five-foot-nine woman stood in front of him. The woman who, without knowing, saved his life with every breath she took, ever since the first time she crawled across a table and transformed their friendship into something more with a single kiss.

"I'll be seeing you in Cancún next month?" he asked.

"Nope."

"So, yes."

She gnawed on her bottom lip and gave him a look that said she either wanted to kiss him or kill him. "I'm only coming because I need a vacation. I'm starting medical school in the fall. Might as well have some fun now."

A group of graduates walked by, waving, and Delilah waved back, promising to "totally catch up" with them later over drinks. Once they were out of earshot, she tipped onto her toes and dropped her voice to a whisper.

"Drinks, who? I'm not leaving my house for those people."

Miguel laughed and took a step closer, stopping short of trapping her against the car. "Why not? They seem nice."

"Guel, I barely talked to them while I was in school when I had to never mind choosing to now. Plus, have you ever curled up, alone, with a good book?"

A breeze tossed the chocolate and honey highlighted strands of her hair about. Once upon a time, reaching out to touch her had been second nature. Now, she wielded an invisible electric fence that threatened decapitation.

His fault.

They'd had seven months of bliss until she realized he was purposefully keeping their relationship a secret. When she asked him about it, he'd lied, which was the worst thing he could have possibly done in that moment.

He wanted to be the man she saw inside him, the man she brought out of him. However, another version of him, dark and pessimistic and brooding, kicked that man's ass and beat him into the ground.

Daily.

"You excited about Johns Hopkins?" he asked.

The corner of her mouth twitched, and another smile touched her mauve-tinted lips. "Excited and nervous. I can't mess this up."

"Why not?"

She looked at him as though he'd asked the question in Ancient Sumerian. "Guel, it's been my dream since forever, and my entire family's counting on me."

"We're all counting on you to do well, but not being perfect and failing are two different things."

"Miguel Reyes, always looking on the bright side, until the bright side shows him a mirror."

"Was that a compliment?"

She shrugged.

On the outside, he was a pillar of optimism. One of the calmest, most easygoing personalities in professional sports. To see Miguel Reyes without a smile on his face was about as likely as seeing Miguel Reyes standing over a campfire, warming his hands next to Bigfoot and their pet Chupacabra. No one knew, including the people closest to him, that his everlasting joy hid among flocks and wore thick layers of wool to hide the lethal predator that lurked underneath.

He poked her stomach, needing a reason to touch her. "Can I come see you in Baltimore? I can fly out, spend some time with my girl."

She poked him back. "I'm not your girl anymore. Besides, what would you fly all the way up from Charlotte to do with a stressed-out med student?"

"Come inside you."

Her lips parted, yet nothing but air came out, quick breaths that took him back to late nights on top of her, her fingers gripping his shoulders and her mouth spilling musical notes of pure pleasure. It was the same gasp she made when he spread her legs and entered her, and she would hold her breath until he was as deep as she could take him. Delilah Daniels, the "innocent" and "quiet" academic scholar, loved when he fucked her like he wanted to destroy her from the inside out.

"I can come fuck you on top of your textbooks," he went on. "Or on top of your 3D heart models. Hell, I'd fuck you next to one of those...plastic skeletons. And I know I'm getting this all wrong. I don't actually know what med students keep in their places. Afterward, we can go to brunch, watch movies, or I can take you shopping. Anything you want. The point is to be with you."

Being with her made him consider the future, and her presence helped to calm the darkest of his thoughts, but she could never know. The amount of pressure it would place on her if she ever found out was something no human being deserved to have to live with.

"Miguel," she sighed, "while we're in Cancún, nothing's going to happen."

He nodded. "Okay."

"I'm serious."

"All I said was 'okay,' Lilah."

She looked left.

He looked right.

Their gazes drifted back together.

"That one guy," he ticked his head toward the graduation ceremony venue, "who is he to you? The one who hugged you and put his hands on what's mine."

"Not your—"

He grabbed her ass through her gown and dragged her up against him. "Like I said, what's mine. Is he more than a friend?"

"You can't ask me those questions if we're not together. FYI, my family thinks I'm going to Cancún with this mysterious group of friends they swear I possess. But that's what you want, right? For no one to know I'll be with you?"

"That's not exactly it."

"Miguel, I would have told the world I was in love with you without batting an eyelash, but you weren't ready for us to take our relationship public. And you still won't tell me why. Yet, here you are, acting like we never broke up."

He raised an eyebrow. "You *were* in love with me?"

"That's what you heard?"

"If you're not anymore, tell me you're not anymore."

"Then what? You'll let me be?"

"No."

A third smile tugged at her pretty mouth, but she fought it, and it was a shame that she did. He loved it when she smiled about as much as he loved when that pretty mouth was pressed against his. Had he polled their friends and family, he was certain he'd still be the last person to ever expect him and Delilah to be the way they were now. To her family, she was something to be protected and handled like glass. With him, she loved being broken in half.

"Miguel, *you* pushed *me* away."

"I know."

"Why?"

"Back to this guy." He tangled his fingers in the ends of her hair and yanked, only using a gentle flick of his wrist to keep her hairstyle mostly intact, angling her face up so they were eye to eye. "Why was he touching you?"

"His name's Bryce," she said, her breaths noticeably more rapid.

"Fine. Why was 'Bryce' touching you?"

"Because...me and Bryce have history."

He momentarily dropped his gaze to her mouth. "Your ex."

"Yep. One of the two relationships I somehow managed to sustain as a college student at Duke while hopelessly in love with my brother's best friend."

"You still haven't answered my question. Why was he touching you?"

They were banking on her family having left when they said they had. If even one of them had remained behind and glanced across the parking lot, there would be a lot of questions to answer come tomorrow morning.

"Bryce is going to Howard to study law. We were going to talk about meeting up in D.C. in the fall, once our programs start, and maybe giving 'us' another try."

"And when the fuck is this conversation supposed to happen?"

She pointed to his face. "See, I don't know how you do that. Even when you're angry, you're still so . . . calm. So, Miguel. You, Carson, and O.B. drop F-bombs like a fighter jet in combat, but yours almost sound like a melody because of that voice of yours."

"*When* Delilah."

She nibbled on her bottom lip. "We're supposed to have dinner—"

"End it."

"End what?"

"The notion, the possibility, and the conversation. Fucking end that shit. There won't be a 'Bryce' when you're in Cancún with me."

"How do you..." She shook her head. "Miguel, I don't get you. You don't want to be with me, but you don't want me to be with anybody else?"

"When did I ever say I don't want to be with you?"

"You showed me, which is much worse."

"Delilah," he took her hand and brought her palm to his chest, "I'm yours. My heart beats for you, and it doesn't beat without you. Do not fucking play with me. End that shit, and I'll see you in Mexico."

She held his gaze.

"You hate me, don't you?" he asked.

"I might start."

"Then let me hear you say it. Tell me you hate me."

It didn't matter what came out of her mouth; he read her face like words on a page. The fingers that had been aimlessly playing with his collar now stroked the silky hair at the back of his neck. She hadn't stepped out of his hold, and she didn't resist when he'd pulled her close enough for their bodies to touch.

"I hate you, Miguel," she quietly said.

"I know." He bent, dropping a soft kiss on her mouth. "And I love you more."

AFTERWORD

Nearly forty percent of victims of domestic violence are male, but males are less likely to report due to stigma, shame, and self-blame.[1]

I wrote this book specifically to highlight both the issue of men in abusive relationships *and* the perception of males, especially Black males, when it comes to seeing them as victims in any way.

On a personal note, in the past, I would blindly assume that women could do no wrong; a woman could never hurt a man. *I* was a woman, and I couldn't fathom having any power or control over someone stronger, heavier, or taller than I am at five-foot-two.

However, I'm not the same person I was ten or even five years ago, and I'm proud to have learned quite a bit since then. I'm also an aunt to several young boys, and I couldn't help but picture them as I wrote O.B.'s character. I know them as sweet, kind, and loving, but a good portion of the world will eventually stop seeing them that way once they've grown old enough. I've also witnessed them question themselves because of other's accusations. Even as a writer, there are still no words for how much that hurts.

If you are a victim of domestic violence or if you know someone you suspect is a victim of domestic violence, the DV Hotline can be reached at 1.800.799.SAFE (7233).

Don't be ashamed of being human.

"If you prick us do we not bleed? If you tickle us do we not laugh? If you poison us do we not die? And if you wrong us shall we not revenge...the villainy you teach me I will execute, and it shall go hard but I will better the instruction."

- The Merchant of Venice

---

1. https://www.mayoclinic.org/healthy-lifestyle/adult-health/in-depth/domestic-violence-against-men/art-20045149

NO FEELINGS ALLOWED - PLAYLIST

1. If I Could - Charlotte Day Wilson
2. VSOP - K. Michelle
3. I Wish I Wasn't - Heather Headley
4. Mine - Bazzi
5. Moral of the Story - Ashe
6. Heard 'Em Say - Kanye & Adam Levine
7. Go Crazy - Chris Brown & Young Thug
8. Rise Up - Andra Day
9. I Need A Dollar - Aloe Blacc
10. The River - Noel Gourdin
11. When The Party's Over - Billie Eilish
12. Savage - Megan Thee Stallion
13. Remedy - Adele
14. Love Will Be Waiting At Home - For Real
15. A Couple of Forevers - Chrisette Michelle

ALSO BY K. ALEX WALKER

The International Mafia Series

Prince of The Brotherhood

Moonlight Retribution

Myths Legends and Monsters Anthology Series

The Gatekeeper

Elias The Wicked

The Game of Love

The Game of Love

The Game of Love - Sequel

Angels and Assassins

The Wolf

The Protector

The Anarchist

The Dark Knight

The Shadow

The Darkest Knight

Hidden In The Shadows

The Boys from Chapel Hill

Seducing The Boss

No Feelings Allowed

More from K. Alex Walker

Fated - A Contemporary Erotic Romance

The Woman He Wanted

The Girl in the Mountains (formerly With a Kiss, I Die)

Jonah's Ghost

ABOUT THE AUTHOR

I'm a creative creature from the Caribbean who likes animals, Star Wars, quirky humor, and any kind of media that deals with people finding love in an otherwise impossible time.

For book updates, blog posts, and TMI ramblings about my monotonous life, join my mailing list by:

- Hitting up my blog at kalexwalker.com
- Clicking **here.**
- Or texting BOOKADDICT to 66866

facebook.com/kalexwalker

instagram.com/kalexwrites

SOURCES AND RESOURCES

Any Black Man Will Do

The Story of Rubin Carter

56 Black Men - Change The Narrative

The Brian Banks Story

9 798727 455111